LOST IN HER

ALSO BY SANDRA OWENS

The Duke's Obsession
The Training of a Marquess
The Letter

K2 Team Series
Crazy for Her
Someone Like Her
Falling for Her

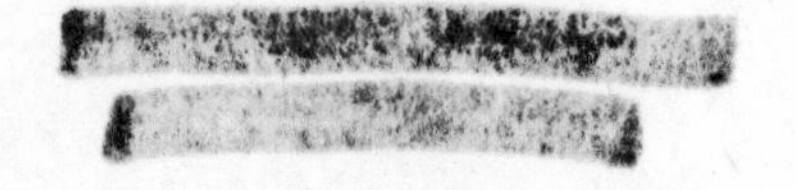

LOST IN HER

A K2 Team Novel

Sandra Owens

This is a work of fiction. Names, characters, organizations, places, events, and incidents are either products of the author's imagination or are used fictitiously.

Published by Montlake Romance, Seattle

www.apub.com

Amazon, the Amazon logo, and Montlake Romance are trademarks of Amazon.com, Inc., or its affiliates.

ISBN-13: 9781503953291
ISBN-10: 1503953297

Cover design by Eileen Carey

Printed in the United States of America

This book is dedicated to all the fans of my K2 Special Services guys. It's awesome that you love my boys as much as I do. You rock!

CHAPTER ONE

One year.

Was that the accepted amount of time to mourn? Ryan O'Connor stared at his reflection in the mirror, debating whether to change out of the black jeans and black T-shirt. Would his hope of getting laid increase if he wore . . . he glanced at the blue T-shirt he'd tossed on his bed. Didn't the brightest-colored male birds get the chick?

Over a year since he'd been with a woman, and five years married before that, which meant he was out of the loop on what women liked these days. A decisive man—he had to be, making life-and-death decisions as the SEAL team's medic and now K2's doc—it annoyed him that he was standing in front of a mirror and dithering on something as stupid as what color to wear.

"To hell with it," he muttered. He wasn't changing again. Someone had told him once that women liked a mysterious, tortured man. If so, he wouldn't have a problem hooking up tonight. The black of his clothes mirrored the condition of his heart these days.

One year and one day ago, he had buried his wife, and then spent the next 365 days mourning her. He missed the hell out of her, but it was time to venture out into the world again. Besides, he needed the soft feel of a woman beneath him, wanting to hear her sweet sighs as he pleasured her.

Ryan turned his gaze to the picture atop his dresser, one of him and Kathleen on their wedding day. The happiest day of his life. After learning her secret and knowing she was gone forever, tears shouldn't still be burning in his eyes.

It was not the time to rehash regrets and obsess over unanswered questions. If he was lucky, in a few hours, he would be buried to the hilt inside the wet heat of a woman. Kathleen stared at him from the photo, sending guilt slithering through him for what he had planned. But why should he feel guilty?

"You're the one who left me," he said. He snatched the frame and stuck it in a drawer, under a pile of T-shirts, burying her.

Again.

"Screw this," Charlene Morgan—call me Charlie—muttered, and unable to concentrate on the story for some reason, she tossed the book aside. Okay, she knew the reason. The emergency landing she'd had to make that morning had unnerved her. It made her think of the things on her bucket list, like her fantasy of having a mind-blowing night of sex with a man she'd never see again.

Her student, a young man whom she'd realized by his second lesson wanted to be anywhere but in the air, had panicked when the plane had sputtered, coughing like it had a chest cold. In between barfing all over her and the plane, he'd actually tried to open his door. Whether he hadn't realized what he was doing or just planned to step out and fall to earth, who knew?

When she was unable to calm him by talking him through his fear, he'd tried to grab the wheel. Not having a better idea, she had balled up her fist and landed a hard punch to his jaw, stunning him enough to bring him to his senses. It had been the only way to safely land the Cessna after the fuel gauge had dropped like a rock. Fortunately, they had just taken off and were able to immediately return to the airport.

His father, an airline pilot determined to see his only son follow in his footsteps, hadn't appreciated it when she'd told him the young man didn't belong anywhere near an airplane. Her only consolation had been the look of relief the kid had shot her when she'd stood up to his father and said there would be no more lessons.

She decided to go to bed and try to forget the whole freakin' day. Thirty minutes later, she gave up on any hope of sleeping. What if she went to a pickup bar and by the time the night was over, was able to check that particular fantasy off her list? Her heart jump-started—it was ready to take off for the finish line, in fact—at the thought of doing something she'd never done before. Sex with a stranger? So not her.

Which was why she wondered if she'd been unknowingly slipped some kind of sex drug as she walked out the door of her house, wearing one of the few dresses she owned, on her way to Buck's on the Beach, the best place in Pensacola to hook up for a one-night stand.

During the twenty minutes it took to get to the ramshackle beach bar, she ordered her car to turn around. Repeatedly. "I do not do one-night stands," she yelled at the Corvette. Her car was apparently deaf.

Choosing a parking spot where she hoped the Corvette would be fairly safe from getting dinged, she sat and watched the people coming and going, some alone and some paired off. A group of six, three men and three women, walked by, talking and laughing, and she tried not to envy them. What would it feel like to have a group of friends?

Although tempted to return home, she instead forced herself to get out of her car. If she could successfully stall a plane in a hammerhead maneuver, she could certainly walk into a bar and survive the experience.

Inside, she paused to survey the scene. The place was jampacked, and she choked down the old fear of being ridiculed or shunned by the beautiful people. A waitress passed with a tray of drinks, and Charlie grabbed one.

"Hey, you can't have that."

Charlie took a quick sip of the drink. Good God, what was in this crap? Lighter fluid? "Sorry," she said over her shoulder as she kept walking. Okay, that wasn't nice to swipe someone else's drink. At the moment, though, she was so mad at herself for even being in a pickup bar that stealing someone's—she tasted it again, wrinkling her nose—whatever the stuff was only counted as a minor sin.

Then she saw him.

He stood near the dance floor, his gaze riveted on someone. Charlie followed his line of sight, then rolled her eyes. So he liked that type? Sheesh, were all men alike? Her ex-boyfriend would've tripped all over his feet to put himself in front of the stacked—every man's fantasy—woman staring back at the man Charlie suddenly wanted.

There was an air of detachment about him, along with a sense that he could be a very dangerous man if he so chose. It was in those eyes that, although focused on the other woman, were watchful of the goings-on around him. It was in the rigid stance of his back, the muscular chest stretching his black T-shirt to its limits, and the way he slanted his head as if listening to the sounds behind him. Like a man who knew better than to let anyone sneak up on him. Even in the crowded bar, those around him had given him space, as if they sensed he was a man best left alone.

Charlie pegged him as military or ex-military. It wasn't just the short cut of his hair, but his very air of being. That Pensacola was a naval base added support to her guess. Normally, she steered clear of any man that hot, but a humming buzzed hungrily under her skin, like a thousand bees scenting honey. Guys like him were the ones who would break a girl's heart, but she only wanted him for one night—didn't even want to know his name—so she could make an exception to her no-super-duper-hot-guys rule.

"Go for it, Charlie," she murmured. The worst he could do was stampede over her to reach his target. Because that was what she guessed the woman was to him, just someone he'd zoned in on. There was no softness in his eyes as he watched her dance, nor was there any hint of possessiveness.

Charlie tipped the glass and downed the contents for courage, then snorted half of it out her nose. Who the hell drank that swill willingly? She grabbed a napkin from the bar, cleaned her face, then quickly touched up her lipstick.

Taking a deep breath, she stepped in front of *him* when the song ended. He moved toward the woman Charlie suddenly hated. As he almost walked right over Charlie, she accepted she'd made a mistake. A man like him would never want a runt—the ex's pet name, one she'd hated from the first time he'd called her that—like her.

Ryan zeroed in on his objective: a tall woman with long black hair, wearing black skintight jeans, and a very low-cut red blouse. She was on the dance floor with some dude, practically humping his leg, all the while holding Ryan's gaze, a come-fuck-me look in her eyes. She would do just fine, and by the way she watched him back, she would be entirely agreeable. The song ended and he stepped forward, intending to separate her from her dance partner.

"Hey, that was my toe!"

With his gaze still on the woman walking toward him, Ryan barely registered the squeak of words, and when he did, he had to look down to see who had spoken.

"What?" he barked, then regretted his outburst. Some guy who came out of nowhere had just swept the woman back onto the dance floor. Damn. He'd have to wait out another dance.

"I said, can I buy you a drink?"

He returned his gaze to the pixie. "You belong on a ceiling."

Blue-gray eyes blinked. "Huh?"

Ryan swiped a hand over his mouth. Man, he really was out of practice. "You look like a cherub." He waved a hand heavenward.

"Huh?"

He felt the beginnings of a smile on his lips. If she'd said something like that to him, he would be saying "Huh?" too. He was definitely out of practice. "Nonsense," he said. "Just spouting nonsense."

He moved to step around the cherub before he lost sight of the woman on the dance floor, who, with her sexy bedroom eyes trained on him, had as much as promised he would get what he wanted. The tiny thing was quick on her feet, though, moving in front of him so that he had no choice but to either stop or run right over her.

"I've never been told I look like a cherub before, so maybe you could tell me why you think that before you go make a mistake." She glanced toward the dance floor where Painted-On Jeans was now crawling all over the man she danced with while watching Ryan.

Was that supposed to turn him on?

"She's gonna eat you alive, you know." Blue-Gray Eyes shook her head as if he were the stupidest man she'd ever met, and he barely refrained from telling her she had that right. She snapped her fingers in front of his face. "Tell me why I'm a cherub . . . I mean, why you think I look like one, and then I'll let her eat you up."

For the first time, Ryan looked at the woman challenging him. Really looked at her. Apparently his dick liked what his eyes saw because he felt the stirring of arousal. "You remind me of those murals the old masters used to paint on ceilings. You could have been a cherub model with your short, blonde hair curling all around your face, and those eyes of yours. They're kind of angelic looking."

Shut your mouth, O'Connor.

An amused grin appeared, bringing his attention to her mouth. A full bottom lip—the kind a man might like to nibble on—disappeared under an even line of teeth as she chewed on it. Then, she laughed.

"What a load of bull." She grabbed his hand and tugged him along behind her. "Forget that hussy showing off for you, humping that guy's leg. I'll buy you that drink, and you can charm me with your clever flirting."

Fascinated by the woman, Ryan followed her to the bar. She ordered a pale ale in the bottle, no mug. "Make it two," he told the bartender. "What's your name?" he asked the cherub.

There was no footrest to help her onto the stool, and when she tried to squirm onto the seat, he bit back a smile of amusement as he put his hands on her waist, lifting her. She was curvy for such a little thing. The sundress she wore inched up, revealing a pair of very nice legs.

After wiggling her butt into a satisfactory position, she shook her head. "No names."

Although he might have been out of the bar scene for several years—or more accurately, never in it—he knew what *no names* meant. She was looking for the same thing as he was. Ryan forgot about the woman he'd first noticed.

He leaned close to the little cherub's ear. "Then give me something to call you, or I'll just make something up." Straightening so he could watch her reaction, he said, "It'll probably be something that will make you blush. Just saying." What he got was a smirk, not what he was expecting, but it told him one thing. The lady didn't easily blush, which made him all the more determined to see her cheeks turn pink.

"Charlie, but have at it, puddin', make me blush."

Charlie? Puddin'? A rare smile crossed his face. The woman wasn't predictable, that was for sure. The bartender slid their drinks in front of them, and Ryan leaned an elbow on the bar after picking up his beer.

"So I'm to call the woman I'm about to make love to *Charlie*? Kinky, but I'm game."

She lifted one pretty brow. "Awfully confident, aren't you? Who says we're going to make love?"

Although he used to be confident, he was no longer. But that was his secret, and not one he was willing to share. He would just have to fake it. He trailed a finger down her cheek, over skin that felt soft and silky.

"Your eyes say so, *Charlie.*" What was her real name? She wasn't going to tell him, and he wouldn't ask again, but he wished he knew.

"Maybe," she conceded. "What should I call you in the throes of passion when I need to yell a name? You are *up* to getting me there, I hope."

A burst of unfamiliar laughter caught him by surprise. "Oh, I'm *up* to it, don't you worry." He liked this woman. "I'm Ry . . ." She'd said no names, yet he wanted her to know his, wanted her to call his out when she came, but she'd set the rules and he would follow them. "Doc. I'm Doc."

He gave her a frank appraisal, his gaze sliding over the swell of breasts peeking out of the top of her little dress, down to those killer legs he'd already noticed. When he raised his eyes back to her face, it was to find her blatantly giving his body a slow perusal. Arousal hit him low and hard when her pink tongue flicked across her bottom lip. He'd almost forgotten how it felt to want a woman.

"Well?" he asked.

She blinked as if coming out of a trance. "Well what?"

"Do I pass inspection?"

Pink tinged her cheeks, and he barely refrained from giving a victory yell. He'd made her blush, and in less than ten minutes of adding it to his list of things he wanted to do to her. Mentally putting a check mark next to the item, he moved on to the next one. Get her out of this bar and someplace private.

"You'll do," she said.

Damn if she hadn't made him want to laugh again. He leaned close and lowered his voice to a whisper. "Did you just challenge me, cherub?" Her scent, something earthy and intoxicating, floated up, and he inhaled her deep into his lungs. Ingrained in his memory was Kathleen's fresh, spring-flowers scent, one he'd once loved. Grateful that Charlie didn't smell anything like his wife, he nuzzled her neck.

A soft, barely discernable sigh drifted past her lips. "Feels good," she murmured, her breath warming his skin.

Another minute and he'd be divesting her of her dress in a crowded bar. "Let's go," he said, lifting her from the seat.

"Wait."

Disappointment stabbed through him that she'd changed her mind. "Sorry, I thought . . . it doesn't matter. Have a nice life, cherub." He turned to go, and she grabbed his hand.

"Don't be an idiot." She caught the bartender's attention and held up two fingers.

There was a first, being called an idiot by a woman. He tipped an imaginary hat. "Sorry ma'am." She gave him an exaggerated eye roll, making him grin. Already, he was realizing she was unlike other women he'd known, which made her all the more fascinating. He'd bet his next paycheck she didn't take shit from anyone. In an argument, she'd probably spit fire. It made him hard just thinking about riling her up and going at it with her.

The new beers were delivered, and she handed him one. "Now, let's go."

Ryan took her free hand—so soft and small in his—and steered her toward the back deck. Halfway to the stairs leading down to the beach, the woman he'd set his sights on earlier stepped in front of them.

After giving Charlie a dismissive glance, she turned a sultry smile his way. "Hey, you. I've been looking for you."

"I've been right here." She really was gorgeous, with her dark brown bedroom eyes and long hair a man would fantasize about wrapping his fist around while he explored her lush body. Up close, she was a little older than he'd thought, maybe even had a few years on him, but she vibrated with sexuality and the confidence that no man could resist her.

Like a cougar separating its prey from the herd, she pushed between him and Charlie and leaned against him, her soft breast pressing into his upper arm. "I saw you watching me. Come dance with me."

CHAPTER TWO

Charlie refused to lower herself to even try to compete with every man's fantasy. To hell with him. Coming to a pickup bar had been her stupidest idea ever. As she passed an empty table, she plopped down her beer and kept going. Once outside, she took a deep breath of the damp, salty air.

More depressed than when she'd left her house, she headed for her car. The moment when he'd forgotten all about her wouldn't have stung if she hadn't liked him so much. "I saw you watching me," she mimicked the she-witch. Of course, he would watch someone like whatever her name was. Probably something adorable like Heather or exotic like Francesca.

Charlie was used to being ignored. On the air show circuit, some of the other aerobatic pilots resented a female who was as good as or better than they were. She'd never understood why it mattered that she was a woman. If you were good, you were good. Plain and simple. And she was damned good at what she did—something no one could deny.

In her personal life, she'd only had one real boyfriend: another show pilot who, in the beginning, she had believed supported her wholeheartedly. Aaron had been new on the circuit when he'd approached her, gushing compliments left and right. She'd fallen for him, and the stars in her eyes had blinded her to his real motivation. Taking him under her wing, she'd spent months teaching him complicated maneuvers.

Lesson learned. Never trust hot guys. As soon as he believed himself as good as she was, he'd ended the relationship. Well, she had news for him. He wasn't near her level, and his arrogance was going to get him killed someday. She just hoped that when it happened, he didn't crash into a crowd of spectators.

On that depressing thought, she hit the remote to unlock the Corvette.

"Nice car, cherub."

Charlie froze when a hard, warm body wrapped around hers from behind, pushing her stomach against the door. He hadn't stayed with the sex goddess?

He put his hands on the vinyl roof, caging her between his arms, and nipped her earlobe. "Leaving without me?"

Unable to find any words, she settled for breathing in his masculine scent, a combination of soap, starch, and a hint of spice. She couldn't think of a more intoxicating, manly smell and had a sudden longing to rub her nose all over him. What would he say if she asked to sniff him from head to toe? Imagining his reaction, a giggle slipped out before she could stop it.

"Wanna share the joke?"

Not even. With his mouth still near her ear, his voice was a low rumble that sent a shiver through her. The man was entirely too potent, and probably more than she could ever handle. But she'd sure like to give it a go for just one night.

"I thought you'd be dancing with the beautiful one." Her voice was no longer hers. It had turned all husky and tremulous.

"I plan on it, beautiful one."

She almost gave him a snarky retort, but when he turned her and took her hands, putting them on the sides of his waist, the words died on her lips. The heat in his eyes as he peered down at her sparked a low-burning fire inside her. No man had ever looked at her like that. A killer smile curved his lips as he spread his fingers over her hips, then began to move them to the music coming from the bar.

Wow! Zip bang bam! Chubby little Charlene Morgan was dancing in the parking lot of Buck's on the Beach with the hottest man to ever touch her. But she wasn't that girl anymore, she reminded herself. She had worked hard to shed the forty extra pounds her body had once carried, and she had worked even harder to make it in the world of aviation, mostly a man's domain. She was Charlie, and Charlie was going to damn well enjoy this moment.

The song was a slow one, "Picture," by Kid Rock and Sheryl Crow. She only caught snatches of the words through the open door whenever someone entered or left, and she wished she'd listened to it more closely whenever they'd played it on the radio. When she got home, she was going to download the song so she'd be reminded of this night every time she listened to it.

"What's your first name?" she asked as he swayed them to the beat of the music. Earlier, she hadn't wanted to know, but now it seemed important.

"Ryan."

"Irish?" Although, inside the bar, she'd been more interested in the muscles stretching his T-shirt, she'd noticed how green his eyes were. There had been something unique about them, but danged if she could remember, considering the strong hands he was stroking over her back.

"All the way down to my Boston-born toes." He pulled her against him. "Come ova heah, sugah."

Hearing him speak with that accent did funny things to her. If she begged, would he talk like that while making love to her? With their bodies pressed against each other, she could feel the hard bulge of his arousal. She wanted to tell him how good it felt, that part of him rubbing against her. She wanted him to know that she was a hair's breadth away from leaping up and wrapping her legs around his waist to get even closer. She wanted him to tear off her clothes and show her all she'd been missing. Because she was positive he could.

All that was too much information, so she settled for pulling his face down, reaching for his lips. He let her play with his mouth for a moment, then he took over. Charlie had never, ever been kissed like that before, and felt as if she were in the middle of a hammerhead stall where she'd cut the engine and was plummeting nose down as her heart raced with the pure thrill of it.

"Jesus, cherub," he gasped when he tore his mouth away. "I wasn't expecting that."

Did he mean that in a good way or a bad one? The bar door opened as a couple came out, and the words to the song floated to them, something about putting her picture away. Ryan stilled, but before she could ask what was wrong, he began moving again. Something had changed, though. She could feel it in the tightening of the abs under her thumbs and in the very air separating them.

The song ended, and he stepped away. "Thank you for the dance, cherub," he said, then brushed his mouth over hers, a fleeting touch before he disappeared into the night.

Charlie stood alone and stared into the dark, wondering if she'd hallucinated him. She touched her tingling lips and knew he'd been real. Or maybe he'd just been a lost ghost who'd somehow managed to materialize for a brief return to earth. Tears leaked from the corners of her eyes at the feeling that she'd just lost something important.

"Utter nonsense," she admonished herself, swiping at the stupid tears with a balled-up fist. Lesson learned. Stay away from bars that men with sexy Boston accents might frequent.

On a whim, she put down the top to her Corvette, then got in and started up her baby. For the next hour, she slow-cruised along US 98 to Navarre before making a U-turn and heading home.

There was now one more thing to add to all the regrets she refused to think about. She would not think about a stepsister who blamed her for so many things. Some rightfully so, some not. She would not think about her mother who'd died brokenhearted.

She would not think of a stepfather habitually writing her from prison the first of every month, swearing his innocence and begging her to recant her testimony. Oh, and postscript, if he *was* guilty, which he wasn't, but if he was, he'd found Jesus and didn't belong there for that reason alone.

She would not think of the hate-filled glares her stepsister had sent her way during the parole board hearing five months earlier when Charlie had spoken against giving Roger Whitmore his freedom.

Most of all, she would not think about a man who'd made her feel beautiful, even if only for one dance.

As she rode home with the wind caressing her hair and the moonlight casting yellow ribbons of light dancing over the gulf, Charlie imagined herself seated in her plane as she pointed its nose up, up, up.

Never was she as happy as when piloting her red-and-white Citabria aerobatic plane, and she didn't need a ghost man who disappeared like a wisp of smoke, making her wonder if he even existed.

Up. Up. Up. She needed no one to soar.

Ryan opened his T-shirt drawer and removed his wife's picture. "I wanted her, Kathleen. More than I'll ever admit to you." He set the photo back on his dresser where it belonged, brushing away a piece of cotton lint. "Are you ever going to let go of me?"

She didn't answer.

Why did that particular song have to be playing? Why had he frozen up like a slab of ice on hearing those words? And after one of the hottest kisses he'd ever experienced, he should be covering a cherub's sweet body about now. Dammit to hell, when would he be able to put the past behind him?

Toeing off his shoes, he kicked them across the room. The heel of one caught the wall just right, leaving a gouge a quarter inch long. "Just great." He'd never had a temper before reading Kathleen's autopsy report, but if anything would unleash it, that fucking did.

His clothes landed in a trail that would have allowed anyone to follow him to the shower. Rage simmered under his skin, feeling like a bed of red ants lived there and were angry with him. So much to be sorry for. So many unanswered questions.

It would have been better if he hadn't read the words on that Goddamned report. Even better, if Kathleen had lived to tell him the truth. The answers had died with her though, leaving him to always wonder. Had she ever loved him?

The lingering smell of Buck's cleansed from his body, he slipped on a pair of sweatpants and, shirtless, walked into his spare bedroom and sat at the corner table. After searching through a box of gemstones, he chose one large gray-blue stone and two small ones. Two hours later, he held up a single polished opal pendant on a thin silver chain and a pair of matching earrings. The set would look great on Charlie, but he would never see her again. Wouldn't ever learn her real name.

He methodically took the jewelry apart.

Ryan breathed through his nose as he ran along the street in the gray light of dawn. Another mile and he could turn and retrace his steps home. Two weeks had passed, and still, he couldn't forget a curly-haired cherub.

Although he'd thought he was ready to venture out of his self-imposed exile from everything but work, he'd learned he wasn't, if the mere words of a song could turn his brain to jelly. Because that was the only excuse he could think of for walking away from the first woman to interest him since the third grade. He smiled, remembering his first sight of Kathleen Donavan.

"Kathleen Donavan!"

Eight-year-old Ryan O'Connor held his breath as Sister Mary Rose, hands on her hips and lips thinned in anger, stared real hard at someone behind him. It was the first day of the new school year, and already she was mad. They had all heard stories about the dragon, and he'd begged his mother to let him go to public school because, really, Sister Mary Rose was worse than having a monster living under your bed.

"Bring your book and that paper you're trying to hide to the front, Kathleen Donavan."

Although he wanted to turn his head and see who had caught Sister Mary Rose's attention, he forced his eyes to remain on a picture just past the nun's shoulder. The scrape of shoes sounded on the room's floor, and he almost smiled at how slow the dragon's victim was moving, but caught himself just in time.

A girl wearing her school uniform of a green-and-black plaid skirt, white blouse, and knee-high white socks entered the corner of his vision. He eased his head a little to the right to see her better. A long braid of hair almost reached her waist, and the color reminded him of the candied apples his mom always made for the school fair. Her eyes were a darker green than his, and they were trying to blink away her tears.

Right then, he hated Sister Mary Rose for making the girl cry. During recess, he approached Kathleen Donavan and told her he was sorry she'd had to stand in the hallway and say the Hail Mary so many times. It was the start of a friendship that led to being inseparable best friends, then boyfriend and girlfriend, then lovers, and finally husband and wife. It was the start of something he'd once believed would never end.

Ryan turned onto the street leading to his apartment. It bothered him that he couldn't remember why she'd been in trouble that day. He should remember, shouldn't he, the thing that brought them together? Already, memories were slipping away; how it felt when he held her, the lilt of her voice, the way her eyes sparkled with amusement when she teased him.

"Why, Kathleen? Just tell me that much."

Halfway up the sidewalk leading to his door, he stopped and put his hands on his knees, inhaling air into his lungs. It was probably time he broke the habit of talking to her, but she'd been a part of his life for so long that not talking to her seemed wrong. He'd loved her for what seemed like forever. He didn't know if he even knew how to love someone else.

Straightening, he did a few stretches before heading inside. With a foot on his bottom step, he stopped and stared. A champagne-colored, nose-twitching, floppy-eared rabbit stared back at him. The creature turned toward the door as if waiting for it to open.

"Not happening. Off with you, bunny." The rabbit didn't shy away when he moved beside it and nudged it toward the steps with his foot. It just hopped right back and pressed its nose against the wood.

Heaving a sigh, he opened his door. Mr. Bunny hopped in as if he lived there. The thing looked as if it had been kept groomed and well fed, and was obviously someone's lost pet. Ryan put a bowl of water down, then rummaged around in his refrigerator, finding two wilted carrots and a head of lettuce he'd forgotten was in there.

Mr. Bunny ate the carrots, then some lettuce, and finished off his meal with a long drink of water. Nose still twitching he—she?—plopped down on the tile floor, and after watching Ryan start the coffeemaker, lowered his chin to his paws, closed his eyes, and went to sleep.

A much-needed cup of coffee in hand, Ryan took a picture of the snoozing rabbit with his phone, and then headed for his computer. Once he'd made a dozen posters, he checked on his guest.

"You stay out all night, Mr. Bunny?" he asked the still-sleeping rabbit. Getting no response, he took his posters with him to the garage, grabbed a hammer and some nails, and spent the next thirty minutes tacking them to trees and light poles around the neighborhood.

Confident he'd soon be getting a phone call from a relieved pet owner, he returned home, showered, and dressed for work while his houseguest slept on. After a bit of deliberation, he decided the bathroom would be the best place to leave his temporary friend. Mr. Bunny barely stirred during the moving process, and Ryan left him, the bowl of water, and the remainder of the lettuce on a large towel he'd placed on the floor.

As he drove to K2 Special Services, he thought about Charlie. Was that even her real name? Not that it mattered since he would never see her again.

CHAPTER THREE

The Citabria's left wing dipped as Charlie angled her plane toward the Gulf of Mexico and the rising sun. It was her favorite time to fly, and over the gulf was her favorite place to practice her aerobatic maneuvers. As one hundred percent concentration was a must, she cleared her mind of all her problems.

Once there was nothing below her except sparkling emerald-green water and nothing above but endless blue sky, she checked her altitude and speed. Satisfied, she searched for a fishing vessel, usually an easy thing to find in the early mornings. Spying a slow-moving trawler, she positioned her plane at a ninety-degree angle to the boat. To warm up herself and her aircraft, she always began with an easy wingover maneuver.

Approaching at a right angle to the trawler, she lowered the plane's nose to allow for acceleration, then pulled up into a climb until the nose was twenty degrees above the horizon. After an eye scan of the area around her to be certain there were no birds or other planes nearby, she focused on the trawler. She rolled the Citabria to a ninety-degree angle, but before she could complete the maneuver, her oil-pressure light came on.

"Damn," she muttered, tapping on the glass. The pressure continued to fall, and she darted her gaze to the oil temperature, which was rising, a clear indication of imminent engine failure. That wasn't good. Not good at all.

"What's wrong with you, baby?" Adrenaline raced through her veins, and she took several calming breaths. Although she'd trained for such a catastrophe, she'd never thought it would happen to her.

Charlie took a deep breath and did nothing because that was what she had been taught to do. She brought to mind the instructor who taught her to fly.

"Pay close attention to this part, Charlie, and you might be one of the lucky ones who lives to see another day," Captain Shafer had said. Even after they'd become friends, he had been Captain Shafer to her. "If you ever have an emergency, you will want to panic. By all means, do that. Yell, scream, curse. Whatever. You can take three seconds to do that. Then do nothing."

"Nothing?" She remembered thinking at the time that maybe she had a stupid instructor.

"Nothing. But only for another few seconds. You're in trouble. You're going to crash and die. But you just might survive if you listen to me."

He had drilled those deceptively lazy brown eyes into hers. He had flown a fighter jet in the Iraq war, the first one—Desert Storm. Since maybe he knew what he was talking about, she had paid attention.

"I'm listening."

"Smart girl. Okay. You've taken the first three seconds to express your rage by yelling words that would make your mother wash out your mouth with soap. Then you've done nothing but take a few calming breaths. Both those done, you're gonna get that emergency checklist you have at the ready, because if you don't, I'll refuse to admit I taught you on the day I read your obit. Got that?"

She'd got it, and two years later when she had attended his funeral after he'd lost his fight against the cancer that had killed him, she'd grieved for the loss of a man who had become a dear friend.

"Emergency checklist, Charlie," his long-gone, smoker's voice rasped in her ear.

"Get a grip," she commanded herself as she grabbed the clipboard. Although she had it memorized, she had been trained to follow the written list so that, in a panic, she didn't forget to do something.

Straightening her spine, she edged up on her seat. Regulations notwithstanding, like any aerobatic pilot with a lick of sense, she wore a parachute, but she refused to ditch her plane unless it was a last resort. She'd worked too hard to own it to see it disappear at the bottom of the gulf.

Throughout her training to become a pilot, it had been drilled into her head that in case of emergency to first aviate, then navigate, and lastly, communicate. She reduced power and then turned the plane toward the airport before radioing the control tower at Pensacola International.

"Mayday. Mayday. Mayday. Pensacola Center. November Three One Golf Hotel declaring an emergency."

"November Three One Golf Hotel, Pensacola Center. State position and emergency," a calm voice answered.

"Center, I'm two point three miles southeast of Santa Rosa Sound. Losing oil pressure and engine temperature's rising. Request you call Pensacola Aviation Center to advise I will be making an emergency landing." There was a pause before the controller responded. She could have called her FBO herself, but it was faster to contact Air Traffic Control than to dial up the frequency for her fixed-base operator—her home base—and she didn't want to divert her attention from what was going on with her plane.

"November Three One Golf Hotel, Pensacola Aviation Center notified. You are cleared for a direct approach."

"Thank you. November Three One Golf Hotel, over and out."

"Good luck."

"Thanks," she whispered. A part of her wanted to keep talking, to keep contact with the voice on the other end of the radio, but getting her plane home would require all her attention.

"You can do this, Charlie. Swear to God you can." She patted the Citabria's dash. "Come on, baby, let's get you back to the barn and see what ails you."

After a quick scan of the next item on the list, she lowered the nose slightly to increase airspeed. The oil-pressure gauge needle was almost flat now, and she knew she had to land on her first try. She breathed a sigh of relief when she sighted the runway. The operations manager, David, stood outside, watching her through binoculars. A fire truck and the line crew guys were positioned alongside the runway. She hoped to God the fire truck wouldn't be needed but she was glad to see it there. As she aligned the nose of the plane with the middle of the runway, the engine quit.

"Shit!" Yelling and panicking wouldn't get her safely on the ground, so she shut everything out of her mind but the feel of her plane and the runway in front of her. An icy calm settled over her as she ticked off the remaining emergency landing procedures.

She raised her flaps to increase her glide range, then flipped off all the switches. Estimating her airspeed and the distance to the runway, her heart almost seized. She wasn't going to make it to the asphalt.

"You don't mind a nice, soft grass landing, do you, baby?" Slightly lifting the nose to get some wind under her, Charlie willed the Citabria to do the impossible. As she'd done everything she could except land, she pulled her seat harness tight, then visualized herself bringing the aircraft down on the field in front of the runway. If she hit any holes or ruts, it was entirely possible the plane would cartwheel, definitely not how she wanted to start her morning.

The next few minutes seemed like forever, but each time her mind tried to examine her life and the mistakes she'd made, she shut it down. Not the time to dwell on regrets.

"No tricks for this one, baby, you hear?" Suddenly the airport's windsock changed direction, indicating she had a tailwind. She made the pitch adjustment required to maintain the proper airspeed. Elation coursed through her when she realized the tailwind was just enough to push the Citabria to the edge of the runway.

"Yes, baby, yes!" She victory yelled when the wheels touched down on the asphalt. "Mama loves you."

Once the plane rolled to a stop, Charlie sat for a moment in an attempt to calm her pounding heart. Funny how it waited until she was safe on the ground before taking off like a greyhound's after crossing the finish line. She held her hands in front of her face and willed them to stop shaking, but they were determined to impersonate a wet dog after a bath.

The door flew open, and David poked his head in. "You okay?"

All she could do was nod as he reached in and released her harness. She grabbed his arm and climbed out of the plane, not letting go of him when her feet hit the pavement because her legs refused to support her without help.

"That was a beautiful landing, Charlie," he said.

Since she was alive, she had to agree. The line crew surrounded them, all talking at once. Even though all she wanted was to find a quiet place to recover her equilibrium, she high-fived them back and grinned a smile she didn't really feel.

"Back to work," David finally said, dispersing them.

When they departed and nothing blocked her view, she saw a local news station's reporter holding up a microphone to one of the firemen. As soon as the reporter realized Charlie wasn't surrounded by a horde of the airport's employees, he rushed over, thrusting the mike in her face.

"Did you think you were going to die?"

Charlie opened her mouth to tell him to get lost, but David, knowing her too well, pushed her behind him. "Did you get that landing on camera? I sure hope so because it was a thing of beauty." He whipped out a business card from somewhere on him and handed it to the reporter. "Call me later, and I'll set you up an interview with her. For now, leave her alone."

She leaned her head against David's back, grateful he'd stopped her from appearing like an ass on that night's news. The last thing she wanted to do was an interview later, but David would insist. Since he'd just given her time to get her act together, she would do it for him.

The reporter and his cameraman climbed into their news van and followed the fire truck back to the exit. "Thanks," Charlie said when it was just her, David, and the plane that had brought her home.

He turned and pulled her under his arm. "You're welcome, but don't think to get out of that interview. They already have it on film so there's no stopping it going on the air. We'll put the right spin on it. It'll be good business."

Of course it would be. She was a well-known aerobatic plane pilot, and she was also one of his flight school instructors. He would make sure that last bit of information was included in the interview, no doubt figuring he would get calls from wannabe pilots asking for her as their instructor.

"Yeah, good business," she sighed. Her student quota had just gone up. Not that she minded. The extra money was always good, and she enjoyed teaching anyone who loved to fly.

Gary, the FBO's head mechanic, rolled up in a tug. "You lost oil pressure?" he asked as he hooked a tow bar to the plane's wheels.

With an affirmative nod, Charlie turned to her plane. "Yeah, then the temperature rose. She's always been steady and reliable. I want to know why."

"I'm on it," Gary said, and then hauled her baby away.

If anyone could identify the problem, it was Gary. Knowing the Citabria was in good hands, Charlie slid onto the golf cart next to David. As if he understood she needed time to herself, he didn't talk to her on their way to the FBO. She settled back onto the seat, closed her eyes, and mentally relived the flight from the moment she'd walked around her plane doing her preflight inspection.

She was a stickler for procedures, and she couldn't see anything she'd missed that would have warned her of a malfunction. Sometimes shit happened, and that would probably turn out to be the case. Every pilot, especially one who flew aerobatics, had a scare or two in their career.

But she'd had two in a week, and that bothered her. Even though it had been in two different planes, with two different problems, what were the odds of that? Now she was being paranoid. It was just bad luck. That was all.

Too keyed up to think about almost dying, she lifted her face to the breeze and closed her eyes. Much nicer to think of a man who had danced with her under the moonlight in the parking lot of a bar. As soon as she'd arrived home that night, she had downloaded the Kid Rock and Sheryl Crow song and had listened to it every night since. Each time she played it, she would close her eyes and think of his kiss.

What had made him walk away? She'd had plenty of time since that night to think about it, and had decided it had something to do with a woman and a picture. After those lyrics played, he'd tensed, and his whole demeanor had changed. Was he married? Had a girlfriend, or broken up with one? It was useless to speculate, and the question would never be answered as she'd never see him again.

Stupid her, she'd even whispered his name late at night in the solitude of her home. *Ryan.* She was going to stop thinking about him, stop playing the song, and most of all stop saying his name just to feel it rolling across her tongue.

"We'll need a medic on this one," said Logan Kincaid, the owner of K2 Special Services, and Ryan's former SEAL commander.

Ryan was ready to get back in the action. He'd come to work at K2 two months earlier, and was happy to be reunited with his old SEAL team. They were all at the conference table except for two. Evan Prescott had been killed on an operation in Afghanistan, and the other missing team member, Cody Roberts, a.k.a. Dog, would be coming onboard in a few months.

The other two at the table were Jake Buchanan—Kincaid's brother-in-law—and Jamie Turner. There was no one Ryan trusted more than the men in that room. He settled in for what would likely be a long session.

The thing he liked most about working at K2 was that they planned the operations, not some behind-the-lines officer who may or may not have ever stepped onto a battlefield. He studied the map, focusing on the city of St. Petersburg. Then his gaze traveled over to Helsinki, Finland, a distance of about 185 miles as the crow flew. Wouldn't be easy getting into Russia, but by staging the operation in Helsinki, they wouldn't have to worry about getting shot at before they crossed the border. Once inside Russia, different story, but he'd take that any day over returning to Afghanistan.

"What's the latest on the daughter?" he asked.

Kincaid thumped a finger on his tablet and scanned the screen. "From what the medical specialist said, she won't last more than six months without a transplant. A congenital heart defect means she was born with the problem, right?"

Ryan nodded. "Yep. I'll need to meet with the doctor and find out what to expect and what particular medicines I need to have with me." He took a sip of coffee as his mind assembled a list of questions.

"The wife's seven months pregnant."

It took a second for Kincaid's words to sink in. Ryan jerked his gaze to the boss. "What?"

Jamie Turner drew something on a piece of paper and turned it toward Ryan. "Pregnant. Means she's going to have a baby."

"You could use some art lessons," Ryan said at seeing the stick figure with a baby bump. Not taking offense, as everyone on the team got off on going at each other, he rolled his eyes. "I know what pregnant means. How come this is the first I'm hearing this?"

"Because we just found out today," Jake, the lead on the operation, said. He crumbled up the stick drawing and hit Jamie with it, right between his eyes. "Sugar's turned your brain to mush."

Jamie—Saint to his teammates because he was about as pure as they came—grinned. "We're pregnant."

"Jesus, Saint, maybe you should move up the wedding," Kincaid said.

"Nah, she and Maria have everything planned. I just keep my mouth shut and show up wherever they tell me. Yesterday, I tasted six cakes 'cause they said my input was required; then they picked the one they both agreed on, a fancy raspberry something or other. Never mind I wanted chocolate." He sat back, his grin growing wider. "We're having a baby. Who cares what kind of cake we have at our wedding?"

Jake, Maria's husband, snorted. "Damn me, Saint. You're my new hero. My wife decided we'd wait one more year."

Ryan tried not to envy his friends. Jake, once known to the team as Romeo, was married to the one woman who had been able to tame him. Kincaid was married to Evan Prescott's widow and happier than Ryan had ever seen the man in all the years he'd known him. Now Jamie was not only about to get married to one of the hottest women Ryan had ever known, but they were having a baby.

He envied them all. They had what he'd once thought was his. As it had turned out, none of it was. Not even the baby. Before he did something stupid like upending the table, he stood. "Pit stop. Back in a minute."

He walked out and headed down the hall to the bathroom. After dowsing his face in cold water, he lifted his head and stared into the mirror. All he saw was a man who barely made it through each day without returning to Boston and tearing the town apart until he found his wife's lover.

Why had she turned to someone else? Why hadn't she tried to talk to him if she was having doubts? Had she ever loved him? Unanswered questions. They were killing him.

Not once had he cheated on her. Had never been tempted to. Kathleen had been his one and only from the day he'd first met her. It had never occurred to him he wasn't hers. Not until he'd read the autopsy report and learned she was two months pregnant. Big problem that. He'd been deployed for eight months. Unless she had been the latest miracle of Immaculate Conception, she'd definitely cheated. As hard as he tried, he couldn't forgive her.

Maybe she'd been lonely. Maybe she'd met someone and fallen in love. Maybe—to hell with the maybes, there was no excuse.

Nothing that could make him forgive her. He wasn't even sure he wanted to. Taking deep breaths, he formed an image of a lockbox in his mind and willed all thoughts of Kathleen into it, then closed the door and turned the key.

It wasn't foolproof. Sometimes she managed to escape, but usually in the deepest hours of the night, bringing back the anger and questions. It was all the talk of pregnant women that had him hanging over the sink gulping air in the middle of the day.

As his breathing slowed, he splashed more cold water onto his face, then wiped it dry with paper towels. With his rage back under control, he returned to the conference room. As he took his seat, he grabbed the dossier on the targets and began reading.

"You okay, Doc?"

Ryan glanced up and met Kincaid's eyes. "Yeah, sure. Why wouldn't I be?"

The boss had a sixth sense, a unique one. He could see things others couldn't. Not in the literal sense, but more like he always knew when something was off. Ryan had learned how to bury his emotions in the past year since Kathleen's death, however, and he spread his arms, palms up, as if he had nothing to hide.

"Just thinking about how to get a sick girl and a pregnant woman out of Russia."

Kincaid gave him a long stare before returning his attention to his tablet. "Here's a brief summary of the intel we have so far. Up until a little over a year ago, Demetri Akulov was a highly placed Russian official. Then he did something to displease Putin. What that was, the CIA isn't saying, and we don't really care. He was banished back to his home in St. Petersburg where he's been under guard ever since."

"Do we know how many he's got watching over him?" Ryan asked, glad the attention was off him.

"Two, around the clock," Jake answered. "Same two during the day, same ones at night. They trade off at eight in the morning and eight at night."

Ryan shook his head. "Stupid not to vary things."

"Yeah, but we're not complaining." Kincaid scrolled to another page on his tablet. "Four months ago, his daughter's heart condition worsened, and she needs a transplant, which is being refused as apparent punishment for his sins. At some point, he managed to get word to our government that if they would promise Sasha a heart transplant he would defect, bringing all his secrets with him. Of course, that was immediately agreed to. He'll only come, though, if his whole family is safely brought to the States. Wife, Tatyana, who we know is pregnant, Sasha, Demetri himself, and their poodle, Valentin."

"You're kidding me, right?" Ryan said.

"About what?"

Kincaid's expression was total innocence, but a slight twitch of his lips gave him away. The man had probably loved dropping the poodle bit on him. *Note to self: get animal tranquilizers from a vet.*

Ryan fell back into his seat. "Oh, I don't know. A pregnant wife close to giving birth, a dying daughter, a damn dog. Take your pick."

"How does a poodle say hello in Russian?" Jamie asked.

Refusing to bite, Ryan kept his mouth shut.

"I give up, how?" Jake asked.

"Beats me, but you two better find out." At that, Jamie burst into laughter. "Rescuing a poodle," he gasped. "You're never going to live it down."

That was probably true. "Swear to God, Saint, you really need to learn some dirty jokes if you ever want to amuse anyone but yourself." For some reason, that made Jamie laugh harder, and Ryan pressed his lips together to keep from smiling.

Kincaid stood. "I'm meeting Dani and the kids for lunch. Jake has all the intel you need to plan the operation." Halfway to the door, he turned. "There were dogs involved when I rescued Dani, but they were manly Dobermans. A poodle, though? That actually is funny." He left then, chuckling his way out of the room.

"Not another word or joke about poodles," Ryan warned when Jamie opened his mouth.

"Woof, woof," Jamie answered. "Oh, wait, they're yappers aren't they?"

Jake snorted, giving Jamie an eye roll. "Fun's over, girls. Let's get to work."

They were deep into the planning when the door opened, and the smell of hamburgers and french fries preceded Maria into the room. Ryan's stomach immediately growled in anticipation, and he glanced at his watch. They'd been so focused on all the details that he hadn't realized it was after one.

"You guys need to take a break." She dumped the bags on the table between them, and then took a seat next to her husband. After giving Jake a kiss on the mouth, she grabbed the sacks and divided up the food, hamburgers and fries for everyone but Jake. He got a broiled chicken sandwich on a multigrain bun and an orange.

The lettuce on his burger reminded Ryan of his guest, and he checked his phone for messages. Not a one from anyone claiming ownership of a rabbit. What was he supposed to do with the thing?

"What do you feed a rabbit?" Three pairs of eyes focused on him as if waiting for the punch line. "Well?" he asked when no one answered.

"What is this, the day for animal jokes?" Jake said. "I don't know. What do you feed a rabbit?"

"No, it's not a joke. I have a rabbit."

An orange slice held halfway to his mouth, Jake lifted one eyebrow as if questioning Ryan's sanity. "The question begs to be asked. Why?"

"It's not like I went out looking for a damn bunny. One found me, came right inside my apartment when I opened the door. It's obviously someone's pet, so I posted fliers around my neighborhood. No one's claiming it." He flicked open his cell and showed them the picture.

"Oh, he's so cute," Maria said. "You need to go to the pet store and buy rabbit food. I've heard you can even train them to go potty in kitty litter."

"What's his name?" Jamie asked.

"How the hell should I know?" He took back his phone and stuffed it into his pocket. "I just call him Mr. Bunny."

"You might want to be careful. Mr. Poodle might get jealous," Jamie quipped.

His three friends dissolved into laughter. "I don't even know why I'm laughing," Maria said. "Who's Mr. Poodle?"

That set Jake and Jamie off again. Ryan tried hard not to crack a smile, but the effort was an epic fail when, unable to help it, he joined in the hilarity. It felt good to be with the team again. Voluntarily isolating himself from family and friends, he had spent the past year devoid of laughter as he'd worked to deal with the hurt of his wife's betrayal.

He felt like he was finally coming home.

CHAPTER FOUR

After stopping at a pet store, Ryan arrived home with several sacks of rabbit supplies, along with a litter box and some kind of clay pellets to go in it. There were also toys in the bag. Who knew a rabbit needed toys? But the clerk had obviously pegged him as an easy mark and had loaded him up with *must-have* stuff for his new pet.

Not if he had anything to say about it. The fat-cheeked furball wasn't his. He hoped the real owners would see one of his posters soon and come claim the thing. They'd better appreciate all the accessories that would accompany their rabbit back home.

After spreading pellets along the bottom of the litter box, he carried it to the bathroom. Mr. Bunny was missing. Ryan finally found him under a pile of clothes intended for the laundry. "Dumb rabbit," he muttered. "I thought you'd escaped and gone home."

The rabbit gave a wide yawn, then hopped to the box Ryan had placed on the floor, jumped in, and did his business. "Someone's trained you. Did you escape when they weren't looking?" Mr. Bunny stared up at Ryan, his ears twitching as if listening.

Then he eyed the open door, crept over to it, peeked around the corner, and hopped away. Ryan followed him down the hall and into the kitchen, where the creature sat and stared expectantly back at him.

"I guess you're hungry." Although he'd never tell a soul he was talking to a rabbit, it was kind of nice having someone . . . rather, something . . . to talk to. Kathleen had filled their home with conversation and laughter, and the quiet had been one of the hardest things to get used to.

While the rabbit ate his dinner, Ryan took a grass ball and an orange rope carrot out of the bag, both of which he'd been assured Mr. Bunny would play with. In another bag was a woven grass tube the clerk said the rabbit would love to hide in. Grabbing a beer from the fridge, Ryan took it, along with the toys, to the living room. The rabbit hopped after him.

When he put the ball and carrot on the floor, the animal's nose twitched in seeming excitement, and he pounced on the rope carrot. Ryan sat on the sofa and tugged off his shoes, then propped his sock-clad feet on the coffee table. He drank his beer, chuckling as he watched the furball play. Still no phone call from a frantic owner, and he wasn't as unhappy about that as he thought he'd be.

At six, he picked up the remote and tuned to the local news channel. His stomach growled, and he debated whether he wanted leftover pizza or the remains of last night's Chinese takeout. Kathleen had been the cook in the family. Her steak and Guinness pie had been almost as good as his mother's.

Except when something reminded him that she had been pregnant—like hearing that Saint and Sugar were going to have a baby—he was finally beginning to think about his wife without rage consuming him or sadness so intense it brought tears to his eyes. He'd fought the urge to return to Boston and track down her lover, too afraid he'd kill the man. To keep his mind occupied with things other than her betrayal, he'd moved to San Diego—about as far away as he could get from the temptation of hunting down a faceless bastard—and taken a job as an EMT at a fire station. During his free time, he'd taken courses at the California Medical College.

It had been a surprise when Logan Kincaid, his former SEAL commander, had shown up one day and offered him a job at K2. Already restless, along with feeling isolated from family and friends—even though it was what he'd thought he wanted at the time—he jumped on Kincaid's offer. It wasn't Boston, but it was the East Coast and close enough to home.

Ryan downed the remainder of his beer, then set the bottle on a coaster. Questions still plagued him, and although he'd thought he never wanted to know more than he already did, he'd recently reached the conclusion that he needed answers. If he could find out why he hadn't been enough for Kathleen, perhaps he could put her to rest. Now that he was finally able to deal with her loss without the urge to do bodily harm, he was considering asking for a few days off to go home. Her lover was there, and Ryan didn't doubt he could find the man. After he came back from his upcoming mission, he'd talk to Kincaid about some time off.

"Forced to make an emergency landing, Charlene Morgan is lucky to be alive."

What the hell?

Ryan grabbed the remote and turned up the sound. He leaned forward, staring hard at *his* Charlie as she stood next to the reporter, a microphone held in front of her face.

"Did you think you were going to die?" the reporter asked.

The glare she turned on the man caused Ryan to grin. "Yeah, Charlie, that was a stupid question." He bumped a fist in the air, saluting her. "So you're a pilot? I'll be damned."

"Never once did I think I was going to die." She glanced at the plane behind her. "My baby always brings me home."

A stunt plane? His Charlie was a stunt plane pilot! Ryan sat back, his attention glued to the screen. In a million years, he never would have guessed it.

The reporter looked into the camera. "Charlene Morgan lost her engine while over the gulf, yet managed to bring the plane home, making a perfect landing. If you missed our lead-in, let's show it again."

"Wow," Ryan murmured when her plane landed on the edge of the runway. She'd caught the right side of the asphalt by a mere two feet. Suddenly, another man appeared on the screen and put his arm around Charlie. Ryan felt like growling.

"Wasn't that amazing?" the man said. "Not only is Ms. Morgan a star on the air show circuit, but she's one of our top flight school instructors at Pensacola Aviation Center."

Ryan tuned out the man and focused on Charlie. She seemed embarrassed by the praise and was inching her way into the background, letting the reporter and the man who introduced himself as the private airport's manager take center stage.

Was there anything between her and the other man? The airport manager had wrapped his arm around her as if he was used to doing so, but Charlie hadn't given any indication of a personal relationship between them. The segment ended, and the news anchor came back on the air. Ryan clicked off the TV.

"Charlene Morgan, you're just full of surprises." Forgetting about dinner, he stared unseeingly at the rabbit as he considered what he wanted to do now that he knew who she was. After a few minutes, he clicked on his phone and did a search for Pensacola Aviation Center. When their web page popped up, he memorized the phone number.

Two days had passed since he'd called and scheduled his first flying lesson. As he walked into the aviation center, Ryan wondered how Charlie would react to seeing him. He also wondered why he was here. Granted, he had thought of her often since that night at Buck's, but he wasn't looking for any kind of relationship with her or anyone else. It was the last thing he was ready for, and it would be a long time—if ever—before he could trust his heart to another woman. Yet, here he was.

And there she was. The woman he hadn't been able to get out of his mind stood at the counter, too intent on writing something in a black notebook to notice him. He paused and studied her. She was a tiny thing, maybe an inch or two over five feet. Her pale blonde hair formed a curly cap around her head, again bringing cherubs to mind. The olive-green T-shirt and tan cargo pants did nothing to hide a curvy body.

"Hello, cherub."

Her back straightened, and she lifted her face, her blue-gray eyes widening at the sight of him. She was even prettier than he remembered. At her confused expression, he shrugged. "I'm your new student."

She grabbed the notebook and stared at it for a few seconds. "You're Ryan O'Connor?"

"In the flesh. It's nice to meet you, Charlene Morgan."

"Ah . . ." Wariness flashed in her eyes. "How did you find me, and more importantly, why?"

Why had he thought she'd be pleased to see him? It had been a mistake to come. "Listen, this was a bad idea." He reached for his wallet. "Let me pay up, then I'll take myself off."

The last person Charlie had expected to see again stood in front of her, holding out a credit card. When she'd seen his name as her first student of the morning, she hadn't connected Ryan O'Connor with *her* Ryan. All she'd thought was that he was her third new student of the past two days, and that David would probably be busy planning another emergency landing for her for the free promotion. Heat spread over her cheeks when she realized she was staring at Ryan like an idiot while he continued to hold out his card.

"Ahem, it's nice to meet you, too." She reached out to shake his hand and ended up with his credit card. That was beyond awkward, she thought as she lifted her gaze to meet his. Dang, he had beautiful eyes. They reminded her of the emerald green of the gulf when the sun shone on it, except they had tiny streaks of orange in the green. Never having seen eyes colored like his, she couldn't help staring.

"It's called heterochromia."

"Huh?"

An amused grin appeared on his face. "It means my eyes have more than one color."

"Oh." What was wrong with her? She'd never been this flustered by a man before. "Well, they're very pretty." Sheesh, now she was telling him he was pretty. What next? Would she blurt out that she'd had an erotic dream about him a few nights ago and then admit to waking up hot and bothered?

"Charlie?"

There was another thing—his voice. It was low and rumbly, and if that wasn't bad enough, his Boston accent about slayed her. She could listen to him talk all day.

"Charlie!"

"What?"

"Are you going to run that?"

She glanced at the card she'd forgotten she was holding. The smart thing to do would have been to give it back to him and send him on his way. The man was just too potent for her peace of mind. But the thought of him walking out that door, never to see him again, made her stomach feel funny, and not in a good way. If she could perform precision spins and snap rolls, she could surely handle a mere man. Except there was nothing mere about him.

"We'll run it after your lesson," she said, handing it back to him. Decision made, she headed for the Cessna, not giving him a chance to respond. She was too afraid he already regretted finding her and would decide to leave.

His footsteps sounded behind her, and she let out the breath she'd been holding. Normally, she spent the first part of a new student's lesson in the classroom before taking them for a brief introductory flight. There was no way she could sit next to him, alone in a room, and speak coherently, so . . . change of plans. Put her in a plane and nothing else mattered. She could ignore hot men who invaded her dreams. She hoped.

As she went through a meticulous checklist—more thorough than usual considering her recent mishaps—Ryan followed closely, asking intelligent questions. It seemed he had prior experience with planes, and curious, she turned to him.

"You've done this before?"

He eyed the plane as if he didn't trust it. "Mostly, I've just jumped out of them. It'll be nice for a change to land in the same one I left in."

Oh, now he'd piqued her interest. "Are you a parachuter?"

"No."

Okay, subject closed. Didn't mean it was closed for her. The man intrigued her, and her imagination went to work as she returned to her inspection of the Cessna. When she'd first met him, she had pegged him as military. If he jumped out of planes, maybe he was a PJ, or had been one. Pararescue Jumpers were heroes, parachuting into war zones to save wounded soldiers. She was dying to ask if her hunch was right, but sensed it wasn't the time.

"Do you want to sit in the pilot's seat?" Although the left seat was the one she normally took for the student's first lesson, it didn't really matter. She could control the plane just as easily from the right if necessary. What she wanted was to give him a choice, if he was a man who needed to feel he was in control, especially if he had the kind of experience she suspected.

"Not even." He glanced at the plane again, and it seemed to her that he gave it the stink eye. "You want to know the truth?"

Yes, she did. Charlie waited for him to look back at her, and she thought she saw a bit of fear in his eyes. It had to be her imagination. "And the truth is?"

"I'm not fond of airplanes. In my experience, they tend to get shot at."

So, it had been fear she had seen in his eyes, and he was or had been military. Something inside her melted a little at knowing this man, who seemed as if he should be afraid of nothing, was, in fact, human.

Not sure where her boldness came from, she slipped her arm through his and tugged him to the side of the plane. "I can almost promise you no one's going to shoot at us. You don't really want a lesson, do you?" She almost fell on her face when he jerked her to a stop.

"I don't, but I'll go up with you if you promise not to yell 'go, go, go,' and then smack me on the back of my thigh."

"And if I do?"

"Then I'll likely jump."

Lord, that grin of his curled her toes. "Then I best put a parachute on you." She didn't want to like him so much, but was finding it hard not to.

After she harnessed both of them into their seats and put their headsets on, she taxied to the end of the runway to prepare for takeoff.

If he didn't want flying lessons, just what was he up to? Had he thought about their kiss as often as she had? Maybe, but she seriously doubted he'd doodled her name along the margins of a romance novel, as she had. The only time she'd been able to put him out of her mind was when she was flying, and that irritated her.

The last thing she expected was to have him next to her in a plane. As she gained altitude, it occurred to her that she should have taken him up in her Citabria, turned the plane upside down, then refused to right them until he confessed his reasons for tracking her down.

"You never said how you found me," she said into her headset's mike.

He'd been looking out the window, and at her question, he turned those amazing eyes on her. "Saw you on the news the other night."

So he hadn't even needed to put any effort into finding her. Just saw her and poof, here he was. He probably hadn't even thought about her between the night he'd given her the most amazing kiss ever and seeing her interview on the news. Did he think he could still get in her panties? She'd certainly given him the impression that was possible at their first meeting—and it would have been if he hadn't vanished like a wisp of smoke—but she was over it.

He smiled, and her body parts called her a liar. Okay, apparently, she wasn't over him, but he didn't need to know that. Turning her attention back to piloting the plane, she flew them out over the gulf, her favorite aerial view. Would he appreciate the beauty below him?

"Look, dolphins," she said, and banked the plane so he could see them better.

"Cool." He pressed his face to the window, watching them until they disappeared, then his attention returned to her. "It's entirely possible you could teach me to like flying. Will you take me up again sometime?"

And there went that killer smile again. Sheesh, how was a girl supposed to resist that? They probably didn't, meaning he probably had a stable full of women's phone numbers stored in his contact list. So why was he seeking her out? That was the big question. All her old insecurities reared their ugly heads, laughing at her for even thinking he could want Charlene Morgan.

"I don't think that's a good idea." She forced herself to look away and turned the plane toward home, doing her best to convince herself that wasn't disappointment she saw in his eyes. There was no way a man like him would give much thought to a refusal from someone like her. He probably had seen her as an easy conquest, one quickly forgotten as soon as he got in his car and drove away.

So why not, Charlie? Bet the man would be crazypants fan . . . tas . . . tic in bed.

Charlie ignored—or did her best to—the voice in her head. She would have argued with it if she'd had a leg to stand on, but as she could only agree with it, she got mad.

When she taxied up to the FBO, David came out and hand signaled the Cessna into its parking space. He gave a careless wave and disappeared back inside when she cut the ignition. Charlie turned to tell Ryan good-bye, fully intending to send him on his way.

Their eyes locked, and before she could say a word, he leaned over and kissed her.

CHAPTER FIVE

As her mouth softened against his, Ryan closed his eyes, savoring the taste of her. He hadn't meant to kiss her. Not after she'd given every sign that she wanted nothing to do with him. But she'd turned to him, and he'd been sure she intended to send him away without ever seeing him again.

There had been such joy in her eyes when they'd been in the air. He hadn't seen that before they'd flown, so he could only chalk it up to how piloting a plane affected her. She'd looked at him with those damn blue-gray eyes and he hadn't been able to resist.

A part of him that he'd thought dead the past year had stirred, seen her passion, and wanted to take it into himself. The kiss surprised him as much as it seemed to surprise her. But he couldn't find it in him to care, especially when she kissed him back. She hadn't at first. Her lips had been firm and unyielding, but then . . . Christ, then, her mouth had softened and she'd leaned into him. Her fingers tentatively touched his cheek, feeling like a caress as gentle as a summer breeze.

The way she responded was almost as if she had tender feelings for him. That wasn't what he wanted, or hadn't thought he wanted.

All he'd sought from her was a few good times. Something that would relieve the need to be with a woman. Any woman.

He supposed the joke was on him because with this kiss, only Charlie would do. Not forever, but for as long as it suited them both. Breaking away, he leaned his forehead against hers and listened for a moment to her breathing, heavier than usual. But then, so was his.

"Have dinner with me tonight."

She pulled away and turned to stare out the pilot's side window. "I don't know if that's wise."

"Since when are we going for wise, Charlie?" He grabbed her clipboard and pen. After writing his cell number at the top of the sheet, he handed it back to her. "If you change your mind, call me."

Walking away without knowing if he'd ever hear from her was the hardest thing he had done in a while. But he managed it. As he drove home to change for work, he tried to figure out what it was about Charlene Morgan that called to something deep inside him. Yes, she was pretty, but not the most beautiful woman he'd ever seen. Yes, he loved the way her pale blonde hair curled itself around her head, and yes, he loved those opal-colored eyes of hers. None of those things were why, though.

As hard as he tried to identify what it was about her that had kept her in his mind since the night they'd met, he just couldn't put his finger on it. Whatever it was that attracted him to her was elusive, but it was there. That much he did know.

Ryan pulled into his parking space, parked his car, then jogged up the sidewalk. Entering his apartment, Mr. Bunny hopped up to him as if happy he was home. He leaned down and scratched the fuzzball under his chin. What did it say about him that he was beginning to like having a silly rabbit for company?

Two days had passed with no word from his favorite pilot. Ryan hung up the phone after talking to his contact in Helsinki and jotted down some notes from the conversation. After getting the important points on paper, his mind veered right back to Charlie. He didn't like that a tiny cherub who obviously never intended to call kept invading his thoughts. Other than her name, two kisses that had rocked his world, and that she was a pilot, he knew nothing about her.

Actually, he did know one other thing. She was as different from Kathleen as night was from day. Where his wife had been tall, Charlie was a tiny thing. Their hair was different; one had long auburn hair, the other a blonde cap of curls. Kathleen had been sweet and soft. He wasn't exactly sure what he meant by soft, but he did know whatever it was, Charlie wasn't it. Strangely, that turned him on.

Comparing the two was a ridiculous exercise, though, and he gave a grunt of annoyance. Thinking of his wife only caused pain, and thinking of Charlie only served to irritate him since she had obviously dismissed him from her life.

When Jake Buchanan and Jamie Turner appeared at his door, each attempting to enter first, playing a game of who could push the other out of the way, Ryan welcomed the intrusion. He sat back and watched them, trying not to laugh.

"Dumb shits," he said. It wasn't lost on him that his friends were intentionally acting like buffoons in an attempt to amuse him. He knew they were worried about him, and knew he wasn't the happy Doc they remembered.

Both thought it was the death of Kathleen that had changed him, and of course it had been. How could it not, when one lost the love of his life? The part that he didn't seem to be able to get over, though, he would never tell them. But he did his best to act like the man he used to be, or as much as he could remember of that man anyway.

"You two should take your act on the road," he said, giving a real laugh when Jamie did that special little trick of his and wrapped a leg around Jake's, putting him stomach down on the floor.

"Son of a bitch," Jake grumbled. "You'll pay for that." Seconds later, the two were wrestling on the floor of Ryan's office. When the boss appeared and leaned against the doorframe, Ryan wondered how he would react to the ruckus. He only knew Kincaid as a SEAL commander; he hadn't worked at K2 long enough to know what the man was like away from the rules and regulations of the military.

Kincaid looked at Ryan and rolled his eyes. "Fucking kindergarteners. When those two clowns finish their playtime, drag their asses to the war room. We just got some new intel."

Interesting, Ryan thought. Unless he missed his guess, Kincaid would have liked nothing more than to join in the fun. Maybe working at K2 might end up being like old times. One of the team's favorite pastimes to burn off tension had been to beat the shit out of each other. They had set up a ring with mats, and whenever they were at their base camp, they would have matches. Their commander had always pretended not to notice, and once, after a particularly frustrating op, Kincaid had even stepped into the ring and taken on two of them at once, coming out on top.

"Children, you heard the boss—time to go to work." Somewhat cheered by being back with his teammates, Ryan walked with his friends to the war room.

"You're set to go a week from today," Kincaid said without preamble when they entered.

Ryan nodded and took a seat across from the boss. "Things are getting dicey in that neck of the woods, so the sooner the better."

"That's why we moved up the date. No telling what Putin might get up to. Best we get the family out ASAP."

Kincaid slid a glossy photo across the table, and Ryan gave a low whistle. "You get us one of these?" The picture was of a boat, one of the latest toys in the SEALs' arsenal. The *Sealion* was a stealth watercraft, low slung, gunmetal gray, and sexy as hell. He glanced up at the boss. "How did you get your hands on it?"

"Let's just say that I'd have to kill you if I told you."

Jake grabbed the photo. "I can't believe we get to play with one of these."

"You'll have one more member added to your team," Kincaid said. "He comes with the boat."

"He got a name?" Ryan asked. An active SEAL on their mission, along with a watercraft that had only been whispered about? The higher-ups wanted their target bad.

"Doesn't everyone?"

There was amusement in Kincaid's eyes, which immediately put Ryan on alert. Was it someone they already knew? He tried to think of who it could be but came up blank. The *Sealion* had only been a rumor, and there hadn't been a hint of a name or names associated with it.

Jake looked up at the boss. "Would you care to share that name?"

"Nope."

"I hate surprises," Jake muttered.

"I'm aware of that." Kincaid met Ryan's gaze and smirked.

The boss was toying with them and loving every minute.

They spent another hour ironing out details, deciding where off the Finnish coast they'd put the *Sealion* into the water, and then where they would enter Russia.

Ryan was glad to get back to doing what he knew best. The past year, he had felt as if he'd been on some kind of autopilot, barely showing up for each day. The adrenaline of something to look forward to was welcome. As he brought the others up to speed with what their Helsinki contact had said, he realized his right leg was bouncing, something it hadn't done since he had learned Kathleen had died.

He was back.

Charlie pressed the last key of Ryan's phone number on her cell, then hit Cancel. He was heartbreak personified, and if she were smart, she would scrub him from her mind. The problem was that her efficiency apartment was closing in on her, and she really, really needed to get out, but she couldn't think of anyone else to call.

She'd dedicated all her time and resources to learning to be an aerobatic pilot, and had relegated herself to a life of doing without. No nice place to live, no friends, no nothing. Well, except for her Corvette, and because it was a bank repo, she'd practically stolen it. Also, she'd bought it right after Aaron had broken up with her, and she considered the rash decision to buy the flashy car akin to eating a five-gallon container of salted caramel chocolate ice cream when depressed. Just a more expensive pity party, that was all.

To hell with it, she would call him. She needed to get out and start having some kind of life outside of flying. Snatching up the phone from where she'd tossed it on the counter, she dialed Ryan's number again and refused to let her finger hit the Cancel button.

"O'Connor," he answered, sounding wary.

Well, she'd let two days pass since he'd given her his number, nor would she be in his caller ID. Guess he had reason to think she was a telemarketer or whatever. She wasn't sure what to say. Why hadn't she practiced something? Honestly, she wasn't even sure why she was calling him. The last thing she needed was a super-duper hot guy complicating her life.

"Hello? If this is a breather, you should know you aren't breathing heavily enough to turn me on. You have three seconds to change my mind. One, two, three. Okay, time's up. Bye."

The man was funny, and she laughed.

"Cherub?"

Sheesh, he knew her laugh? "Yeah." That was all she could think to say.

"Give me an address, and I'll come pick you up and take you to dinner," he said.

Wow, maybe she didn't need to talk. She kind of liked that. "No, I'll meet you. How does Dockside sound? Say in an hour?"

That way, she could leave whenever she wanted. He sounded disappointed but agreed. Hanging up, she raced to her small closet and tore through it, looking for something that wasn't a flight suit, jeans, or a T-shirt. She should've gone shopping before calling him. Would he remember the dress she'd worn the night they met? Probably not, but what if he was observant?

At the very back of her closet, she found a pair of white slacks and a blue silk blouse she had forgotten about, still with the tags on them. She had bought the outfit in anticipation of a celebratory one-year anniversary dinner with Aaron, but since that little event hadn't occurred, she'd never worn the clothes.

"Perfect," she said, and laid the slacks and blouse on the bed. Since the pants were white, that meant she'd have to wear nude panties. One quirk she owned up to was her love of sexy underwear. So what if no one saw what she had on under her clothes, she knew what was there. As soon as she'd lost weight, she had bought a supply of matching lacy panties and bras. Not that Ryan was going to see them anytime soon. At least, she didn't think so. The one night she'd been willing, he had walked away. He had some work to do to get her out of her sexy panties this time around.

"Whoa, Charlie, getting ahead of yourself." Who knew if he even wanted *in* her panties? After a quick shower and leg and underarm shave, she toweled off, glad she'd washed her hair the night before and didn't have to mess with blow-drying it. Her natural curls never frizzed—something she often thanked her mother for passing on to her—and all her hair needed was a quick brushing.

Which body lotion? She uncapped both of the ones in her cabinet and sniffed the vanilla chai scented one. "Nice, but too sweet." She didn't want to be sweet for Ryan, not on this particular night. She brought the second bottle up to her nose and inhaled. Not bad. She read the label. *A day at the beach sunshine fresh* was in script across the bottom. It did have a fresh, sunshiny smell.

Thirty minutes later, she stood in front of the mirror and assessed her sunshine-fresh-smelling self. Something was missing, but she couldn't figure out what. Maybe she should use more makeup. All she'd put on was a little eye shadow, mascara, blush, and lipstick. No, even that was more than she usually wore. What about jewelry? Other than the delicate silver cross her mother had given her on her thirteenth birthday, she rarely wore anything else. Earrings! The blue-beaded ones in her jewelry box would be perfect with the blouse.

Just the right touch, she decided, eyeing the earrings dangling from her ears. Time to go meet Mr. Hot Guy, and she absolutely wouldn't be disappointed when nothing came of it. The drive to Dockside only took fifteen minutes, and she pulled into the parking lot fifty-five minutes after agreeing to meet Ryan. She put her hand on the door handle, then stopped, grabbed her purse, and fished around for her lipstick. Sheesh, she was acting like a teenager on her first date. Even so, she applied another layer of color on her lips.

As she stepped around puddles left by an earlier rain, she noticed her toes, the nails clearly visible because of the white sandals she wore. Dang, she should have painted them. Not used to acting girly, it hadn't occurred to her.

"Enough, Charlie," she grumbled. She was what she was, and if he didn't like that, to hell with him. Satisfied she'd gotten her head on straight, she entered Dockside. The foyer was crowded, and why hadn't she thought of how popular the place was when she picked it? Not seeing Ryan among the people waiting for a table, she approached the hostess, thinking to add her name to the wait list.

"I have us a table, cherub."

Charlie almost jumped out of her skin, then she about melted as Ryan's warm breath wafted over the back of her neck. She turned and lifted her head, then lifted it some more. "Hi."

Those beautifully strange eyes of his crinkled at the corners. "Hi back."

He slipped his hand around hers and started walking. Unable to do anything else for more than one reason—like because he was big and strong, and because she suddenly wanted her hand in his—she meekly followed along. Which was damned strange. Charlie didn't do meek for anyone. Oh, she once had, but that had changed the day she found the courage to get on a witness stand and send her stepfather to prison. But she wasn't going there, not while her hand was engulfed by the hottest man she'd ever known.

"I got us a table on the deck. Thought you'd like that."

Okay, give Hot Guy bonus points. How he'd gotten them a table at the railing, looking out over the gulf when so many people were waiting, she didn't know. Apparently, he was a magic man. Their only two kisses had certainly been magic. Charlie wondered if she was so far out of her element that she'd somehow entered the stratosphere.

"Thank you for coming," he said, sounding as if he really meant it.

"I tried not to call you," she answered, then bit down on her bottom lip, sorry she'd admitted that much.

Green eyes with streaks of orange in the irises zeroed in on hers. He smiled at her oh so slowly. "Maybe I shouldn't tell you this, but I checked my messages probably a hundred times hoping to see one from you."

Oh. Oh, well then. Either he really had thought of her, or he was like one of those basket cobras that gently swayed to the soft tune of a flute, charmed the daylights out of you, then bit you. Warning bells went off in her head, and she decided she'd best keep her guard up. More than likely, Hot Guy was a player—definitely not what she wanted in a man, even short-term.

"Well, here I am," she said, then stared out over the water so she wouldn't drown in the eyes focused on her with an intensity she had never experienced from any man.

The reflection of the moon shimmered over the gulf, and out of nowhere she wished she were alone in her plane, just her up there in the night sky. Why hadn't she thought of doing that before she'd dialed his number?

She didn't belong anywhere near the man sitting across the table. He was too much. Too much man, too much for her to ever handle. What had she been thinking?

She stood. "I'm sorry. This was a mistake." Without waiting for a response, she fled.

CHAPTER SIX

What the hell? Ryan threw a twenty on the table, then followed his little cherub. "We have an emergency," he said to their waitress as he passed her. With his long strides, it was easy to catch up with Charlie.

"Where we going?" he asked, matching his pace to hers. She stumbled, and he clasped her elbow.

"Stop sneaking up on me like that." She pulled her elbow away, giving him a disgruntled glare. "*We're* not going anywhere."

"What did I do wrong, Charlene?" They reached her car and he blocked the driver's door with his body. "I'm just asking. I don't have experience at dating, you see." He glanced away, hiding the pain he knew showed in his eyes. There had only ever been Kathleen for him, and he'd never learned how to play the game.

"Yeah, right." She tried to push him away, sighing when he didn't move.

"Yes, that *is* right." He smiled at her expression of disbelief. Ryan knew he was considered good-looking, fit, and halfway intelligent. It did sound far-fetched, even to him, who knew it as the truth. "One thing you need to know about me, cherub. I'll never lie to you, and that's a promise."

Her gaze roamed his body, from his face on down, then back up. "Look at you. How can you stand there and say you never dated? Were you a monk or something like that, then decided you didn't like it?"

After the past year, he certainly felt like a monk. At what point when you met a woman you liked did you tell her you had been married? Just another thing he didn't know. What he did know was that he didn't want to have that kind of conversation standing in the middle of a parking lot.

"If you want to know why I haven't dated, let's go for a ride." He stepped away from the door and eyed the car. "I've never ridden in a Vette. Come on, Charlie, take me for a spin up the beach road."

"Are you a serial killer?"

Ryan sputtered a laugh. "I'm a lot of things, but that's not one of them." When she seemed undecided, he said, "I have no way to prove that, I guess, other than my word. But you don't know me, so let's do this. We'll go inside and ask for the manager. I'll give him my driver's license to copy, and we'll tell him that if you're not back in an hour to call the cops."

That seemed to satisfy her, and the tension lines around her eyes smoothed.

"Okay, you're not a murderer. I didn't think you were, anyway." She smiled and dangled her keys. "Wanna drive?"

"Hell, yeah!"

She dropped the keys into his hand, a smirk on her face. "I'm not stupid, you know. If you're driving, you can't strangle me." With that, she laughed and skirted around the back of the car.

Ryan grinned. His tiny cherub was going to be a handful. As

she opened the passenger door, he leaned over the roof. "Can we put the top down?"

Her face lit up. "Hell, yeah."

Once on the beach road, she turned on the radio, tuning it to an oldies station. When she turned up the volume to where it made talking impossible, Ryan relaxed. Maybe he wouldn't have to talk about his marriage after all. Marvin Gaye's "Let's Get It On" came on, and as he drove one of the coolest cars on the road with a woman he really liked sitting next to him, and the night wind blew across his face, Ryan felt something he hadn't experienced since losing Kathleen. He'd all but forgotten how light in spirit happiness made one feel.

Charlie sang along with Marvin, and although she didn't have a great voice, it wasn't terrible either. Unable to resist showing off, he joined in. The surprised look she gave him made him laugh. His family members were singing fools, and blessed with a beautiful voice, Kathleen had fit right in. At family gatherings—whether cookouts, at Christmas time, or for no reason at all—he and his wife had been the stars of the show with their duets.

No, not gonna think about Kathleen, not when he was with Charlie. Taking a chance, he reached over and wrapped his hand around hers. Either she was too caught up in the song to notice, or it was okay with her to hold hands. He hoped it was the latter. As the high-performance Vette cruised up US 98 under the moonlight, Ryan couldn't think of anywhere else he'd rather be right then. Not even with Kathleen, and that was epic.

"Turn in there," Charlie said, pointing to the access road leading to a state-owned picnic area. The place was empty except for two cars parked right in front of the pavilion. Two couples with five kids between them sat together at one of the tables, enjoying a dinner at the beach. Ryan parked the Vette away from them, at the far corner. He turned off the ignition and waited to see what Charlie wanted to do.

"Let's walk on the beach." Without waiting for his agreement, she slipped off her sandals, then opened her door. Halfway out, she glanced over her shoulder. "Coming?"

"Give me a sec," he said as he struggled to remove his shoes and socks in the cramped space.

"You can catch up with me," she tossed back, and off she went.

He watched her dance-hop over the rocky pavement, smiling as she skipped over the first sand dune the same way a child of six would. "I like her, Kathleen. A lot."

Not expecting an answer from his wife, he rolled up his pants, then did his own hopping over the stones. As he passed the families at the picnic table, the smell of hamburgers caught his attention, and his stomach growled. Did dating include giving up one's dinner when the date decided the restaurant *she* had picked didn't suit her?

Apparently, yes.

Since he wouldn't die from missing one meal, he dismissed that particular rule as insignificant. There was a cherub somewhere out there in the dark, and he intended to find her. He reached the top of the sand dune and paused to get his bearings. The moon was still low on the horizon, but bright enough to see Charlie standing at the edge of the water, looking up at the stars. He jogged down to the beach and came up beside her.

"You're wishing you were up there, flying among the stars, aren't you?"

She lifted her face toward his. "How did you know?" Then she grinned. "Stop sneaking up on me like that."

It was too dark to see her eye color as she looked at him, but it made no difference. He had their blue gray memorized. "I watched you when you took me flying. You love it. You live for it."

"Flying's my life." She returned her attention to the sky. "Sometimes when I'm in my plane at night, I just want to keep going up until I can touch one of those stars. I don't care which one." She turned in a full circle, and fascinated, he watched her. "Maybe that one," she said, pointing at Sirius. "Sirius, the dog day of summer. I'll touch him, I think."

Ryan stepped in front of her, blocking her view of the sky. "This is just dream talk, right? You're never going to point the nose of your plane up, knowing you'll not come down in one piece?" Something ripped at him, thinking she would even consider such a thing. "Right?"

Her gaze returned to him. "Every time I fly, Ryan, I point the nose of my plane up, never one hundred percent sure how I'll come down. No, I would never purposely do something like that. I'm just dreaming, that's all. If I ever have to go out, though, I want it to be when I'm reaching for the stars."

Jesus walked on water! Ryan was floored by this woman. "I was married," he said, surprising them both if the expression on her face was any indication. He didn't doubt his face showed surprise at what he'd just blurted. "I was married to the woman I had loved since the third grade." He turned away from her and headed down the beach. How was it that he was heartbroken by the loss of his wife, yet felt like he was ready to step off a cliff for the woman scurrying to keep up with him?

"You said *were*. Are you still?"

He walked faster, yet he didn't seem to be able to leave Kathleen behind. "She died."

"Oh God, I'm so sorry."

If he hadn't realized Charlie was two-stepping to keep up with him, he would have run. Away from her, away from Kathleen's ghost, away from a baby that wasn't his.

"She was pregnant," he said, then wished to God he could take those words back. They weren't meant for anyone's ears but his. He started walking again. The woman must be stupid. Instead of turning her back on him, she grabbed his arm and tugged him to a stop.

"Ryan, God, I don't know what to say. I can't imagine how hard it was for you to lose your wife and your child."

"The baby wasn't mine," the mouth he wished would shut up said.

"Holy shit."

Not quite his exact words when he'd read the autopsy report, but close. Done with talking, he turned and walked down the beach. The water cooled his temper as the cold waves lapped at his feet. It wasn't Charlie's fault his wife had been pregnant with another man's baby, and that fact slowly sank in. Letting out a deep breath, he stopped and waited for her to catch up.

"I sent my stepfather to prison," she said, coming up beside him. "It tore my family apart, and now my stepsister hates me. My mom . . ."

Ryan turned to face her when she hesitated. "Go on."

"My mom, she died believing I lied about seeing him molest my best friend. She refused to accept that Roger would do such a thing. My friend, she got a rope out of her father's shed, went into her closet, and hung herself. She did that after I went to my guidance counselor and told her what he had done. Mrs. Bronson . . . my guidance counselor, she called the police. The same day my friend killed herself, she mailed me a letter. She wanted me to know that she hated me for telling what I'd seen, that she had never wanted anyone to know. Because of me, she said everyone would talk about her, that our other friends would think she asked for Roger to do what he did and would say she was a slut."

Christ. Ryan took Charlie's hand and led her up to dry sand, then sat, pulling her down beside him. "Why would they think that?"

"You know how kids are, but I think that it was more like how she saw herself in her own mind. She thought Roger was handsome and worldly, and she had this weird crush on him. Whenever she came over, if he was around, she would flirt with him. Sometimes she would joke about taking him away from my mother, but I never took the whole thing seriously. If I had, maybe I could have done something to stop what happened."

There was regret and self-blame in her voice. "How old were the two of you?"

"Fifteen. I guess I didn't think much of it. At the time, I had a major crush on my biology teacher. I thought he was the hottest thing ever, but it never occurred to me to do anything but stare at him with dreamy eyes. I thought it was the same with her."

"Good God, Charlie, no fifteen-year-old is responsible for what a grown man does. He was the one who should have known better than to touch a young girl."

She huffed a weary-sounding sigh. "I know that now, but back then, it felt like I was the one who put that rope around her neck. On top of that, I tore my family apart, and my mom died of a broken heart. She never forgave me for talking to the police."

"You did the right thing, you know, even considering the consequences, ones you couldn't have guessed at when you reported him. If he would molest one child, he would do it again. You get that, right?" She flopped back onto the sand, and he followed her down.

"I get it, but if I had known the consequences as you say, I would have kept my mouth shut. Then five months ago, my stepfather came up for parole and I went and spoke against his release. Now Ashley . . . that's my stepsister . . . hates me more than ever. If not for me, her father would be out of prison."

"Why are you telling me all this?" A falling star shot across the sky and he followed its progress until it disappeared from sight. The night hadn't gone at all like he had envisioned when she had agreed to meet him for dinner.

"Because you shared a secret with me, and I'm guessing it's one you've never told anyone. Because I wanted you to know that you're not the only one whose heart hurts. But most of all, because I like you, and I don't want you to feel so alone. Because I think you do. Feel alone, that is."

Ryan kept his gaze on the night sky until he was sure he could speak without a catch in his throat. Why had he told her so much? All she had needed to know was that he had been married to his childhood sweetheart, just enough to explain why he didn't have dating experience. Her response made him feel as if she could see into his soul, a place he no longer invited anyone.

When he was sure he had control of his emotions, he lifted onto an elbow and stared down at the woman who seemed to see too much. "That's a lot of becauses, cherub."

He lowered his head until their mouths met, then paused, giving her time to push him away. Her hand snaked around his neck and he took that as permission. Like their previous two kisses, this one knocked his socks off. Or maybe it was because Charlie was only the second woman he'd ever kissed, and it was the novelty of it. He didn't think so, though. He thought it more likely that it had everything to do with the girl who didn't want him to feel alone.

Charlie tightened her hold on Ryan's neck, letting him know she wanted this, wanted his mouth on hers. His tongue slid across the seam of her lips, and she opened her mouth, welcoming him in. He groaned and covered the right side of her body with his. Warmth seeped into her at all the parts he touched.

Although she had only been intimate with one man—her ratfink ex-boyfriend—in high school, she had kissed a lot of boys. Most had bumbled their way through the experience, a learning process for them as much as her. One though, Levi Greenberg, had definitely known what he was doing, or so she had thought at the time. She mentally struck him off her one-person list of all-time great kissers and replaced him with Ryan's name.

"Ahhh," she said, her mind going blank when he nibbled his way to her earlobe and sucked it into his mouth.

His chuckle vibrated against her skin. "Was that a good ahhh, cherub?"

Was he kidding? "Mmm." Sheesh, not only had he stolen all the thoughts in her head but all her words right along with them.

Another chuckle as his warm breath tickled the hairs along her neck. From her ear, he made his way to the vee of her blouse, then his tongue did a long lick down to the first button. She fisted her hands to keep from ripping her shirt apart to give him better access.

"You taste so good." He swiped his tongue over her skin once more.

"Fresh," she said, then gave an inward groan. *Real sophisticated there, Charlie.*

He lifted his head and grinned down at her. "That, too."

"No, the lotion, it's some kind of sunshiny-fresh beachy stuff. Or maybe it's beachy-fresh sunshine. I can't think too good right now." If she stopped talking, maybe he would go back to what he had been doing. Actually, she should stop talking altogether, because nothing but nonsense was coming out of her mouth.

His grin morphed into laughter, and he flopped back onto the sand. What was wrong with her? Why couldn't she keep her mouth shut? Now he was laughing at her. Mr. Hot Guy probably wished he'd let her walk out of Dockside and into the night where he'd never have to see her again.

He reached over, picked up her hand, brought it to his mouth, and kissed the top of her palm, near her wrist. "I like you, Charlene Morgan. A lot. Can I see you again?"

Oh, not what she'd expected to hear, and her heart did a somersault while screaming, *"Yes!"* She rolled onto her side and the big hand he had wrapped around hers caught her gaze where their hands rested against his chest. She could feel his strong heartbeat, the *thump, thump* of it, under her palm.

"I'd like that," she said, lifting her eyes to his. Was he done with kissing her?

A smile curved his lips as he tugged on her hand. "Come here, cherub."

"And do what?"

"Whatever you want."

That was an invitation to sin if there ever was one. She pulled her hand from under his, then traced the outline of his lips with her finger. His smile faded, and he watched her face with an intensity that was both unnerving and exciting. She lowered her mouth to his.

She equated letting him into her life with shutting down the engine of her plane at the top of a hammerhead stall. Anything could happen, and it could be the most thrilling ride of her life, or she could crash and burn. Either way, she would have no regrets. That she promised herself.

One thing she'd fantasized about doing since the first night they'd met was exploring all those muscled parts of him. He dropped his hands to his sides, and other than their tangled tongues—busy tasting each other—he remained still. She understood his message that she was in charge.

With their mouths locked together, she unbuttoned his shirt down to where it was tucked into his pants, then slipped her hand under the material. His skin was smooth, taut, and hot. The little hum he gave when she trailed her fingers along his side encouraged her to be bolder, and she found the arrow of hair leading down his stomach to his belt.

She had never touched a man as muscle hard as Ryan, and all that power was sexy as hell. With her hand poised at his belt buckle, she asked herself if she was ready to go that far with him. From the time she had flown her first aerobatic plane, she had found her passion, discovering a strength and courage inside her she had never known existed. "Reach for the stars" had become her life's motto. This man was a shining star, one she couldn't resist. Refusing to allow her fear of rejection to keep her from what she wanted, she began to unbuckle his belt.

So fast that she yelped, he had her under him. "Not tonight, cherub. I promised to have you back in an hour and time's up."

Confused, she blinked up at the face hovering over hers. "I don't understand."

"What? That I'm not taking you on a public beach where anyone could come by, even though it's night? Here's the thing. I thought . . . no, I hoped, we would end up in bed, yours or mine, didn't matter. Then I thought we probably wouldn't see each other again once we both got what we wanted."

"But?" she asked when he paused and looked out over the gulf. If he said he didn't want to see her again, she might cry.

"But," he said, returning his gaze to hers, "what I said earlier. I want to see you again. I'm not looking for another wife, but I'm also not a man who gets off on seeing how many women I can sleep with."

He laughed. "At least, I don't think I am. Never had a chance to find that one out. I want a girlfriend, someone I can spend time with, someone who wants to be with me. So, before we go and screw up the chance of that happening by having a one-night stand, I want to tell you that I think I'd like for you to be my girlfriend. If you're interested, that is." Another laugh, one that sounded as if he were embarrassed. “Christ, I sound like a high school kid. You wanna go steady?”

Charlie was charmed down to her toes by his little speech. No boy in her high school had ever asked her to go steady, even though she had kissed more than her fair share of them.

“Well, do you?” he asked.

CHAPTER SEVEN

Ryan kissed his new girlfriend good-bye, then watched her Corvette until the taillights disappeared. Damned weird night, and damned weird stuff had come out of his mouth. He wasn't even sure he was ready for a girlfriend. But when Charlie had said all those *because*s, he couldn't imagine not seeing her again.

When her fingers had traced a circle over his belt, he'd come close to removing it for her so she could get her hand inside his pants. He had stopped her because he feared once they made love, she wouldn't agree to see him again.

So he had asked his dumb question, and surprise, it appeared they were going steady. He looked up at the stars that his pilot girl loved. "What a night," he said to them, then got in his car and headed straight for the closest hamburger drive-thru.

When he arrived home and walked inside his apartment, Mr. Bunny was at the door as usual to greet him. The rabbit hopped along behind him as Ryan made his way to the bathroom. After a quick shower, he grabbed a beer from the fridge, then decided he should call his new girlfriend to make sure she had arrived home safely. Slouched on the sofa with his beer, and a rabbit nestled between his legs, he dialed Charlie's number.

"Hey, cherub," he said when she answered. "Wanna have phone sex?"

"Not until I have your class ring hanging on a chain around my neck," she fired back.

"I knew I was forgetting something. You want my letter sweater, too?"

"You got one?"

He smiled as he pulled a throw pillow up behind his head. "No, but I could give you my dad's."

"Is he as cute as you?"

"You think I'm cute?" A little snort sounded in his ear, and he took that as a yes. "Stop that, Mr. Bunny." He pushed the rabbit's mouth away from where he was nibbling on Ryan's sweatpants.

"Hey, Ryan?"

"Yeah?" Was she going to say something sexy?

"If you tell me you have a giant, invisible rabbit as a friend, then I'm breaking up with you."

Laughter burst from him, and it felt good. "Nope, just a normal-sized living and breathing one."

"Sheesh, you had me worried there for a minute. Seriously, though, you have a rabbit for a pet? That's kinda weird, isn't it?"

"Not gonna argue with that, but in my defense, he adopted me. Showed up on my doorstep one day and refuses to leave."

"Softie," she whispered.

"Mmm, not always," he said, but doubted she'd get his double meaning. Even though their conversation wasn't sexually charged, he was getting turned on just talking to her.

"No dirty talk, Mr. Hot Guy, until I see that class ring." She ruined her stern voice by laughing.

"Tomorrow," he said. "Come here for dinner. I'll put it around your neck myself." Where the hell was the ring?

"Do I get to meet Mr. Bunny?"

"Absolutely." They agreed on a time, and he gave her his address. "Charlie?"

"Yeah?"

"I really do like you."

She made a *pfff*ing noise. "I should hope so. You did ask me to go steady, after all."

After he disconnected the call, he stared at the phone as doubt crept in. Was he going too fast with her, committing to something he wasn't sure he was ready for? After thinking about it for a few minutes, he waved away his misgivings. The going-steady thing wasn't real, just a game. And he did want to see her more than once, and more than just for sex. Whether that made her his girlfriend, who knew?

"We have a ring to find, Mr. Bunny," he said, as he carried the rabbit with him to the bedroom. An hour later, his closet torn apart, and the rabbit lost somewhere in the mess strewn on the floor, he found the ring in a shoebox. Also in the box were pictures of him and Kathleen.

Other than the one photo of her he kept on his dresser, he hadn't looked at any pictures of her since he had watched her coffin being lowered into the ground. Hadn't wanted to. He shuffled through them, stopping at one taken by his mom the night of the senior prom.

Kathleen had been beautiful, and he touched a finger to her hair, tracing the auburn locks down to where they disappeared behind her back. She had grown into her beauty. When they had decided to be best friends, she had hated her hair, the freckles across her nose, and the way her front teeth protruded. By her fifteenth birthday, her hair had taken on its deep auburn color, her freckles—which he had loved—had been easily hidden by a little makeup, and braces had given her perfect teeth.

He remembered the dress in the picture. She had dragged him with her to shop for it, so no surprise he could close his eyes and recall that afternoon. He had wanted her to take his mother instead, but Kathleen wasn't having it. "You have to like it, too," she'd said.

So he had sat in a chair outside the dressing rooms of some downtown Boston department store. The first two times she had walked out, he'd shaken his head. The third time when she appeared in front of him, he sucked in a breath. His Kathleen was stunning.

Two years earlier, his parents had finally saved enough money to take the family on a vacation to the home country. The dress was the same deep green as the hills of Ireland that he could still see in his mind's eye. The bodice, held up by thin straps over her shoulders, gave a bare hint of what was covered by the material, and the skirt swirled around the tops of her knees as she pivoted for him.

He reached out a hand and fingered the soft fabric. "This one." She had been his best friend since the third grade, they had talked about it and decided to be boyfriend and girlfriend in the ninth grade, and he fell in love with her on that day in a Boston department store.

It wasn't until he felt his eyes burning that he realized tears were falling down his cheeks. Angry that he still cried for her, he tossed the photos back into the box and slammed on the lid. He slipped his class ring onto his finger, than began putting his closet back in order. Under an old sweatshirt, he found a sleeping rabbit.

Ryan checked his watch to see he had a little over an hour before the grocery store closed. Leaving his new pet to his dreams, he went to the kitchen and made a list of the items he would need to make his new girlfriend an authentic Irish meal. Lots of new things in his life, he thought as he grabbed his keys. He hoped they were good ones—the job, the girlfriend, the rabbit—because he could certainly use some good.

Charlie fisted her hands at her sides to keep from putting a hole in the nearby wall. "I want my plane moved into the hangar." She poked a finger into David's chest. "Today." She had kept it stored on the tarmac, tied down at night like all the other planes because it was cheaper. Hangar space would take a bigger bite out of her funds, but she didn't care. With a nail driven into each of the tires, she could no longer deny someone was messing with her plane.

The airport manager spread out his hands. "We're full in here, you know that."

"Don't give me your bull crap. I've seen you squeeze in an overnight plane before. Squeeze mine in." David was a genius at making room when a pilot slipped him a few extra bucks.

"Fine, but only for a few days."

She kicked at one of the flat tires. "No, until we find out who's screwing with my plane, or would you rather attend my funeral?"

His face paled. "Jesus, Charlie, you know better'n that. Don't even talk that way, it's bad luck."

It was going to be someone's bad luck whenever she found out who was playing their nasty games. She eyed David. He gave her a blank look, then his eyes widened.

"You're not thinking . . . seriously, you don't think . . . dammit, you couldn't possibly think . . ."

"You're sputtering, David." She sighed. "No, not really. It's just that it could be anyone, you know. I don't know who to be suspicious of."

Her gaze roamed around the hangar, stopping on Gary. The top half of his body was invisible as he stood on the far side of a Learjet. As the head mechanic, he would definitely have the know-how, but what had she ever done to him that would make him want to kill her? Three other mechanics and five of the line crew guys huddled in a corner, drinking coffee as they waited for their day to begin. Charlie glanced at the clock. God forbid they started three minutes early.

Her first student wasn't scheduled until eleven because she had marked out time to start choreographing her performance for the air show. As her aerobatic plane now had flat tires, practicing was out. Whoever was doing these things had declared open warfare with the nails. She only had two weeks before the show, and although that was plenty of time, she hated leaving preparations until the last minute.

"Well, it's not me, so get that idea out of your head," David said, bringing her attention back to him.

She patted his arm. "I know. I'm just frustrated. No, actually I'm royally pissed off. Don't pay me any mind. You need to call the police and file a report about this."

"Ahh . . ." He kicked the toe of his shoe across the cement floor.

"Right. Bad publicity. Well, hear this. One more incident, and I'm calling them myself." Not waiting for an answer, she said, "I guess I'll go catch up on paperwork." Halfway across the hangar, she paused and turned. "I better see my plane tucked up in here all safe and sound tonight." Satisfied with his nod, she headed to her cubicle.

As she passed the other flight instructor cubicles, she began ticking them off. Scott? Had she ever done anything to him that would give him reason enough to mess with her plane? Rob? Hank? Derrick?

She ruled out her ex-boyfriend. What would he have to gain? Aaron had been the one to break up with her, so why would he be angry with her?

Then there was her stepfather, who had found Jesus right after she had testified against him at his parole hearing. If true—which she doubted—wouldn't Jesus frown on murder? Plus, he'd have to somehow get an outsider to do his dirty work.

The only person she knew who truly hated her was her stepsister. Charlie couldn't imagine Ashley deciding to commit murder, though. Nor would she know how to sabotage a plane.

"Gah!" She hated being suspicious of everyone. Who was she supposed to trust?

At her desk, the framed photo of her family before everything had fallen apart caught her eye. It had been taken at Christmas in front of the last tree they would ever decorate together. She'd been such a brat that day, mad because her friends were going to the movies while she had to stay home so her mother could get the perfect holiday picture of the family wearing stupid matching red sweaters.

They always decorated the tree exactly one week before Christmas, a tradition her mother insisted on. Charlie picked up the photo and stared at her fifteen-year-old chubby self. Still pouting when it was taken, she had refused to smile, and suddenly she was embarrassed by her behavior, especially all these years later.

Her stepsister, Ashley, always perfect, smiled brightly at the camera. They'd never had a great relationship, but they had mostly tolerated each other. Until it all fell to pieces, anyway. Did Ashley hate her so much that she would concoct some kind of stupid scheme? Charlie tapped her fingers on her desk for a moment, then made up her mind. Last she had heard, Ashley was still living in her father's house, and fishing her phone from her purse, Charlie dialed a number she still remembered.

"Hello, this is Ashley."

Half expecting that Ashley would have changed her number, Charlie squeezed her eyes shut. Her stepsister's voice was as perky as ever. "I-it's Charlene." Silence. "I just wondered . . . ah, I just wondered how you were doing." She should have thought out what to say first.

"What do you care?"

Okay, Ashley still hated her, but enough to want to kill her? "I just . . . I dunno. You left the parole hearing before I got a chance to talk to you. We're still family, you know, and I—"

"We're not family."

The line went dead, and Charlie dropped her phone on her desk. "Nice talking to you, too, sis."

The day Ashley's father had been convicted, she had confronted Charlie outside the courtroom. "How could you?" she had screamed, her face inches from Charlie's.

"So you think what he did was okay? Shannon hung herself because of him."

"No, she killed herself because of you and your big mouth. I wish my dad had never met your mother, then none of this would be happening. You ruined our lives. I'll always hate you for that."

Those were the last words her stepsister had spoken to her until a few minutes ago. At the parole board hearing, all her stepsister had graced her with were looks that said Charlie was no better than dirt. Charlie opened a drawer and put the photo in it, wanting it out of sight. If she hadn't said anything to her guidance counselor, would she still have her family and would her mother still be alive? One question had plagued her in the years since then. Had she really been the reason Shannon decided to put a rope around her neck?

Charlie hadn't meant to tell the guidance counselor. Troubled by what she had seen her stepfather doing to Shannon, she'd felt mad at everyone, and mouthed off to a teacher. Sent to the office, then to the guidance counselor, Mrs. Bronson had somehow gotten the ry out of Charlie. From there, her world had crumbled around ıer when the police got involved.

Guilt over destroying her family, and even worse guilt over Shannon's suicide, had ruined her appetite. To avoid the accusing eyes of her mother and stepsister, she'd stayed in her room when not at school. Even her friends avoided her, as if she had some kind of contagious disease.

Hurt and lonely, self-hatred drove her to consider taking her own life. Her father had been a commercial airline pilot, but he'd been killed in a car accident when she was nine. The lure of being with her dad had been strong, but in the end, she hadn't been able to take that final step. Her greatest worry had been that she would go to hell if she really were the reason Shannon had hung herself, and then she would never get to see her daddy again.

Then one day her jeans were so loose that they barely stayed on. She had stood in front of a mirror for a long time and stared at the girl reflected back at her. Her hair was dirty and stringy, there were shadows under her eyes, and she was at least ten pounds lighter than she had been before life as she had known it changed.

Charlene hadn't recognized herself, and something inside her said she could transform herself into a different person, one who hadn't caused so much carnage. She began to run every morning before school, she studied hard, and she decided to be a pilot like her father, except the new her wanted something more exciting than flying commercial airliners around the country.

Her phone buzzed, bringing her back to the present. When she saw Ryan's name on the screen, she smiled.

"No, I'm still not going to have phone sex with you," she said as a greeting.

"You're breaking my heart, cherub."

She doubted that, but she heard the smile in his voice. "What can I do for you, Mr. O'Connor?"

"Well, if you're not going to have phone sex with me, I guess nothing."

Her heart skipped a beat. Was he going to cancel their date? "Okay, so you're calling because?"

"Maybe I just wanted to tell my new girlfriend to have a nice day. We still on for tonight?"

"Oh, yeah," she said as her heart seemed to sigh in relief and return to its normal pace. "Can I bring anything?"

"Just your lovely self. I've got the rest covered. See you tonight, girlfriend."

"No ring, no girlfriend," she said. She had never been able to flirt so easily with other men, and wasn't sure what was different about Ryan that she didn't have to take ten minutes to think of a response. Weird, but nice. Definitely nice.

"Got that covered, too," he said before hanging up.

"Bye," she said to dead air, smiling.

Derrick popped his head up from the other side of the cubicle and waggled his brows. "I'll have phone sex with you."

"In your dreams. No, ewww, not even there. And stop listening to my conversations."

"Hard not to when I'm sitting right here, and, anyway, don't wanna stop when you get dirty phone calls. You expecting any more?"

Charlie shot him a bird on her way out to do an extracareful preflight of the Cessna before her student arrived. On second thought, she went to the schedule and signed out a different plane than the one in the book next to her name.

CHAPTER EIGHT

The aroma of an authentic shepherd's pie filled Ryan's apartment. It was the one Irish dish he knew how to make. He'd only had to call his mother twice regarding the meal he had planned for Charlie. Although his mother was happy he had a date, the first time he had called was tough as they both skirted any mention of Kathleen. She and his mother had been thick as thieves, and he couldn't help wondering what his mom would think if she knew the truth about his wife.

It had been one reason he'd fled to San Diego, to keep from seeing his family every day and at some point blurting out the truth. Although Kathleen had betrayed him in the worst possible way, he couldn't bring himself to tarnish her image in their eyes.

At the end of his second call, he had promised to come home as soon as he could manage a few days off, something he already intended to do for an entirely different reason than she could ever guess.

His plan for the evening was to give Charlie a taste of Ireland, as much as he could in a one-bedroom apartment in Pensacola, Florida. Irish music played on the stereo, and the pie was baking in the oven. For dessert, he would make her a coffee with Baileys and whipped cream.

He'd had a moment of indecision when deciding what to wear, then realized he was getting a little too crazy about his date night. "I have a date," he bragged to Mr. Bunny. The rabbit twitched his nose, and Ryan figured if the fuzzball could talk, he'd say, "About time." Couldn't argue with that, Ryan thought, as he eyed the contents of his closet.

Finally, he settled on a pair of comfortable jeans and a white button-down shirt that he left untucked. He rolled up the sleeves, then picked up his class ring—now on a silver chain he'd bought on his lunch hour—and tucked it in his pocket.

The doorbell rang and he walked barefoot to the door. Mr. Bunny sat in front of it as if waiting to see who was on the other side. Ryan picked up the rabbit and opened the door. "Look, Mr. Bunny, it's my girlfriend." And she looked entirely edible wearing white jeans shorts and a teal T-shirt that said, *Save a horse, ride a pilot.* Worked for him.

"Oh my God, you really do have a rabbit," she said, holding out her arms.

"That I do." Ryan handed over his pet, then brushed his lips across hers. "Follow me." He led her into the kitchen and waved a hand at his small table. In the center was a plate with some fancy cheeses and crackers he'd added to the grocery cart at the last minute.

"He's such a cutie," she said, rubbing noses with the rabbit. "What's his name?"

"Mr. Bunny."

She gave him a disbelieving look, then burst into laughter. "I heard you say that on the phone, but I just thought you were calling him that, you know, generically. Like, because he's a rabbit. He is a he, right?"

"Hell if I know."

"No kidding? You haven't looked?"

It hadn't occurred to him to wonder what sex the rabbit was, but if it was a female, it had better not be pregnant. He watched as she flipped Mr. Bunny over in her arms and separated the fur with her fingers. "I dunno. Kind of hard to tell, but I think these are little balls."

Ryan bent over the rabbit that had better be a boy and eyed the suspect balls. "Beats me," he said. "I guess I should take it to the vet, find out. Can you neuter a rabbit?"

"No, I can't," she said and chuckled. "Whether a vet can, I don't know."

"Smart-ass girl."

She lifted her face, and their mouths were inches apart. Suddenly, he didn't care about rabbits and balls. All he cared about was kissing Charlie. He put his hands on the back of the chair, caging her, and lowered his mouth to hers. Her lips were soft and warm, and he just kissed her, no tongue, no touching anywhere but their mouths. It was sexy as hell.

Keeping one hand on the rabbit in her lap, she lifted her other one and flattened her palm against his cheek. It was something Kathleen used to do, and he almost jerked away. "Charlene," he murmured to ground himself.

His cell phone buzzed, and he lifted his head. "I'm sorry, I have to answer that. Might be a work call." Kincaid had never called him at home, but with the way the planned operation was suddenly popping, it was a possibility.

He stepped back to the counter and picked up the cell. "O'Connor." As he listened, he glanced at the rabbit nestled in Charlie's lap and frowned. "What color was it?" He'd forgotten about the posters he had put up around the neighborhood. The relief at the man's answer surprised him. "No, it's not him." After hanging up, he made a mental note to go out and take all the posters down after Charlie left.

"Someone trying to claim Mr. Bunny?" she asked.

"Yeah, but he said his was white. I don't think he ever owned a rabbit because he hesitated when I asked him what color. The posters I printed were in black and white, so I guess Mr. Bunny could've looked white in them. Weird. Why would he want a rabbit?"

"Rabbit stew?"

"The hell you say." No one was making a stew out of his rabbit. "Listen, dinner will be ready in about a half hour. I'd planned for us to have a glass of wine," he waved a hand at the cheese and crackers, "while we snacked a little on those and talked. But I need to take the lost-and-found posters down." The thought of Mr. Bunny going into a pot was intolerable. He grabbed the wine bottle he had opened earlier and set it on the table. "Have some wine and play with him. It won't take me long."

"I'll come with you."

He walked over and gave her a quick kiss. "No, I'm going to run, and your beautiful legs won't be able to keep up. I'll be back in fifteen." After a detour to his bedroom to put on a pair of sneakers, he went back to the kitchen, and kissed Charlie again. "Be here when I get back, cherub."

"I'm not going anywhere until I get my ring," she said, smiling.

"Then we can have phone sex?"

"Sheesh, you have a one-track mind, Hot Guy."

"What can I say? I'm a man."

She gave him a push. "Go. I'm just going to sit here and get drunk with Mr. Bunny."

"Don't you dare get my rabbit drunk. Back soon."

Charlie watched him jog toward the door, admiring his very fine butt until it disappeared from sight. She picked up the rabbit and held him in front of her face. "I don't blame you for refusing to leave. He's definitely a keeper."

Mr. Bunny twitched his adorable nose, and she laughed. Setting him back in her lap, she poured a glass of wine. It had been an interesting evening so far. No man she knew would adopt a stray rabbit and then worry that someone might eat it. There had to be something wrong with him, some flaw she hadn't seen yet. In her experience, men just weren't that perfect.

Curious about him, she picked up her wine and, with Mr. Bunny nestled in one arm, went into the living room. The furniture was minimal, and there were only a few personal items. Some books stacked on a side table caught her attention, and she walked over and scanned the spines. Tom Clancy, Daniel Silva, and Lee Child. "So you like spies and adventure, Hot Guy." She liked Lee Child's Jack Reacher series, so that would give them something to talk about.

The left side of the sofa was more indented, and she decided that was where he sat to watch TV. The next time he called her from home, she would be able to imagine him sitting there, and she liked that. There wasn't much else in the living room that would give her a clue about him, and she eyed the hallway. She wouldn't snoop, but she was curious about his bedroom and would just take a quick peek from the doorway.

The bed was made up, and a cozy-looking deep-blue comforter covered it. Would she end up in that bed later? Still believing that he was too much man for her to handle, she wasn't sure that would be a good idea. Yet, the thought of never seeing him again didn't sit well either. Just as she turned to head back to the kitchen, a photo on his dresser caught her attention.

He said he would be back in fifteen minutes, and he'd been gone about five. Unable to resist, she walked to the dresser and stared at Ryan and the beautiful woman in a silver frame. She wore a gorgeous wedding gown, and her smile was one of pure happiness. Her green eyes, so much like his, sparkled with life. In the photo, Ryan was looking not at the camera but at his wife, and there was so much love in his eyes that Charlie felt as if she had been punched in the stomach.

What was she doing in an apartment with the hottest guy she'd ever known, one who would never look at her with stars in his eyes? Backing away, she spun and carried the rabbit to the kitchen and set him down. Where had she dropped her purse? The front door opened at the same moment she located her purse on the floor in the living room.

"Got them all," Ryan said, walking past her with a handful of posters.

Charlie swiveled and watched him dump the pages into a garbage pail. She didn't know what to do. What reason could she give him for leaving? *Hey, I snooped around while you were gone, and I've decided I don't belong here. I think I'll just go now and try to forget I ever met you?*

After he had disposed of the offending posters, he glanced at her, then stilled. "Charlie?"

"What?"

His eyes narrowed, and he stalked toward her, stopping so close that she could feel his warm breath on her cheeks. "Were you leaving?"

Yes, that had been her intention, but she couldn't bring herself to turn away from him and do just that. She also couldn't bring herself to lie to him. "I think it would be best."

"Why?"

"Because you loved her, and I think you still do," she blurted, and as the words fell like an unmovable boulder between them, she would have given anything if she could take them back. His eyes glittered, and all she could think was that she had poked a dangerous lion.

"I told you I was married, so of course I loved my wife. What brought this on, Charlene?"

The way he said her name told her she had ventured into forbidden territory. "I think I should just go," she said as she backed up.

He put an arm over her shoulder and flattened his left hand against the door. "No."

Hadn't she already decided he was a man she couldn't possibly handle? So why did the totally alpha male breathing fire at her excite her? Well, she had always loved the thrill of living on the edge in her plane, so maybe he gave her the same kind of buzz. "No? You don't get to say no to me, Ryan." She was taunting him, and she knew it.

"Then I'll just have to change your mind, cherub," he said right before his mouth covered hers.

Oh yes, playing with fire was about as good as performing one of her death-defying tricks. His right arm flashed in her eyesight as he put that hand against the door on the other side of her face. She was blocked in, and she loved that he seemed to want her to stay.

Then he backed away. "That was wrong of me. If you want to leave, I won't stop you. Just know that . . ." His eyes focused on a spot somewhere over her shoulder. "Know that I want you to stay."

"Okay," she said, apparently willing to jump into the fire feet-first, or was it headfirst? There had been something in his expression that had tugged at her, like maybe he didn't just want her to stay, but needed her to. At her agreement, a beautiful smile bloomed on his face, one that took her breath away.

He grabbed her hand. "Come with me. I'm taking you to Ireland tonight. It's a land of magic, and who knows, you might even see an enchanted bunny." At the entrance to the kitchen, he stopped and focused his unique green eyes on her. "But you have to let your imagination soar, Charlene. Can you do that?"

Charlie was a person who saw things in black and white. Not only that, but they had to be there in the first place for her to see. A part of her nature came from her training as a pilot where facts were crucial to one's survival. It had begun, though, on the day her beloved father was killed. That was about as black and white as one could get, and his death had stolen any imagination she might have had.

Yet, the man waiting for an answer made her want that lost imagination back. Not sure how to handle the depth of emotions swirling around inside her, she laughed. "I've always heard the Irish were whimsical. Guess it's true." She stepped up to him and pressed against his chest, laying her cheek over his heart. "No one has ever invited me to a magical land before."

He wrapped his arms around her and nuzzled her neck. "Then I'm your man."

If only, but she couldn't get the picture of Ryan and his wife out of her head. It just wasn't possible for a man to love like that twice in his lifetime. What didn't make any sense was his claim that she was pregnant and the baby wasn't his. If he really were her man, Charlie would never look at anyone else.

Trained to make quick decisions, she made one. It didn't matter that he would never love her the way he had his wife because love wasn't up for discussion for either of them. She would view him as a time in her life when she had caught the interest of an honest-to-God hot guy. She would just go with it and have fun. Then in a few days, or maybe a month, he would move on, and she would return to her comfortable existence.

So close to him, she could smell the spice of his aftershave, she took a deep breath, memorizing his scent. "Take me to Ireland, Ryan."

"Aye, cherub, I'd love to." He led her back to the table. "Sit here and prepare to enjoy my amazing culinary skills." The plate of untouched cheese and crackers was taken away. "You up for the whole experience? If you ordered our meal in an Irish pub, you'd get laughed out of the place if you drank anything but a good Ireland-brewed beer. I have wine, though, if you'd prefer."

"Oh no, I'm not going to get laughed out of here before I get my dinner. Whatever it is, it smells divine." And it did, so much so that her mouth watered. It seemed her choice of beer to drink pleased him because he grinned. Two frosted mugs were whisked from the freezer, and then the beer was expertly poured into them.

"To my new girlfriend and magic nights," he said, standing near her as he raised his mug.

Charlie tapped her glass against his, while furtively squeezing her thighs together because of the way he looked at her, as if he wanted her for dinner. "I'm good with both of those," she said, wishing she were cleverer with comebacks. Sometime later, probably around two when she was in her bed and unable to sleep, she would think of the perfect thing she should have said.

"And I'm definitely good with your being good." He set down his glass and put his hands on the table, then lowered his mouth to within an inch of hers. "Actually, I'd be even better with us both being bad." Not giving her a chance to answer, he covered her lips with his just as a buzzer went off. "Damn," he muttered.

She sat back and worked on catching her breath when he left her to turn off the timer. He put on oven mitts, then opened the oven door. "What is it?" she asked, when he set a baking dish between their plates, pleased that her voice was only a little shaky.

"Shepherd's pie. The real Irish kind." After dishing a healthy amount onto her plate, he sat back and watched her expectantly.

"Oh. My. God," she said after swallowing a forkful. "This is amazing, Ryan."

He took a bite. "Mmm, not bad. Not bad at all."

"You can make this for me anytime you want." The pleased smile he gave her sent little flutters through her. As they ate, the conversation centered around the rabbit and how he had showed up one day on Ryan's doorstep.

"I have to go out of town in a week, and I'm not sure what to do with him. Maybe I can find a vet I can board him with," he said.

"Oh, where you going?" And just like that his face blanked. Weird.

"I can't say." He stood and gathered their empty plates, set them in the sink, and ran water over them. Turning, he leaned back against the counter. "I should have made something up, said I was going home to Boston or something. But I promised I would never lie to you."

Although he didn't owe her any explanation, she appreciated that he hadn't tried to lie, but he'd certainly sparked her curiosity. "Exactly what do you do?"

He seemed to consider the question for a few seconds. "I work for K2 Special Services."

That told her nothing. "Never heard of them. What do they do?"

Again, he took his time answering. "Lots of stuff. We work with companies, helping them secure their computers against hackers. We teach drivers for CEOs how to keep their bosses safe when they're in a car."

"Defensive driving?"

"Defensive and offensive, and how to know which needs to be done when. Ah, let's see, we help companies through the legalities of doing business overseas."

Nothing there that would prevent him from telling her where he was going. That meant the company must do secret stuff.

"Does K2 also take jobs from the government, say, like the CIA or maybe agencies I've never even heard of?" Wow, he was good at blanking his face, but that alone was a tell. She waved a hand in the air. "No, don't tell me 'cause then you'd have to kill me, right?"

"And that would be a damn shame, especially since we haven't had phone sex yet."

Charlie burst into laughter. "Sheesh, Hot Guy, I thought you'd forget about that." He'd kicked off his shoes when he came back from collecting his posters, and standing there barefooted, wearing jeans and a white button-down shirt with the sleeves rolled up, he was just downright sexy.

"Not gonna forget."

She wiggled her fingers. "No ring."

"I already told you I had that covered." He reached into his pocket, and then held out his fisted hand. "Come here, cherub."

Was he kidding? The whole ring thing had just been a joke between them, hadn't it?

CHAPTER NINE

The surprise on Charlie's face delighted Ryan. He raised a brow when she just sat there gaping at him. "You're going to have to come to me if you want it." Would she? Although the whole ring thing had begun as a game between them, somehow it had come to mean something to him. What, he wasn't sure, and why he—a man of twenty-eight—wanted to go steady, he also didn't know. All he knew was that he liked her, and didn't want her seeing anyone else.

Was she seeing someone else? He'd never asked. They really hadn't known each other long enough to commit to any kind of a relationship, but the idea of sharing her made him want to hurt someone.

Yes! Barely refraining from making a victory fist, Ryan smiled when she came to him.

"Hello, girlfriend," he said when she stopped in front of him. She was a sexy little thing, and he also barely refrained from scooping her up and carrying her to his bedroom, where he would strip off her clothes and do wicked things to her body. Another thing he refrained from doing was blatantly reaching down and adjusting himself in an attempt to find more room in his pants.

"So this is real then?"

He trailed his knuckles down a baby-soft cheek. "Do you want it to be?" She chewed on her bottom lip, drawing his attention to them. They were full lips. Kissable lips. That much he already knew.

Finally, she gave a little shrug. "Why not?"

"You're such a romantic, Charlie," he said, grinning when she narrowed her eyes. "Stand still." He slipped the chain around her neck. He'd bought a long one so that she could keep the ring tucked inside her clothes if she preferred.

She picked it up and studied it. "This really is your class ring, isn't it?"

"Yep."

Blue-gray eyes lifted and met his. "Does this mean you won't be dating anyone but me?"

"Yes, that's what it means, and no one but me for you, right?"

"Right," she said, and surprised him by tugging him back to his chair, then straddling him.

"If I'd known I'd get this reaction, I would've given that to you as soon as you walked in the door."

"I guess we'll just have to make up for lost time." She wrapped her arms around his neck and kissed him.

Ryan clamped down on his need to take over, letting her explore his mouth. Her tongue scraped over his, and he loved the taste of her. Suddenly, she sucked his bottom lip into her mouth. Total turn-on.

Sitting on a hard kitchen chair wasn't where he wanted to be though. He stood with her still wrapped around him, and on his way out of the room, he reached over to the coffeepot and flipped it on. Ryan wasn't even sure she had noticed that they were on the move as she had her face buried in his neck and was licking his skin as if he were a lollypop.

"Coffee?" she murmured.

Okay, she was somewhat aware of her surroundings. "Yeah. Gonna make you a coffee and Baileys."

"With whipped cream?"

"Uh-huh." He fell onto the sofa with Charlie still glued to him.

"I love whipped cream."

All kinds of visions popped into his head, all of them X-rated. "Then next time, I'll buy the store out."

Her pelvis rested on his erection, and if she didn't stop moving, he was going to flip them both over and claim her as his. "Charlene, I'm one breath away from losing control here. I don't think either of us is ready for that." Had those words really come from his mouth?

She stilled, her eyebrows furrowing as she studied him. "I thought . . . I guess I thought this was what you wanted."

Ryan didn't know what he wanted. Not true. He did know. Her. Right then. Right there on his couch. "Believe me, it is."

"But?"

"What you just said is the *but*." He hadn't realized it until she'd said it, but it was the reason for the big stop sign flashing in his head. "You guess this is what I want, and I won't even attempt to deny it. But you have to want it, too, just as bad."

Troubled eyes stared back at him. "I do. It's just that . . ."

He waited, not willing to let her off the hook. He wanted to know her, to know her secrets and her dreams. Their relationship—whatever it was exactly—had started strangely from the beginning. They'd almost had a one-night affair, and he thought she had been more than willing for her own reasons, yet, he believed she had never done anything like that before. Why had she been willing to sleep with him when she hadn't known him, but hesitant after agreeing to be his girlfriend?

Her gaze lowered to his chest, and she sat back onto his knees. "I don't know how to explain this."

"Just say what you're thinking, Charlie."

"Can we have that coffee now?"

Ryan sputtered a laugh. "That's what you were thinking? Maybe I'm not as good at kissing as I thought I was."

Wide eyes lifted to his. "Are you kidding me? I've kissed tons of guys and trust me, not one of them was as good at it as you."

"Tons?" Just how many men had she kissed to think in terms of tons?

Her cheeks turned pink. "Sheesh. I didn't mean to tell you that."

She tried to push away, and he wrapped his hands around her waist, holding her still. "Well, you did, and now that that cat's out of the bag, you've got my curiosity in high gear. How many is *tons*?"

It didn't really matter to him if she'd kissed a thousand guys as long as she didn't kiss any man but him while they were together. The sense, though, that she needed to get something off her chest drove him to probe deeper.

"I knew I was going to screw this up," she said. "I mean, you can have any woman you want." She waved a hand in the air as if there were women surrounding them for him to choose from. "Why would you want me?"

What minefield had he stepped onto? The safest thing to do when that happened was to backtrack on the exact footsteps that got you in that fix, but just maybe Charlie was worth the danger of going forward. No way to know until he made it out the other side or something went *boom*. But he was a man who thrived on danger, so he pressed onward.

"Tell you what. You get your thoughts together while I make us that coffee. Then we're going to have a nice long talk. Before we're done, I'm going to tell you exactly why I like you. Okay?"

The nod she gave him was halfhearted, telling him she would probably rather be anywhere else about then. He lifted her onto the sofa next to him, then brushed his lips over hers. "Be right back."

Coffee made with a little extra Baileys to hopefully relax them both for what he suspected was a heavy conversation about to happen, Ryan paused before picking up the cups from the counter. His living room and kitchen were one big room, with a half wall separating the spaces, allowing him to see Charlie. Curled up in the corner of the sofa, she studiously examined her fingernails.

Why would she think she wasn't desirable? Although she was petite, she had a perfect body for her size. The short, blonde hair that curled around her head fascinated him, and he wanted to play with it, wanted to know if the curls would bounce back into place if he tugged on them. Between the hair and her blue-gray eyes, she really did remind him of a cherub.

That she was a stunt plane pilot performing death-defying tricks about blew his mind. Meeting her on the street, if asked what she did, that would be the last thing he would have guessed. He honestly couldn't wait to introduce her to his teammates, then watch their reactions when he told them she flew a stunt plane in air shows.

The woman was damn hot, but apparently had no clue. Why was that? He picked up the cups and returned to the living room. "Here you go," he said, handing her one.

"Thanks." She grinned. "Wow, that's a lot of whipped cream piled up on there."

He sat beside her. "Correct me if I'm wrong, but you did say you loved the stuff."

"I do."

She stuck out her pink tongue and licked up the top of the cream. Ryan stifled a groan. "You're killing me, cherub."

The woman who had no clue of her effect on him peered up at him. "Is that good?"

"Jesus, Charlie, who screwed with your mind?" Some asshole had to have done a number on her if she had to ask. That had to be the answer to what puzzled him about her insecurities. If the man was still bothering her, he wouldn't be for long.

Instead of answering, she wrapped her fingers around the spoon he had put in the cup and stirred the whipped cream into the coffee. "This is so good."

He tapped his cup against hers. "To secrets revealed. Tell me yours, Charlie."

Like a sailor in a bar after four months at sea, she tipped up the cup and practically chugged the contents. When she finished, a whipped-cream mustache lined her upper lip. He swiped his thumb over her mouth, tidying her up.

"Tell me about the tons of men you kissed."

Wary eyes searched his. "Why do you want to know?"

"Because you brought it up, so I think it's something you want to tell me. Remember, I said I'd tell you why I like you?" She nodded. "If you want to know, start talking."

"You drive a hard bargain, Hot Guy." With a drawn-out sigh, she set her cup on the table, then laid her head back on the sofa and closed her eyes. "In high school, I let any guy kiss me who wanted to. I was what the boys called a tease. I'd make out with them, but I'd never put out."

"Why was that?" He resisted putting his hand over the thumbs she furiously twirled around each other.

Yeah, why was that? Charlie thought back to her high school days and analyzed her behavior from an older, wiser perspective. She had been an insecure, overweight, stupid teen, trying to figure out how to be as cool as Ashley. When her stepsister had first entered her life, Charlie had been in awe. Ashley was everything Charlie wasn't. Beautiful, popular, and the boys liked her.

Charlie had wanted the boys to like her, too, but she hadn't known how to go about getting that from them other than to let them kiss her. The stupid girl she had been had thought she would find a boyfriend that way. A boy who would look at her like a dozen or so boys looked at Ashley. All she had actually accomplished was the claim to kissing more than her fair share of boys who wouldn't even acknowledge her the next time they saw her. Remembering those days now, she was embarrassed for the girl she had been, but she refused to make excuses.

Wondering how Ryan had gotten her to talk about a time in her life she'd rather forget, Charlie opened her eyes and saw only interest in Ryan's green ones. When she had admitted to Aaron that she had kissed several boys during her high school years, he hadn't been as forgiving.

"Which? The tons of kisses or never putting out?" She thought she would rather eat three green peppers in a row—the food she hated most—than have a conversation about her teenage years. How had Ryan even picked up on the careless comment she had tossed out? The man was entirely too perceptive, something she would have to remember.

He curled his fingers over the thumbs she hadn't realized she was twirling around each other. "Just because you kissed boys didn't mean you had to put out. If they thought otherwise, that was their bad, not yours. Do you want to tell me about that time in your life?"

If she wasn't careful, she could fall in love with her Hot Guy. "Yeah, I do." Which was a surprise because it was a time she'd tried hard to forget. "Long story short, I was a fat, geeky kid with a beautiful, popular stepsister. All the boys liked her, but she was a snob and only hung out with the"—she made air quotes—"'in crowd.' I dunno, I guess in my warped, insecure mind, I thought letting boys kiss me proved they liked me. That maybe I was popular like Ashley."

"Did they? Like you, I mean?" he asked, and by the softness in his eyes, she understood that he already knew the answer.

"No. A boy I might've made out with the night before under the bleachers would walk right by me the next day and not even see me."

He pressed his palm against hers, and held up their joined hands. "Look how small yours is compared to mine."

Hers was half the size of his, and as warmth seeped into her skin from his heat, a sudden longing to have the right to hold his hand anytime made her feel like crying. He might claim she was his girlfriend, but it was only a game to him, and games always ended with someone losing. From prior experience, that would be her.

She put her free hand over her face and groaned. "This is so embarrassing."

"Come here, Charlene."

Peeking through her fingers, she asked, "Why?"

A grin that seemed totally wicked curved his lips. "Because I want to make out with my new girlfriend."

"You gonna pretend you don't know me tomorrow?"

"Silly girl. I'll be proud to know you tomorrow and the day after that."

Oh, okay then. "No more talking?"

"Not unless you still want to know why I like you, then I'll have to talk, won't I?" He patted his legs.

Relieved he wasn't going to persist with his questions, she climbed onto his lap, facing him. "So?" she asked. His oddly colored eyes flicked over her, the heat in them making every nerve in her body tingle. The man had a killer smile, one that made her feel it was meant just for her. *Dangerous thinking, there, Charlie.* He might speak the truth when he claimed he wasn't a player, but she had no doubt he could sneak his way into her heart with little effort. She had best keep her guard up.

He tugged on a strand of her hair and then let it go. "It does bounce back. I've been dying of curiosity about that. So, why do I like you?" The corners of his eyes crinkled, and she would swear the little streaks of orange in his irises brightened in pure deviltry. "It's your ears. I'm wicked hot for them."

Laughter spilled out of her. Before she could catch her breath, she was flipped onto her back on the sofa, and Ryan was braced on his elbows over her.

"You think that's funny, cherub?"

Well, she had, but with his hard male body pressed against hers, and his mouth just inches away, her breath hitched as desire swept through her. His grin faded, and his eyes darkened to the green of leaves wet from rain. The scent of him washed over her, and she inhaled his smell deep into her lungs. She didn't think he wore cologne, but the spice of his aftershave and the clean smell of what she thought might be bay-scented soap made her want to press her face against his neck and lick him.

Caught in his intense gaze, Charlie slid her hands up his arms. Firm muscles flexed under her palms, and certain there was much to admire under the cotton material, she wished she had the nerve to ask him to take off his shirt.

He nudged her legs apart and settled between her thighs. She kicked off her sandals and rubbed her feet over the backs of his calves. She wished he would take off his jeans, too. With a grunt of what sounded like approval, his mouth claimed hers.

His kiss was playful, nipping at her lips—quick tongue licks at the corners, then brushes as soft as the feathery wings of a butterfly.

She had never been kissed like that before. In her experience, men were quick to go right for the tongue. Ryan toyed with her mouth as if she were a delicious dessert that he wanted to savor.

Deciding she wanted to play, too, she sucked his bottom lip into her mouth and held on to it with her teeth. A chuckle rumbled through him, and when she let go, he kissed a trail over her cheek to the side of her neck.

"Such a pretty pink shell of an ear you have, Charlene. No wonder I'm hot for it," he said right before his tongue swirled, damp and hot, around it.

Shivers rippled through her, and her body shook from the sensation. Heat pooled deep inside her, and she heard herself moan. In response, and even through the thick denim of his jeans, she felt his erection pulse against her stomach where he lay over her.

His mouth found hers again, and this time, his tongue swept inside. He tasted delicious, like coffee and Baileys Irish Cream. God, she wanted him. The man was melt-her-bones hot, and past caring if she was too forward, she unbuttoned his shirt, tugging on it.

"Off," she said.

Breaking their kiss long enough to yank off his shirt, his mouth came down on hers again as soon as he tossed it away. There were any number of stunts she performed in her plane that gave her a thrill, but this man topped them all. She wasn't even sure of her name anymore.

The naked hard chest hovering over her was even more than her imagination had conjured. She began at his shoulders and worked her way down to his nipples. Each place she touched on his skin seemed to grow hot under her fingertips. When she lightly scraped her nails over his broad back, then trailed her hands down to the curve of his spine, he grunted. He rocked his hips against her, the hardness of his erection rubbing her in places that made her feel hot and bothered.

With his tongue still making love to hers, she slid her hands down his sides, over his rib bones, and then ended her quest at the round metal button of his jeans.

"No, cherub."

His hand wrapped over hers, and she wanted to scream in frustration. "I'm not saying no." She almost cringed at how begging that sounded. It was impossible that she had mistaken his desire, not with the bulge in his jeans even now.

"I am," he said, taking his marvelous heat away when he stood. "I'm saying no."

CHAPTER TEN

He must be crazy. That was the only answer as to why he was standing there when a beautiful woman was on his couch, offering herself to him. Ryan fisted his hands and tried to get a grip on his raging lust.

The last thing he wanted to be to her was one of those boys who had kissed her, then ignored her. He sat on the edge of the coffee table and picked up her hand. It really was small compared to his, and so baby soft.

"You really are beautiful, and don't doubt I want you. I just . . . I just—"

She pushed herself up, and grabbed a pillow, holding it to her chest like body armor. "You just what?"

"We're not ready for this, not yet."

"I can't figure you out, Ryan. You're not like any man I've ever known."

"Is that bad?" He hadn't explained a thing, and it was no wonder he was a puzzle to her. Hell, he even puzzled himself.

Instead of answering his question, her gaze roamed over him, then her eyes lifted to his and she grinned. "It's kind of weird. You know, like our roles are reversed. Makes it interesting if you want to know the truth."

Her perusal of his body reminded him he was shirtless, and he caught himself contracting the muscles in his arms like a damned peacock showing off his tail feathers to a hot chick. For the first time, he resented that he hadn't spent his teen years learning about women and how to act around them. How to date them. He was sure he was screwing up with Charlie.

His rabbit hopped out of the kitchen and across the room, landing with a thud on his bare feet.

"Mr. Bunny, where've you been?" Charlie said, reaching down to scratch him under his chin.

Ryan peered down at the fuzzy creature sitting on his toes. "He likes to sleep in the kitchen next to the oven when it's warm."

She trailed her hand over Mr. Bunny's back, and the rabbit arched into her touch. Ryan remembered doing the same thing mere minutes ago when she had slid her hand over his back. Why had he gone and ruined that moment and what might have followed?

"I should go. I have to get up early tomorrow," she said, and stood, moving away before he could touch her.

He reached out and caught her arm, pulling her next to him. "Call me when you get home so I know you're all tucked in safe and sound. Okay?" When she nodded, Ryan lowered his mouth to hers, needing one last taste of her.

After seeing Charlie to her car and watching her drive away, he went back inside to wait for her call. Going into his bedroom, he stood in front of his wedding-day photograph and studied his wife's features. Pain slashed his heart to look at the two of them, remembering how happy they both had been that day. He was tired of hurting because of things he couldn't change.

At the buzz of his cell phone, Ryan picked up the photograph and put it in a drawer where it would stay until he stored it away somewhere. That he was finally able to take that step felt like some kind of milestone. A positive one. It was time to move on, time to make new memories, and he would do that with a pretty little cherub. He fished the phone from his pocket, then sprawled onto his back on his bed.

"Happy anniversary, girlfriend," he said.

There was a hesitation on the other end. "Anniversary?"

"Yeah." He looked at his watch. "Three hours we've been going steady. Does that mean we can have phone sex now?"

Silence, then laughter. "Sheesh, Hot Guy, you really do have a one-track mind."

He loved the way she laughed, spontaneous and carefree. "I think I've admitted that to you already."

"I've never had phone sex," she said in almost a whisper.

He sat up and stuffed a pillow behind his back. "No kidding? You're a phone sex virgin?"

Her soft chuckle floated through the phone. "I guess I am."

"Maybe we should correct that, Charlene. Mmm?" *Please say yes.* Growing hard at the thought of having phone sex with his cherub, he rubbed his palm along the inside of his thigh, and then over the zipper of his jeans.

"I don't know what to do."

"Ah, but you have me to guide you, so that objection has been obliterated. Any other reasons to say no you want to toss at me? You'll like it, I promise. Even better, you'll sleep like a baby afterwards."

"Okay."

Ryan laughed. "That was downright erotic there, Charlene."

"Now you're making fun of me."

"A little, *A mhuirnín.*"

"You sound so Irish when you say that. What did that mean?"

"*Tá mé an Gaeilge.*"

"I don't know what you just said, but it sounded sexy."

"I said that I am Irish, and *A mhuirnín* means darling." That was the extent of his Gaelic, but if she thought it sounded sexy, he might need to learn more Irish phrases. "Back to the phone sex." Her laughter was pure and long lasting, and he found himself laughing along with her.

"One track," she said between gasps.

"We've established that." It struck him that he hadn't felt this happy in over a year. If that was guilt he felt for experiencing a bit of happiness, he chose to ignore it.

"So we have," she said. "Well, phone sex instructor, start instructing."

She sounded so businesslike that he almost laughed again, but she'd agreed, and he wasn't going to do anything to divert her attention elsewhere. "What are you wearing, cherub?"

"Wow, your voice changed. Got all low and raspy. Sexy like."

"Does that turn you on?"

"Kinda."

Kinda wasn't good enough. "Tell me what you're wearing."

"The clothes you saw me in. I called you as soon as I walked in the door."

For what they were going to do together, she needed to be relaxed, almost sleepy.

"Here's what I want you to do. Do you have wine?"

"Yeah."

Keeping his voice low and intimate, he said, "Okay. Pour yourself a glass, then go take a shower. I'm hoping you have something scented to bathe with so you can tell me how sweet you smell. After you're all scented up, put on some sexy lingerie. If you don't have any, lie to me when I ask what you're wearing. Take whatever wine you haven't finished with you and get in your bed. Ah, before you do that, light some candles and turn out your lights. Then call me back. You and me, we're going to have the most burning phone sex on record." When she didn't respond, he pulled the phone away and looked at it to make sure they were still connected. They were. "Charlene?"

"I'm here. I have to tell you, what you just said . . . that's the hottest thing any man has ever said to me. Call you back in thirty."

Ryan tossed his phone on the bed and made a fist pump as he headed for the shower. As he soaped up, he played her last words through his mind. That no man had appreciated her enough to say hot things to her puzzled him. She was amazing in so many ways, and how had the men in her life not seen that?

Charlie sniffed her elbow as she read the back of the jasmine-vanilla-scented body lotion bottle. "Jasmine inspires sexy self-confidence while the vanilla scent soothes the soul," she read aloud. Well, she could sure use some sexy self-confidence, not to mention some soul soothing. Ryan had told her to put on something sexy, and she just happened to have a little teddy that she had bought to wear for Aaron shortly before he broke up with her. One she'd never had the chance to wear, and best of all, she wouldn't have to make up something when Ryan asked what she had on.

Bathed, scented, sexy lingerie on, candles lit, she climbed into her bed and picked up her phone. Nerves struck her then, and she chewed on her bottom lip as her finger hovered over the keypad. This would be the first time doing such a thing, and although the idea of it excited her, she wasn't sure she could go through with it.

Sex with Aaron had been okay, but her vibrator worked just as well. She had a feeling that making love with Ryan would blow her mind to smithereens. But phone sex? The whole idea of a man listening to her pleasure herself was just weird.

Maybe she could pretend. He would never know, would he? Experimentally, she tried moaning to see if it sounded real. At hearing the fake moan, she burst out laughing. God, she sounded exactly like a woman faking it. She tried once more, deepening her voice. Gah! That one was even worse. Nope, he wouldn't fall for it.

"You've never been a coward, Charlie, don't start now." Pep talk done, she lowered her finger to punch in his number. The ring! Shouldn't she be wearing it? Rolling out of bed, she returned to the bathroom and picked up the pretty silver chain. It still amazed her that he'd given her his class ring. She held it up to the light, admiring the emerald-green stone, then noticed writing on the inside.

May all your dreams come true, son. Love, Mom and Dad.

The inscription made her sad. From what Ryan had angrily admitted the first night she'd met him, it didn't seem as if his dreams had come true. Turning away, she slipped the chain over her neck, then returned to bed. Half surprised he hadn't grown impatient and called her, she picked up her cell phone and speed-dialed Ryan's number.

"I thought you weren't going to call," he said, sounding happy to hear from her.

Charlie glanced at the clock. Fifty minutes had passed since she had said she would call in thirty. "I almost didn't."

"Why's that?"

"Because I don't think I can do this." She stuck a finger through his ring and toyed with it. The rustle of bedcovers sounded in her ear, and she closed her eyes and imagined him in his bed. Was he wearing anything?

"Charlene, tell me what you smell like," he said, his voice soft and intimate.

Glad that he had ignored her misgivings, not making her explain herself, she lifted her arm to her nose. "Sweet, like the way night-blooming jasmine smells, with a hint of vanilla."

"And if I licked you, would you taste like vanilla?"

Sheesh, he would make a fortune if he could bottle that sexy bedtime voice. "I don't know."

"Close your eyes and run the tip of your tongue along the inside of your wrist. Pretend it's my tongue licking you."

Even though she thought it was a silly thing to do, she did as instructed. Holy Mama Mia! Her fingers tingled to their very ends when she thought of him doing that to her.

"Charlene?"

"Mmm?"

"What do you taste like?"

"Vanilla. I taste like vanilla, and a little like . . ." She licked her wrist again. "I dunno, like a flower, maybe."

He gave a satisfied sounding hum. "Just so you know, next time that will be my tongue on your skin. Now tell me what you're wearing."

The man was melting her bones and he wasn't even in the same room with her. "Ahem, well, I have on a pale blue . . . when I bought it, the description said it was angel blue, whatever color that is."

"Your eyes are angel blue, so I can see the color."

She had angel-blue eyes? "My ex said my eyes were ghost eyes." Why had she admitted that?

"Your ex was an ass, so forget about him. What you're wearing, is it transparent?"

Although she already knew the answer, she glanced down, then did a double take. Her nipples were puckered and she thought it was the first time they had ever done that. At least, it was the first time she was aware that they had. The man on the other end of the phone was clearly lethal.

"Are you looking at yourself, Charlene?"

How did he know? And oh God, she loved how he said her name, all raspy and drawn out, as if he savored saying it. "Yes," she whispered, a little embarrassed.

"Describe what you have on."

"Okay. Like I said, it's pale blue and see-through. The panty part barely covers my bottom and has a row of lace around the legs. The top has spaghetti straps, then there's some lace that stops right above my breasts, and the rest is silk."

"You're killing me, cherub," he said, and by the sound of his voice, maybe she was.

Charlie couldn't stop her smile. She'd never come close to *killing* any man in that way before Ryan. "What are you wearing?" she asked.

"Nothing."

The word hung between them as she tried to imagine his beautiful body—what she had seen of it was beautiful—sprawled out on his bed. "Where's your hand?" The question had blurted right out of her mouth before she could stop it. Even as she'd asked it, she knew the answer.

"Where do you think?"

Had she forgotten to turn the air on? Because suddenly she felt like she was on fire. "Ryan?" The nerves she'd felt earlier had disappeared, and she wanted to get in her car and drive right back over to his place so she could watch as he touched himself.

"Mmm?"

Her landline rang and she glanced at the caller ID. Why was David calling her so late at night? He never had before. "Hold on a sec." She set her cell aside and picked up her home phone. "I'll be there shortly," she said after listening to what he had to say.

She sighed in frustration. Her conversation with Ryan had ventured into foreign lands—for her, anyway—and she wanted nothing more than to stay and see just where his phone sex would take her. But someone had broken into the hangar and gotten to her plane. Damn. Damn. Damn.

"Ryan, that was the FBO manager on the phone. I have to go."

"What happened?"

His sexy, intimate voice had disappeared, replaced by an alert, *what dragon do I need to slay for you* one.

No way she would involve him in her problems. This thing between them was only a game, and he owed her nothing. "Not your problem," she said. "I'll call you tomorrow."

"Are you headed over to the airport?"

"Yes. Gotta go." She clicked off before he could ask any more questions, and before she found herself telling him her problems and leaning on him to take care of them. They weren't his responsibility.

CHAPTER ELEVEN

The airport's lobby was locked and it was dark inside when Ryan arrived, but he had noticed light pouring out of an open hangar door along the side of the building. Heading that way, he slowed at the entrance and studied the scene before him.

Charlie squatted under what he guessed was her stunt plane, peering up at the underbelly. Two men—one he recognized from the news segment as the airport manager—stood by with their hands on their hips. Each had the look of a man wary of what might come their way.

"What the hell?" Charlie said, her voice muffled.

In unison, the two men took a step back. They were afraid of his Charlie, and that made Ryan smile. He eased up behind them. "Someone mess with her plane?" he asked, and both men startled, swiveling as one to gape at him. "I'm Ryan O'Connor, a friend of Charlene's," he said, and held out his hand to the one he knew was the airport's manager.

"Who's Charlene?" the other man asked.

"He means Charlie, you idiot," the airport manager said, shaking Ryan's hand. "I'm David Haydon, the manager of this place."

"I know." Ignoring Haydon's surprised reaction, Ryan turned to the second man. "And you are?"

"Gary Thomas, the head mechanic."

"Is that the cops you're talking to?" Charlie asked from under the plane.

Ryan shook his head at the men to keep quiet, then scooted up behind her. Anticipating her reaction, he held his hand over her head to keep her from banging into the plane. "There a problem here, Charlie?"

She jerked back and plowed her head into his palm. "Ryan? What're you doing here?"

"You're my girlfriend. Where else should I be when you've got trouble?" Something flickered in her eyes, and if he wasn't mistaken, there was gratitude to go with her surprise. He caught her scent, and breathed her in. She was right, she did smell like jasmine with a hint of vanilla, and he did want to lick her. That would have to wait, however.

"What's going on?" he asked. Her eyes shifted to the bottom of her plane, and he followed her gaze. What the hell? "Why is there a black pentagram spray-painted on your plane?"

"Because someone wants me to crash and burn maybe? So they're putting a curse on me?" Her voice trembled as she spoke.

Ryan took her hand and pulled her out from under the aircraft. "There's no such thing as curses; you know that, right?"

"I know, but things have been happening to my plane, and now they're trying to mess with my mind."

"Whoa. Back up a minute. What's this about things happening?"

Instead of answering, she turned to the airport manager. "You called the police, right?"

The man crossed his arms over his chest, and shook his head. "No."

"Why not, David? Someone broke in. How do you know they haven't done something to any of the other planes?"

"Gary will check them out, but I'm sure it's only yours they messed with."

Ryan swallowed a grin as she got in Haydon's face, backing up a man twice her size. "You're avoiding my question," she said, poking him in the chest. "Why didn't you call the cops?"

The woman was amazing. Where Kathleen would have turned to him to fight her battles, Charlie seemed perfectly capable of fighting her own. Who knew he would like that? What he did know was that the cops would more or less yawn over someone's amateur attempt to curse her.

"It's bad PR, Charlie. I'm not calling the cops." Haydon took another step back. "I'll hire a nighttime security guard, okay?"

"Not okay," Charlie said, her voice rising. "Forget it. I'll call them myself."

Ryan decided it was time to step between them before she completely lost her temper. He wrapped his arms around her waist, pulling her away from her assault on Haydon. "I can help, but you need to tell me what's been going on from the beginning."

She leaned her head against him and sighed. "I'm not your problem, Ryan."

Seriously? He lowered his mouth to her ear. "You will never be a problem, cherub." He put his hand on her elbow, and then turned to the airport manager. "Take us to your office."

Close to an hour later, Ryan sat back in his chair. "And you didn't think to tell me any of this?" he asked, looking straight at Charlie, wanting to shake her for not trusting him enough to tell him what was going on in her life.

"It's not your problem," she answered, apparently fascinated by the hem of her T-shirt where she twisted it around a finger.

That burned. "I'm getting tired of hearing you say that." He lifted a chin toward Haydon, and the man took the hint and left, towing the head mechanic with him. When they were alone, he turned his chair so he was facing her. "Charlie, who in your life do you trust?"

"Myself."

He was struck by how fast she answered, with no hesitation. If ever he was in trouble and he wanted his family's help, all he had to do was pick up the phone. Within a day of his call, his parents and all of his siblings would be on his doorstep. Just because he hadn't chosen to burden them with his secrets didn't mean he didn't know they were there for him if he ever needed them. That she didn't feel she had anyone to lean on made him that much more determined to prove he was there for her.

"Do you know who would do something like that?" he asked.

Still picking at her shirt, she looked up at him. "You really don't have to bother yourself with this. I don't see what you can do about it anyway."

Quelling his temper, he leaned back in his chair. "I want to bother myself with whatever this is all about. As for what I can do, you might be surprised. I don't think I've mentioned my talents. I'm a former SEAL, and if you know anything about the SEALs, then you know we're highly trained, not to mention, we're kick-ass bad." He smiled when she widened her eyes. "I told you I work for K2 Special Services, and we . . . well, I can't tell you exactly what we do as most of it's classified, but I'm still highly trained and still kick-ass bad. I can help you, Charlie."

He hesitated a moment before continuing. "If someone hadn't actually tried to sabotage not just your personal plane, but your instructor one, I'd chalk the pentagram up to a prank. But this is serious shit, and you need me."

The woman who tried not to need anyone let out a sigh, one that sounded like relief. For a moment there, he'd thought she was going to refuse his offer, and when she did, he was going to run right over her refusal. Thankful it hadn't come to that, he leaned forward and took both her hands in his.

"Whoever's doing this wants to scare you. You get that, right?"

"I get it," she said as she stared down at their joined hands. "And he's doing a damn good job of it if you want the truth."

"Charlie," he said and waited for her to look up at him. "I'll kill him before I'll let him hurt you. We never got to finish our phone sex, and no asshole's gonna take that away from us. Okay?"

Giving him a little smile, which was what he'd been going for, she nodded. "Okay. What do we need to do?"

The trust in those blue-gray eyes about floored him, and he felt a very male need to be a hero to her. "We need to make a list of everyone you suspect." He reached over and grabbed a notepad and pen from the nearby desk.

Thirty minutes later, he sat back and eyed the short list of three names. With each one, he'd urged her to tell him why she might suspect that person. He no longer wondered if she was alone in this world. She had been. But now she had him.

"Okay, cherub, there's nothing more we can do about this tonight, so I'm going to follow you home. You need to get some rest. Tomorrow, I'll start doing a little investigating. Okay?"

A soft sigh and a weary nod told him she was tired, and seemed to be grateful he was taking charge. He stood and pulled her up, then wrapped his arms around her and held her close for a few moments. The only reason he didn't scoop her up and carry her to her car was because he knew it would embarrass her in front of her coworkers. Instead, he tucked her under his arm and walked with her back into the hangar.

"Gary found some red paint that almost matches your plane," Haydon said as they approached.

She pulled away and went to her plane, then bent at the waist and peered underneath. Apparently, she was more than pleased with the result as she practically threw herself at Gary and hugged him.

Without taking his gaze from her, Ryan asked Haydon, "Do you trust him?"

"Who? Gary?"

Ryan nodded.

"He would never do anything to hurt Charlie."

For her sake, he hoped that was true. It was obvious that she really liked both men, but Ryan would hold his opinion of them until he checked them out. In his line of work, he'd learned never to trust anyone, and Kathleen had taught him a new lesson. Even those you believed you could trust would betray you.

Charlie backed out from under her plane. Just seeing the pentagram painted over and gone from sight eased her mind. "Thanks, man," she said, giving Gary one more hug.

His cheeks turned pink, and he shrugged. "Not that I believe in any of that shit, but it was creepy, you know?"

Yeah, she knew. Whoever was out to get her had apparently given up on trying to damage her plane and had turned to trying to mess with her mind. Was it a coincidence that it was happening right before the upcoming air show? Aaron had waited too late to get his application in—something she used to do for him—so he wasn't on the program. Instead of blaming himself for that, maybe he worked it around in his mind until he could reason out blaming her. But to want to kill her?

As she turned from Gary, her gaze fell on Ryan. Although talking quietly to David, he focused his attention on her. What was he thinking? That he'd gotten more than he bargained for where she was concerned? Did he think she was nothing but trouble? If so, both her stepsister and stepfather would agree with him. Her stepfather was counting on wearing her down until she recanted her testimony, so she didn't think he wanted her dead. But Ashley? She would be ecstatic if Charlie disappeared from the face of the earth.

The man patiently waiting for her, though, was the only person orbiting her world right then that she trusted. As she paused to take him in, it occurred to her that she'd never been tempted before to literally drool over a man, but that one, sheesh, she could give a slobbering hound dog a run for his money. With those awesome colored eyes, the broad shoulders, trim waist, and lean hips, he was definitely Hot Guy. One side of his lips curved up as if he knew she was drinking him in, and he winked.

How sexy was that? A smile that she was sure was high-school-girl silly curved her own lips, and she went to him like a woman in a trance.

When she reached him, he pulled her to him and tucked her up under his arm, a place he seemed to like her being, and she loved it there. Aaron had never tucked her next to him as if she were the most important thing in his life.

"Ready to go home, cherub?" he asked.

"Yeah, I'm tired." And she was. Of whoever wanted to see her dead, of a stepsister who hated her, of a stepfather who wouldn't leave her alone, and of an ex-boyfriend who had never held her close the way Ryan did.

Even though she told him he didn't need to follow her home, he insisted. As his headlights reflected in her rearview mirror, she thought back to the moment when she became aware of him under the plane, squatting next to her. She had almost fallen on her butt from the surprise of hearing his voice near her ear.

A part of her had wanted to send him away, the part that had been forced to take care of herself from the time she was fifteen years old. The other half, the side she hadn't known existed until then, wanted to lean into him and put her troubles into his obviously capable hands. And as she'd felt the comforting heat of him next to her, she couldn't bring herself to tell him that she didn't need him.

When she pulled into her driveway, she expected him to blink his lights and go on his way. Once again, he surprised her by pulling up behind her, turning off his car, and walking up to her door. She didn't miss how he scanned the area around them, his body reminding her of a sleek jungle cat, tense and ready to pounce. Once he seemed satisfied that all was well, he opened her car door.

As he liked to do, he tucked her into him, but this time she had the impression he was making himself a body shield. Not since her father had died had anyone, including her mother, acted as her protector, and tears stung her eyes that it was a man she barely knew who had stepped into the role.

Her efficiency apartment was up one flight of stairs, and when they came around the corner and she saw her front door, she stumbled. The pentagram painted in ominous black was just too much, and she tried to back up.

Ryan tightened his arm around her. "Give me your key," he said.

It was then she noticed the gun he held down by his right leg.

"Whoa, cowboy, do you really need that?"

"Let's hope not."

Her hands shook as she dug into her purse, and that just pissed her off. Seriously, who drew pentagrams, anyway? Pretend witches? She'd never met one in her life, and the only person on her list of suspects who would play this kind of game was her stepsister.

From the first, when Charlie's mother and Ashley's father had decided their relationship was serious enough to introduce their daughters to each other, Ashley had made it clear she found Charlie lacking and had reveled in screwing with Charlie's mind. Sometimes it had been to steal a page of homework, always from the middle so Charlie wouldn't notice; other times, she would invite Charlie places, then leave without her.

The worst was the day she had asked if Charlie wanted to have lunch with her and her friends. When a smiling Charlie brought her tray to their table and took a seat, every girl picked up their lunches and walked away. Kids at the nearby tables snickered, and dying of embarrassment, she had forced herself to stay seated and eat her food while wishing the floor would open up and swallow her. Yes, Ashley was her prime suspect, but if it was her stepsister, she had to have help.

Once Ryan opened her door, he put an arm out, blocking her way. "Let me go in first. You stay right behind me." With his gun still down at his side, he stepped inside and stilled.

Not expecting him to stop, Charlie ended up with her nose pressed against his spine. Sheesh, the man smelled yummy. Not only that, but his back was washboard hard. She had the urge to slip her hands under his shirt and run them over all those taut muscles. Giving in to the need to touch him, she put her hands on his waist, right above his jeans. There wasn't an ounce of fat on him and she'd bet her small savings account that naked, he'd look just like those hot guy pictures women posted on Facebook, the ones where the guy had the V-line that women called sex lines.

His hand settled over one of hers. "Cherub, I'll take a definite rain check on your exploring my body, but now's not the time. Pay attention."

Embarrassed, she snatched her hands away.

He chuckled. "You can put your hands back on my waist if you want, *A mhuirnín.*"

Whenever he called her that, she felt as if she'd stepped into a romance novel where there was always a happy ending. It wasn't going to happen, and she'd best not forget that. Still, she put her hands back over his shirt, very much liking them there.

"Is that your bathroom?" He lifted his chin toward the only closed door in her efficiency apartment.

"Yes."

He stood off to the side when he opened the door, and brought up his gun with the familiarity of one who was accustomed to using a weapon. An alpha warrior type had never been on her hot guy radar screen before, but this one might change her mind about what it took to be on her hot guy list.

He turned and gave her a look that brooked no argument. "Pack whatever you need for the next few days. You're coming with me."

"I'm fine staying here."

His eyes glittered with a hardness she'd never seen in them before. "No. You're not. Are you going to pack a go bag or should I?"

Huh? "What's a go bag?"

After swiping his hand over his face, clearly signaling his exasperation with her, he sighed. "Sorry if I'm going all macho on you, but you can't stay here. Not if whoever's painting witches' symbols on your plane obviously knows where you live. Pack enough stuff for a few days, okay?" He put his fingers under her chin and lifted her face so that she had no choice but to look at him. "Please."

The man wore macho well, but it was the soft please that had her giving in. He was right, though, whoever the creep was knew where she lived. Besides, Ryan had a gun and she didn't. "I guess a motel's better than staying here."

"No motel. You're coming home with me."

CHAPTER TWELVE

Ryan toed Mr. Bunny out of the doorway as he led Charlie into his apartment. She moved to the center of his living room, crossing her arms over her chest. "Not one more word that you're imposing," he said when she opened her mouth. Like he was going to put her in his car and drop her off at some motel. He bit back a smile when she snapped her mouth closed and glared at him.

On the drive back, he'd debated the sleeping arrangements. His apartment was a one bedroom, and his preference would have been to have her in his bed, but not when he thought she might jump out of her skin if he touched her.

"I'll take the couch, and you can have my bed." He'd purposely bought an oversized sofa that would fit him for stretching out and watching weekend ball games. Besides, he was used to sleeping on any surface from the rocky ground to the hood of a Humvee.

"No. I'm small. I'll sleep on the couch." She marched over and sat in the middle as if claiming the space.

Well, that answered that. She had no intention of sleeping with him. Although he wanted to argue that she should take his bed, the defiant lift of her chin kept him quiet. "Okay, I'll get you a pillow and throw."

At some point, they had lost the easy camaraderie that had existed between them earlier. Whether it was because she was upset over her plane, or that she resented his pushing his way into her problems, he didn't know, as she wasn't talking. After snatching the extra pillow from his bed, he grabbed a blanket from the linen closet.

"Here you go. The bathroom's down the hall on the left. If you're hungry or thirsty, help yourself to anything you can find." Realizing his words were coming out clipped, he took a deep breath. She was so petite, and the cover and pillow he'd tossed at her almost buried her. "Is there anything you need, Charlie?" *Like talking about what you're thinking or just letting me hold you?*

"No thanks, I'm fine."

It sounded like a dismissal, and he could take a hint. "I guess I'll see you in the morning then."

"Okay."

"Goodnight, cherub."

"Nite."

At the hallway, he almost said to hell with it, went back and scooped her up, and carried her to bed with him. But she'd made it clear she didn't want his company, so he forced himself to keep going to his bedroom. Mr. Bunny hopped along beside him, and he picked the rabbit up, closing the door behind him. After tossing his furry pet onto the bed, Ryan changed into a pair of loose sweatpants. Laptop in hand, he nudged Mr. Bunny over and settled on top of the covers.

With the three names of the people she suspected, he started with the ex-boyfriend. Aaron Gardner had no priors that he could find, and bringing up his Facebook page, Ryan studied the man's photo, memorizing his face. "Cocky bastard," he muttered. In the picture, the man stood next to his stunt plane, wearing a flight suit and reflective sunglasses. There was something about his pose that told Ryan he thought he was hot shit. Scanning Gardner's posts, Ryan's already low opinion took a dive to the basement. In almost every one, there seemed to be only one goal—attract women.

What had Charlie seen in the man? Ryan had gone as far as he knew how to go, so he picked up his cell phone and called the Buchanans' number.

"I'm naked in the hot tub with my wife, so keep it short," Jake said in greeting. "What's up, Doc?"

Ryan shook his head at the old joke. "Are you ever going to get tired of asking me that?"

"Probably not."

"I was afraid of that," Ryan said, laughing. "I need to talk to your wife."

"Yeah? Why?"

"Just put her on the phone. She can tell you why after she hangs up."

Whenever they needed to dig up information, Maria Buchanan was their go-to person. If she couldn't find something on a computer, then it wasn't there. After telling her what little he knew of the three people on Charlie's list, he thanked her and went back to his own search.

Ashley Whitmore's Facebook photo showed a pretty, young woman with shoulder-length light brown hair. Her brown eyes had a hard glitter to them, though. Her lips seemed to be sneering, as if she looked down on those around her. Maybe it was his imagination, influenced by the way she had treated Charlie. Even so, Ryan took an instant dislike to her. Her posts were all about hair, makeup, and clothes—pretty much what Charlie had told him held her stepsister's interest.

It was difficult to pin attempted murder and curses on her, however. How would a woman who had bullied Charlie into doing her homework for her be smart enough to know how to sabotage a plane? Unless she had an accomplice. There was always that possibility, so he wouldn't rule her out. Other than a minor accident report, he couldn't find any dirt on her.

The last one, Roger Whitmore, Charlie's stepfather, wasn't on Facebook. No surprise there as he was in prison. Ryan read the newspaper reports of the arrest and subsequent trial. The pictures of him coming and going from the courthouse were of a man Ryan guessed women would find good-looking. Charlie had told him Whitmore was thirty-five when he'd been arrested. His full head of sandy-blond hair touched his collar, and he had the look of a man who worked out. On his right, holding his hand, was a woman Ryan was sure was Charlie's mother, an older version of Charlie. On his other side, also holding his hand, was Ashley.

Charlie was nowhere in sight in any of the photos. He made a mental note to ask her about that. Had she been separated from her family? It was obvious the man's wife and daughter supported him, which meant even Charlie's own mother had chosen her husband over her daughter.

"Who held your hand, Charlene?" he murmured.

Ryan tried to find the trial transcript, but wasn't sure where to look. He yawned and glanced at the clock to see it was after midnight. It was past his bedtime, and knowing Maria would find the transcript, he shut down his laptop.

With his hand halfway to the lamp to turn it off, he paused. Was Charlie comfortable on the couch? Mr. Bunny, curled up next to Ryan's side, squeaked, then made a little snoring noise. Ryan glanced at the rabbit and wondered what he was dreaming that made his nose twitch as if there were a dozen carrots dangling just in front of his face.

"Silly wabbit," he said. Quietly chuckling, he eased out of the bed so as not to wake Mr. Bunny.

At the end of the hallway, Ryan paused and observed his girlfriend. Was she still his girlfriend? He wasn't sure anymore, not after the way she had brushed him off. She was awake, sitting on the couch. The TV was on with the sound muted. He glanced at it to see what she was watching. Bull riding? With a grin at how she continued to surprise him, he decided she belonged in a bed. With him.

Charlie's gaze flickered to the eight-second clock off to the side of the screen as the rider flew up and his body flipped end over end. Dang, one more second and he would have made the bell. Chase Outlaw was up next—sheesh, that couldn't be his real name, but it was a kickass bull rider's name—and he would show them how it was done.

Without her even noticing his approach, Ryan was suddenly in front of her. He scooped her up, and then lowered his body with her cradled in his arms, and punched the Off button on the remote.

She wrapped her arms around his neck. "What are you doing?"

"Taking you to my bed."

Okay then. Charlie had thought because he'd first said he'd sleep on the couch, that he didn't want her in his bed. That had left her floundering, asking herself if he'd already tired of her. If he had, she wouldn't blame him. She was a hot mess of trouble.

He stopped halfway down the hallway and peered down at her. "If you have a problem with that, tell me now. If you don't . . . have a problem, that is, then don't say a word."

Charlie said not a word.

At the edge of his bed, they both looked down at the rabbit snuggled in a nest of covers. "Don't disturb him," she said.

"Either he goes, or you go back to the couch." The sexiest grin she'd ever seen in her life curved his lips. "Please say he goes."

"He goes."

"Thank you, God," he said. After lowering her down opposite his rabbit, he picked up Mr. Bunny and cuddled him in his arms.

As he carried his pet away in the crook of his elbow, she drank him in. Wearing only a pair of sweatpants that hung low on lean hips, he was without doubt the sexiest sight in her limited experience. His back was even broader than she'd imagined when her face had been pressed against it. There were freckles scattered haphazardly over his shoulders that she credited to the Irish in him, and before the night was over, she hoped she'd have the chance to count each one using her tongue.

He set the rabbit on the hallway floor, then turned, closing the door behind him. His gaze settled on her with an intensity that sent scorching heat through all parts of her, to places she was aware of and to places she'd never known existed.

"You look like you're going to eat me," she said as he prowled toward her. As soon as the words were out of her mouth, she realized what she'd said, and heat spread from her neck to her cheeks. "I mean—"

"No, cherub, don't be taking it back." The orange streaks in his eyes seemed like pure flames of fire. "Where shall I start my feast?"

"Ah . . ." Wherever he wanted was good with her.

"Yeah, ah." He smiled as he looked down at her. "Remove before flight. Sounds like a great plan."

She glanced down at the logo on her shirt. In her haste to throw some things into an overnight bag, all she'd tossed into it for night wear was an old pair of comfortable boxers and the faded blue T-shirt.

Stretching out next to her, he cradled the side of her face with his hand, then lowered his mouth to hers, and with nothing but his lips touching hers, he seduced her with his kisses. Before she'd had enough of kissing him, he leaned away and slipped his fingers under the hem of her shirt.

"May I?" he asked even as he tugged the material up.

"Yes." Because that didn't sound adequate enough, she said, "Yes, please." His answering smile sent an arrow through her heart, where it lodged, most likely a permanent affliction. The T-shirt was tossed over his shoulder, then he pulled her against him, her bare breasts to his bare chest.

He lifted the ring dangling at the end of the silver chain and studied it. "Are you all right with this?"

Wearing his ring? "I'll admit I thought you were just kidding around, but I like pretending I belong to someone. So yes, I'm all right with it for as long as you want. Just let me know when you want your ring back," she said to make sure he knew that she understood the ring was not hers to keep.

"I'm not even sure which one of those things you said to address first." He lowered the ring and tucked it into the valley of her breasts. "Looks good there."

There was warmth in his eyes as he put his hand on the side of her waist, then glided his palm up her body. At the curve of her breast, he paused and rubbed his thumb over her skin, the barest of touches that gave her goose bumps.

"Okay, Charlene, here's the truth. Maybe I was playing a game with you in the beginning, but no more. I want you for a real girlfriend, not a pretend one. Let's make that for as long as we both want."

When he paused, seeming to wait for a response, she nodded. "I'd like that." Understatement there. She'd freaking love it.

"Good." His hand moved up and over, until his fingers were spread over her left breast. "As for pretending you belong to someone, stop it. Until being together no longer feels right to us, you belong to me, and I belong to you. Okay?"

Another nod was all she could give him. If she tried to speak, he would hear her voice tremble.

"And last but definitely not least, when I asked if you were all right with this, I wasn't talking about my ring. I meant making love with me tonight. Are you?"

At some point, she was going to have to talk, but the lump in her throat was still there, so she nodded. Again. Although she hadn't missed his caveat that their time together would only last as long as it felt right for both of them, she decided to throw caution to the wind. Wasn't that how she lived her life every time she pointed her aerobatic plane nose up?

"Have you forgotten how to talk?"

From the laughter she heard in his voice, she knew he was teasing her. It was so novel to have someone tease her that the lump in her throat doubled in size. To keep from answering, she attacked him.

"Okay then," he said, spreading out his arms when she straddled him. "Have at me. Just think of me as your boy toy."

That made her laugh. "How about that. You just handed me the keys to the candy store, Hot Guy." Yay her, she could talk again. She ground her pelvis against the bulge in his sweatpants. "Did I tell you I have an insatiable sweet tooth?" Where was that flirting coming from? If this was a new her, she liked it. No, she loved it.

"No, you neglected to mention that, and you should have. It seems like an important fact about you." Faster than she could blink, he flipped her underneath him. "Let's stop playing, Charlie, and go for the real thing, okay?"

"Yes. Okay." His heat surrounded her body, warming her. Anything he asked of her at that moment would be okay with her. More than okay.

"Wicked good, girlfriend of mine," he said in his Boston accent, and if he knew how much that turned her on, he would always use it to get his way with her. He kissed her then, his mouth hot and wet on hers. Although it wasn't their first kiss, it was different—devouring—as if he couldn't get enough of her. When he pulled away, she tried to follow him, wanting more.

He chuckled. "Easy, cherub. We'll get there. We have a problem, though."

"I don't have a problem, I promise." Sex had never been a big deal to her, but he'd changed that. Made her want it. And she wanted it immediately. She clamped down on her bottom lip to keep from begging.

"Ah, but you do. You still have too many clothes on." Sitting back on his heels, he put his hands on her hips and pushed her up to a sitting position.

Sheesh, the man was strong. Was she just supposed to rip off her boxers while he watched?

"Take them off."

Okay, right. That was what she was supposed to do. Except he was Hot Guy and would look glorious nude. She, on the other hand, was the chubby girl she still saw in the mirror.

"Now, Charlene."

Her Hot Guy sure knew how to put a command in his voice. She barely refrained from saluting and snapping a smart "Yes, sir." With a mix of excitement thrumming through her, and the thought that she was just going to die of embarrassment, she slid the boxers off.

"Look at me," he said when she looked everywhere but at him.

She lifted her gaze from the glossy wood floor of his bedroom—did he have a maid who kept it that shiny?—and sucked in air at the heat in his eyes.

"You're beautiful. All of you."

Maybe it was the huskiness in his voice, but dang if she didn't believe him. "Now you," she said, then lifted a foot and, with her toes, tugged on the waist of his sweats.

"Yes, ma'am." He slid off the bed and pushed his pants over his hips, letting them fall to the floor.

She tried not to stare, but he was magnificent. And more man down there than she'd ever imagined a man could be.

"You keep looking at me like that, Charlene, and I'm going to embarrass myself."

Just like that, he'd let her know what kind of power she had over him. It was a first, and it was heady. It could even be addicting.

CHAPTER THIRTEEN

As sexy as Charlie was—laid out in front of him like a feast offered to a starving man—he had to look away. Twenty-eight years old and he had never made love to any woman but his wife. The guilt he felt didn't seem fair and it made him angry.

"Ryan?"

The uncertainty in her voice drew his attention back to the woman in his bed. "I'm here, cherub, I'm here." And dammit, he was.

"It was like you left . . . I don't mean physically, but you got a really faraway look in your eyes. Were you thinking about her?" She pulled the sheet over her stomach and chest, hiding herself from him.

Was he that transparent? "I . . ." He sat on the edge of the bed, not sure what to say, only knowing he didn't want Kathleen in this room with them. "I was just—"

"You promised you'd never lie to me." She twisted the hem of the sheet in her hand, winding it around her fingers.

So he had. He put his hand over her busy one. "In a way I was. We're going to make love, and it will be the first time for me since Kathleen. I guess I'm a little nervous is all." Okay, so he wouldn't tell her the entire truth. She didn't need to know that he'd had a guilty moment.

"It's been how long?"

"Over a year." A long, lonely, angry year.

Her eyes widened, and she let out a little whistle. "That long, huh?"

The skin on the top of her hand was silky smooth, and he focused on the back and forth movement of his thumb. "Yeah, that long." Lifting his eyes to hers he said, "But that's not why I want you." He needed her to know that.

"That first night, though? At the bar? You were there to get laid, weren't you?"

How had they gotten into this conversation? Uncomfortable, he just nodded.

"I wish . . ."

"You wish what?" She had beautiful eyes, and he thought of the earrings he'd made for her, then taken apart. The opals would have been perfect on her, and he wished he had them now to give to her.

She blew out a breath. "I wish I wasn't going to be your first after her . . . your wife, I mean. I think you're going to be disappointed." She pulled her hand away, and held the sheet close to her breasts. "Maybe this isn't a good idea. You and me."

"No, cherub, you and me, we're a good idea. I'll prove it to you." He stood, swallowing a smile at the way her gaze roamed over him. When she flicked her pink tongue over her bottom lip he almost groaned. They were definitely a good idea, the two of them.

"I'll be right back." He barely resisted looking over his shoulder to see if she was staring at his ass as he walked out of the bedroom. He didn't need to, though. He could feel her eyes on him.

In the kitchen, he grabbed two candles he kept for power outages and a box of matches. As an afterthought, he poured one glass of red wine.

"Do all men just walk around naked, you know, not embarrassed?" she asked when he walked back into the room.

"Is that a problem for you, Charlene?" At the vigorous shake of her head, he grinned. Too bad she wasn't as at ease with her body. That sheet she had wrapped around her like a shroud had to go. Setting the candles and matches on the nightstand, he sat next to her again. After taking a drink of the wine, he turned the glass so she would have to put her mouth where his had been, and handed it to her.

She eyed the rim, then lifted her gaze to his, a soft smile on her pretty face. The sexy effect was ruined though when she downed half the glass, confirming his guess that she was also nervous. It settled him that they were both feeling edgy. Put them on equal footing. Before the night was over, he hoped neither one of them could remember their names.

After lighting the candles, he turned off the lamp. Taking the glass from her and making a point of drinking where her lips had been, he swallowed a healthy amount, then handed it back to her to finish. While she drank, he tugged the sheet from under her arms and pushed it aside.

"Don't be hiding this beautiful body from me." With his finger, he traced a line down the valley of her breast, pausing a moment when he touched his class ring, then on down to her belly button. At her shiver, he was satisfied that she wasn't unaffected by his touch. He took the empty glass from her and set it aside, then gave a moment's thought as to where he should begin. From the bottom up, he decided.

"Take your legs out from under the covers." At her immediate compliance, he wondered if it was the command in his voice that had her obeying, or if the wine had loosened her up. "Good girl."

That earned him a somewhat loopy but adorable smile, and he felt a little tug in his chest, in the vicinity of his heart. Not a welcome feeling. He liked her, he wanted her, he enjoyed being with her, but he had no intention of falling in love with her—or any woman, for that matter. He'd learned his lesson the hard way. Since he wasn't going to allow himself to develop deep feelings for her, he decided whatever he'd felt there for a few seconds wasn't anything to worry about.

"Now, what have we here?" He scooted to the end of the bed, picked up her small foot, and slid his fingers down the sole just enough to give her a little tickle. Her toes wiggled, and she tried to pull away, although she was laughing. Damn, if she didn't have a sexy laugh, deep and throaty. But he didn't want her laughing. He wanted her moaning and begging.

Keeping his touch light, he danced his fingers over her ankles and up to her knees. She was no longer laughing. With a glance to see that she watched him with eyes gone darker, he leaned over and nipped at the inside of her thighs, then licked a path halfway up to his goal before stopping.

"You taste so good, Charlene. There's not a place on your body safe from my tongue."

"That's okay," she said, then leaned her head back and closed her eyes.

"Just okay?" He chuckled. "Let's see if we can get better than that out of you."

"If you didn't talk so much, you'd have more time for all that exploring."

"I'm Irish, talking is what we do. When our tongues aren't otherwise occupied, that is. Which mine's about to be." He moved between her legs and put his hands on her thighs, spreading them. She was pink and wet, a glistening gem, as pretty as any in his collection.

Lowering his body to the bed, he slid his thumb through her folds, then parted them. Her scent, a sweet musk combined with the fragrance of the jasmine she'd said she favored, floated up, making his mouth water. It had been so long since he'd had his mouth on a woman there, and he hesitated, savoring the anticipation.

"If you start talking now, Hot Guy, I might die." With that pronouncement, she wrapped her legs around his back and pushed his head down with her hands.

"Can't have that," he said just to get the last word in. Then he plunged his face down, aching to taste her. A wicked shudder traveled through her when his tongue circled her clit, and already hard, he throbbed with need. He had expected her to taste good, but she was delicious. It didn't take long to bring her to a climax, and that was a good thing. He almost came just from having his mouth on her.

"Oh. My. God," she said.

He liked how she didn't seem to be able to speak in a complete sentence. Good to know he hadn't lost his touch. But he wasn't done with her yet. He made a slow slide up her body, his tongue leading the way as he licked a path to her breasts, next on his list of must-haves in his mouth. Her nipples fascinated him. The color reminded him of raspberries and they were peaked, as if begging for his attention. Cradling one breast, a perfect fit in his hand, he swirled his tongue around her pert little nipple, then closed his teeth over it.

"Ahhh," she said.

"Like that, do you? You're so responsive," he added without waiting for her to give the obvious answer to his question. As he suckled her, his other hand was busy roaming over her body. Everywhere he touched felt like silk under his palm, her skin so soft and warm.

As much as he wanted to spend hours learning her, he was too close to losing control. Reaching over to the nightstand, he dug into the new box of condoms he'd bought before he had gone to Buck's on the Beach. As he sat back on his legs, Charlie opened her eyes, and watched him roll on the condom. Damn turn-on that was.

"Let's make some magic, girlfriend," he said, and lowered himself over her. She was small compared to him, and he didn't want to hurt her, so he eased his way in, stopping to let her adjust to him. Apparently that didn't work for her because she put the heels of her feet on his ass and pushed.

He laughed. "Impatient little thing, aren't you?"

"I know what I want," she snapped, sounding miffed.

The woman amused the hell out of him. "Okay, okay." He pushed the rest of the way in until he was buried to the hilt. "Jesus," he murmured. How had he gone over a year without this?

Burying his nose in the soft skin below her ear, he breathed her in. She sent his senses into a frenzy. Her touch, her scent, her taste, the sight of her all flushed and eyes darkened from desire, the sound of her breaths growing heavy as he began the push-pull rhythm where their bodies were joined. He wanted to go on like that for hours, but it wasn't going to happen. He was too turned on, too close.

"You feel so good. I want to make love to you all night. How many times do you think I can make you come?" He felt her smile against the side of his cheek.

"Dang, Ryan, you do like to talk."

True, he did, and he was a talker when making love. "From the first time we kissed, I've dreamed of making love to a girl named Charlie. My imagination was lacking." He thrust into her.

"Yes, like that."

"Like what?"

"Hard. Like you're doing."

His girlfriend was a tiger in bed, and he wondered how he'd gotten so lucky on his first venture out. Needing to be connected to her in every way possible, he sank his tongue into the wet heat of her mouth. Her tongue fought with his with a fierceness that sent him over the edge.

"Come, Charlie. Now!"

Her inner muscles squeezed around him, and he lost all the air in his lungs. For the first time ever while making love, white spots danced in front of his eyes. Spent, drained dry, he fell heavily onto her, gulping in huge amounts of air.

When reason returned, he realized he was squashing her and lifted himself onto his elbows. She tried to pull him back down. He let her. What had just happened?

"Wow, that was amazing," his cherub said.

Lifting up again, he stared down at her. The short, curly cap of hair he loved was damp, her lips were red and swollen, and the pupils of her eyes were dilated. She had the look of a woman who'd just been thoroughly made love to, and had loved every minute of the experience. She was also a very dangerous woman. To him. To his resolve to never again put himself in the position of being destroyed.

"I've never had an orgasm with a man before, only with my trusty little vibrator."

"Seriously?"

"Seriously, and it was amazing. Thank you."

There it was again. That little tug in his chest he didn't want. He rolled onto his back and pulled her into the crook of his arm. Would he be an ass if he warned her not to fall in love with him? He gave an inward snort—there was an ego bigger than the Pentagon. She'd never given any indication that he meant more to her than he wanted to mean. Hadn't she even said to let her know when he wanted his ring back? For a man who liked to talk, he was at a loss as to what to say. Did they need to agree on the conditions of their time together?

He glanced down at her, surprised to see her sound asleep. Actually, that was good. It would give him time to think about what he wanted from her. The last thing he wanted was to hurt her. She didn't deserve that. They needed to talk, and they would. If she understood and agreed to his rules, they were good to go for however long the fun lasted. If not . . . he didn't know how to finish that thought.

Had he really been the first man to give her an orgasm?

Charlie was only pretending to be asleep. She had felt him tense when she'd let her secret spill, something she hadn't meant to tell him, nor wanted to, and she sensed he was preparing his little speech. Imagine his surprise if she gave it for him. "There's no future for us, Charlie, but let's enjoy our time together while it lasts. Okay?" And she would nod, all agreeable while trying to keep tears from flowing down her cheeks, betraying her. It was not okay.

The way he had made love to her had blown her away. Into another world. One she had never visited before. It had felt as if he treasured her, which had given her the courage to step out of her comfort zone. Making love with Ryan had been as thrilling as pointing the nose of her plane at the stars. He had sent her heart to soaring the way it did when performing a perfect hammerhead stall, and she had given herself free rein to take what she wanted.

She didn't doubt that it had been good for him, too. That had been obvious. But maybe it had been too good between them. If she was beginning to understand him—and she thought she was—that scared him.

So she pretended to be asleep to avoid the awkward conversation she knew was brewing in his mind. When minutes later, he eased his body away from hers and slipped out of bed, she didn't stir. The bedroom door opened, and she peeked under her lashes to see the most amazing butt in the world disappear from sight. Because the hall light was on, she saw his rabbit hop after him.

Damn him. Damn him. Damn him. She had two choices as she saw it. Keep on seeing him while pretending he wasn't worming his way into her heart, or call it off immediately before she could say she really was in love with him. Because she already was, a little. Ending it now would be less painful, but then it would be over. No more man with a silly rabbit, no more kisses that sent shivers down to her toes, no more orgasms unless it was with her vibrator. That last one sucked.

It came down to one question. Was she willing to risk a broken heart just to spend however much time with her Hot Guy as he was willing to give her?

"There's a dilemma for you, Charlie," she said as her eyelids grew heavy.

CHAPTER FOURTEEN

Ryan held up the earrings and ran a critical eye over them. Although they were similar to the ones he'd made before, they were slightly different. More Charlie. Knowing she wouldn't like anything flashy, he had used the same opals as before, but had made the settings a little smaller and more delicate than the first ones. They would be sexy dangling from her ears.

Mr. Bunny sat on top of the worktable, and when Ryan held them in front of the rabbit, he sniffed them. "You think she'll like them?" The rabbit's nose twitched, and Ryan took that as a yes.

The lamp flickered, and he tapped the bulb. It flickered again, and he wondered if he was going to lose power. The hallway light hadn't gone off though. When he checked the cord to make sure it was plugged in securely, he sighed.

"Mr. Bunny, if you don't stop eating the cords, you're going to find yourself served up as rabbit stew." Both he and the bunny knew he didn't mean it, but it worried him that the fuzzy menace might electrocute himself if he didn't stop chewing on electrical cords. Ryan had already put protective covers on the others, but had forgotten about the lamp on his worktable. The rabbit stuck his nose into the tray of gemstones.

"Hey, you. That's not food or toys." He picked up his pet and went to the kitchen. Pouring a small amount of Cheerios onto the floor, he left Mr. Bunny to his favorite treat. Back at his worktable, he took a small white box out of a drawer and put the earrings in it. Someday, he might make the matching necklace, but he thought it would be too soon to give Charlie a set.

As he tidied up, he vowed to spend more time at his hobby. Because it had reminded him too much of Kathleen, he'd not touched a piece of jewelry until making something for Charlie, and he had forgotten how much he enjoyed it.

The Star of Life he'd bought before his last deployment caught his eye. A symbol of paramedics, the silver piece was a six-pointed star featuring the rod of Asclepius in the center with a serpent curled around it. He picked it up and studied it.

The past year, he'd lost sight of who he was. There wasn't an MD after his name, but he was a certified paramedic, trained to save lives on a battlefield. Although he had once considered going for a medical degree, he'd realized that wasn't what he wanted. The kind of work he'd done as a SEAL and now with K2—being a member of a team who did what few others could, combined with the saving of lives—that was Ryan O'Connor. His wife had never understood that.

While he had everything out, he took a strip of black leather and cut it to fit his wrist. After putting a clasp on the ends, he added the Star of Life to the front. When he finished, he tried it on. As he admired his handiwork, something inside him that had been wound tight since Kathleen's death loosened. The knot was still there, but it was unraveling.

"There's a cherub in my bed, Mr. Bunny, and I'm wondering why I'm in here."

He flipped off the hall light and returned to the bedroom, where he set the box on the nightstand. Mr. Bunny hopped into the room, and he put the rabbit on the bed. After blowing out the candles, he eased his way under the covers, and inched over until he was spooning Charlie. She gave a little sigh when he spread his fingers over a breast.

Mr. Bunny snuggled up against his legs, and as Ryan lay there in the dark, holding his girlfriend and listening to the rabbit making little snoring noises, it struck him that it had been a long time since he'd felt such a sense of contentment.

The next morning, he awoke to an empty bed. The irresistible aroma of coffee and bacon had him up and slipping on a pair of jeans. A pity his cherub wasn't still in bed so he could wake her up. There was nothing better than morning sex, and now that he'd broken his sex fast, he wanted more. Grabbing the little white box from his nightstand, he stuffed it into a front pocket.

At the end of the hall, he stilled and took in the scene in front of him. Wrapped in a towel, her hair wet and curling around her head, Charlie held his rabbit in the crook of her arm while flipping bacon.

"You don't eat bacon, do you, Mr. Bunny?" She looked at the rabbit as if waiting for an answer. "No, of course you don't. What do you eat, anyway?" she asked, then kissed his little twitching nose.

There went that heart tug again. "Rabbit food and Cheerios."

She squeaked and spun around. "Dang, you're a sneaky one."

Like a puppet on a string, he was drawn to her. "Good morning," he said, and then wrapped his arms around her and soundly kissed her. "Best way to greet the day, an almost naked woman in my kitchen making me breakfast."

A shy smile appeared on her face. "I just kind of made myself at home. Hope that's okay."

"It is, but I don't expect you to cook for me." It really was nice having her there, someone to talk to and start the day with.

"Here, feed your rabbit while I cook some eggs." She handed him his pet. "How do you like them?"

"Any way you want to make them." After feeding Mr. Bunny, Ryan set the table, then poured a cup of coffee. She was efficient in the kitchen, and he leaned against the counter and watched her whip the eggs.

The toast popped up as she spooned the eggs onto their plates. He pulled out a chair for her, then sat across from her. "What's your plan for the day?" he asked as he slathered butter over his toast.

"Me and my baby are going flying."

He paused, a forkful of eggs halfway to his mouth. "Your baby?" There was that laugh he loved.

"If you could see the look on your face. No, there's no secret baby. My plane. She's my baby."

The demand that she not take her plane up almost slipped out of his mouth before he caught the words. He had no right to tell her what she could and couldn't do, but he wanted to. Finally, he settled on saying, "Are you sure that's a good idea?"

Her eyes narrowed, and she set down her fork, aligning it precisely alongside her knife. "Flying is my life. It's what I live for. I refuse to let some demented asshole stop me." The hard glitter in her eyes softened. "I know you think it's not a good idea. You're probably about to bite your tongue off to keep from grounding me, am I right?"

Damn straight. It seemed a good time to retreat before he did order her to keep her feet on the ground. "Just be careful, okay?"

Ignoring the confusion clearly visible on her face, he walked out. He had a mission to prepare for, a dangerous one considering the upheaval in the Baltics. The last thing he needed on his mind was a pretty stunt plane pilot. Halfway down the hall, he stopped and swore. Then he went into his bedroom, found his cell phone, and called Buchanan to tell him he would be a few hours late coming in. He took a quick shower, dressed, moved the little white box from his jeans to his cargo pants, and was at the front door only a few minutes before Charlie walked up.

She had on a T-shirt that said *Real pilots don't need runways.* Too close to the truth where she was concerned. She was also sexy as hell, and he'd like nothing more than to scoop her up into his arms and take her back to bed. But it seemed he was about to go flying instead, and in a stunt plane no less.

The hell if she was taking off without him. He was a good parachutist, and if the worst happened, he would make sure she ended up with her feet planted on the ground or he would die trying.

"I'm coming with you."

"Coming with me where?"

There was a hint of a barely suppressed eye roll. "Flying."

That, Charlie wasn't expecting. "Why?" He seemed to take great interest in his shoe as he toed a line over the wood floor, and she wondered what was going through his mind.

"Beats me. When I figure out the answer, I'll let you know." He stuck his hands in his pockets, then frowned as he pulled out a box and held it out to her. "I meant to give it to you at breakfast."

"What's this?" She took it from him and opened the lid. Okay, another thing she wasn't expecting. "Oh, Ryan, they're beautiful." A sudden thought struck her. Was this like a kiss-off gift? "You don't need to be buying me anything." She tried to hand the box back, but he wouldn't take it.

"I made them. For you."

Made them? "Why?" She braced herself to hear a *it's been nice, but . . .*

He took the box from her and lifted the earrings, easing them through her pierced earlobes as if he'd done such a thing many times before. Then he put his hands on her shoulders and turned her. They ended up in the bathroom, and when she faced the mirror, with Ryan standing so close behind her, his heat and the scent of the soap from his shower surrounded her. He inched up until his hips pressed against her bottom.

"They're perfect for you," he said, twirling one with his finger. "They match your beautiful eyes. That's why I made them for you. You know, the early Arabians believed opals were magical stones that fell from the heavens. I hope that's true and they keep you safe for me."

Amazed her legs didn't crumble, landing her in a pile at his feet, she met his gaze in the mirror. "I love them. Thank you." The orange streaks in his eyes flared, and going on instinct, Charlie turned and lifted onto her toes. She wrapped her hands around his neck and pulled him down to meet her mouth.

"You're welcome," he said against her lips. Then he took control of the kiss.

It was definitely not a brush-off kiss, nor did the earrings seem to be a good-bye gift. Understanding that, her heart went crazy. Or maybe it was the curl-her-toes kiss that sent the thing into a frenzy.

Pressed back against the counter by Ryan's warrior-hard body, she closed her eyes as the sensation of his hands roaming over her skin consumed her. He rocked his hips, and his erection rubbed her in all the right places. She moaned, and he echoed her.

"We're never going to leave this house if we keep this up," he said, pulling away.

"I'm good with that."

The corners of his eyes crinkled in amusement, and he winked at her. "If a certain someone had stayed in bed a little longer this morning . . ."

He trailed off as if leaving the rest of his sentence to her imagination, and for some reason that seemed sexier than anything he could have said. "Won't happen again, I swear. I learn from my mistakes." The way he smiled then, as if she'd pleased him, sent her heart to fluttering again.

Stop it, heart! Falling for him was so not a good idea. To keep from begging him to kiss her again, she turned back to the mirror. "They're beautiful." She fingered one, admiring the small pear-shaped opal encased in a delicate silver setting, loving how they dangled at just the right length.

"I can't believe you made these. That's amazing you can do that. How'd you learn?"

If she hadn't been watching him in the mirror, she would have missed whatever it was that flashed in his eyes. Regret? Sadness?

"My wife was a jeweler. She taught me. Come on, let's go." Not waiting for her, he walked out of the bathroom.

Great, Charlie, go and remind him of the woman he said was having another man's baby. Angry that her eyes filled with tears, she squeezed them shut and took a minute for a few calming breaths.

"Okay," she said as she swiped her fingers over the few tears that insisted on falling. "We know the score so we're good, right?" She gave a brisk nod, confirming she got it, then went to find the man she refused to fall in love with.

Charlie was tempted to point the plane's nose up for a few thousand feet and then point it straight down to the ground in a death-defying dive just to get a response from the man sitting silent in the seat behind her. She wished she could see him, see if he was turning green. The only thing that kept her from performing the rolls and dives she had planned was that she didn't want to embarrass him if it might make him sick.

He had driven her to the airport in silence and followed along behind her in silence while she did her preflight checklist—a more detailed one than she'd ever done before. She did have to give him credit for his intense focus when she gave him an overview of what she had planned, along with instructions on what she expected from him.

But she was tired of having a passenger who seemed to wish that she forgot he was there. So she had said something to remind him of his wife. How was she supposed to know who had taught him how to make jewelry?

Because of the earphones she wore when flying, she didn't wear earrings during working hours, but she might never remove Ryan's gift. He'd said that opals were magical . . . okay, he'd actually said the Arabians had believed they were magical, but that was just semantics. They would keep her safe for him, he'd said. *For him.*

That sounded promising, but that was before he'd gone comatose on her. She didn't resent that he'd loved his wife; in fact, she respected him for it. The nagging worry, though, was could he ever get over her loss? Because he obviously still had issues about it. Not that Charlie was expecting a forever from him, but competing with a ghost for however long they were together didn't sit well. Would she have to filter everything she said? That wouldn't be good because things tended to pop out of her mouth before she thought better of it.

"Borrring!"

Startled by his voice unexpectedly booming through her earphones, she yelped. When he laughed, it was a welcome sound. Maybe he was over his pique.

"Didn't mean to scare you, but seriously, this isn't much better than riding a merry-go-round. This the best you got?"

Infuriating man. "I was afraid you'd get sick."

"I *do not* get sick."

Uh-oh. She'd insulted him. All righty then. Time to do some serious flying. Following her tradition before beginning her first trick of the day, she patted the plane's panel. "Let's have some fun, baby."

To ease Ryan into the routine she was planning for the air show, she decided to start with an easy maneuver, the wingover. After scanning the sky to make sure there were no other aircraft in the vicinity, she checked to make sure she was at the right power, then positioned the plane at a ninety-degree angle to the straight line of the coast. Basically, she would maneuver so that her left wing was pointing up and her right wing pointing down as she rolled the plane into a curve, almost making a U-turn.

"Kid's play," Ryan said as she came out of the turn.

Ha! *See what you think of this one, Hot Guy.* She applied forward pressure so that she was accelerating downward to gain speed, then went straight into a barrel roll.

"Yee-haw!"

Charlie laughed. He sounded like a kid on an amusement park ride. "That was nothing," she said. "Tighten your harness, Hot Guy."

"Yee-haw!" they yelled in unison as the plane dived toward earth.

An hour later, she touched the wheels down on the runway, the exhilaration of the stunts she had performed still strumming through her veins. Because Ryan had told her he hated planes, she'd expected to do nothing more than take him for an easy ride, wasting what little time she had left to prepare for the air show. But her boyfriend had surprised her. She could picture herself taking him up for a lifetime of flying just to hear his *yee-haw* over and over.

They rolled to a stop, and she turned, peering around the back of her seat to see him grinning at her as if he'd just had the best time of his life. Her stupid heart liked seeing that grin way too much.

"When can we do that again?" he said.

We. She liked the sound of that. "Whenever you want, Hot Guy."

"I want."

The look he gave her was so full of heat that it sent a fire burning through her, one so out of control that if she combusted on the spot it wouldn't surprise her. "I want, too."

The orange streaks in his eyes flared. "If we weren't in a plane that doesn't even have seats side by side, and if we weren't buttoned up in our flight suits like a swaddled baby, and if we didn't have parachutes on our backs, and if your airport manger wasn't standing next to your plane, bouncing up and down because he has something to tell you, and if I wasn't harnessed down to the point where I need you and at least one other to get me out of this seat, I would bury myself so deep inside you right now, Charlene, and love you so hard, you wouldn't know what day it was. That's how much of a turn-on that was. Seeing you in your element, I mean."

Charlie tried to remember how to breathe. "That was a really long sentence, but I have to admit, I really liked it," she finally managed. Her hot guy did like to talk when he was turned on.

"You were amazing up there, pilot girl. I hadn't a clue."

Okay, that did it. She was halfway in love with him.

CHAPTER FIFTEEN

All Ryan wanted to do was lay Charlie down somewhere in her plane and have his way with her, but the thought of the airport manager watching them nixed that idea. Who knew flying with her, watching her handle her plane as if she had been born at the controls, would make him hard and wanting?

It was all that power she harnessed in such a small body, the way the plane became a part of her. It was her peals of laughter that followed the end of a stunt, as if she were the happiest person in the world. He wanted to wrap his body around her and draw all that joy inside her into the pores of his skin and the air he breathed.

Unsnapping his harness, he followed Charlie out of the plane and stepped beside her, putting an arm around her shoulders, tucking her next to him.

"What the hell were you thinking, Charlie?" David said without preamble.

"About what?" Charlie slipped out from under Ryan's arm and faced him. "Help me out of this thing."

Ryan began to work on the straps of her parachute.

"About buzzing that family on the beach. They said you scared the hell out of them, and now there's a complaint filed against you." David swiped a hand through his hair. "Are you even listening to me?"

"What're you talking about?" She turned back to David. "I didn't buzz anyone."

"Nope, she didn't," Ryan said, as he began working on his own straps.

"Well, they had your tail number. Said you came so close to them, they had to duck."

"That's bullshit. Who's saying that?"

"Doesn't matter. You're grounded until this gets straightened out."

By the fire flashing in her eyes, Ryan figured she was seconds away from losing her cool, and he stepped back to enjoy the show. The urge to take charge and fight her battle for her surprised him, though.

Not disappointing him, she got in David's face. "You. Can. Not. Ground. Me." Each word accompanied by a poke to his chest the way Ryan had seen her do before. "I own this plane, and you're not the FAA. If someone's telling lies about me, I want to know who."

"I can damn well ground you from the flight school plane and I am. If you're smart, you'll lie low for a while and let me get to the bottom of this."

"Screw this," she said over her shoulder as she stomped away.

"She didn't buzz anyone," Ryan said. "I was with her, and I'm a witness that she didn't do it. Why would someone even claim something like that?"

"Trust me, O'Connor, I know her, and it's the kind of thing she would do. She's just lucky you're backing up her story. Of course, you could be covering for her."

Ryan was close to losing his cool with the man and was tempted to mimic Charlie and poke him in the chest. If he did, though, it would be with a lot more strength than Charlie had, and someone was going to end up on his ass. And it wasn't going to be Ryan.

"Are you calling me a liar? Because if you are, I take exception to that." He also took exception to the way the man's gaze seemed to be on Charlie's ass as she headed for the hangar. Stepping in front of the airport manager to block his view of her, Ryan crossed his arms over his chest. "Something doesn't smell right about all this. I want to see the report."

"I'm handling it," David said, then walked around Ryan.

Ryan turned and watched him head back to the airport office. Something was definitely off, and he made a mental note to ask Maria to run a check on the man.

"I don't know why I can't just go home and sulk."

Ryan grinned at the woman pacing the confines of his office like an agitated tiger. She was cute when she was mad. Sexy, too. "Because then I'd have to spend the rest of the day worrying about you. As long as you're with me, you're safe."

She stopped midstride and turned to him. "That's really sweet. The last time anyone cared enough to worry about me was before my mom met my stepdad."

"You're killing me with confessions like that, Charlie." She was. If his mom was ever in the position of being single and met a man she fell in love with, he and his siblings would still always come first for her. He knew that to the bottom of his heart.

"I'm sorry. I shouldn't have told you that. I don't want your pity."

Silly girl. He stood and went to her, twirling around his finger a strand of the hair that had fascinated him from the night he'd met her. "I don't pity you, Charlene Morgan. I'm not even close to that.

Do I like you? Yes. Do I fantasize about all the things I want to do with you? Yes. Do I want to keep you safe? Yes. But if you think I'm keeping you with me today because I pity you, you're wrong."

"Sheesh, Hot Guy, you really do like to talk."

"You keep saying that," he said, then kissed her. Because he had to. Because he couldn't get enough of the taste of her.

"Oh, sorry. Didn't mean to interrupt."

Ryan laughed when Charlie squealed and backpedaled until she hit the wall. "Come on in, Maria. I was just kissing my girlfriend, but you just saw that, so I'm stating the obvious. Charlie, this is Maria Buchanan, second in charge here at K2 Special Services. Maria, Charlene Morgan, pilot extraordinaire."

After the two women exchanged pleasantries, Ryan asked, "What you got for us?"

Maria handed him the folder she held, then sat in a chair across from his desk, patting the seat next to her. "Come sit, Charlene."

Giving Ryan a wary glance, Charlie sat next to Maria. "It's Charlie. I mean my real name's Charlene, but everyone calls me Charlie." She gave a little snort. "Except for him. He has all kinds of names for me."

Maria laughed. "Do tell."

"They're all good ones," Ryan said. Half listening to the two women chat, he opened the folder and began to read. Silently thanking Maria for turning the conversation to Charlie being a stunt plane pilot, giving him time to finish the report on their suspects, he quickly scanned through the contents.

Frowning, he glanced up at Charlie. "Did you know your ex-boyfriend was married?"

She stopped midsentence in what she was telling Maria and turned to him, her eyes narrowing. "Aaron?"

"Yes. Did you know?"

"I've got some things to finish up if I'm going to take the afternoon off," Maria said, standing. "I'll be back in a little while to kidnap you, Charlie. We're going to have a girl's afternoon with Dani and Sugar while the boys get some work done."

Charlie's head swiveled from him to Maria. "Who're Dani and Sugar?"

"Along with me, your soon-to-be new friends. Right now, I think Ryan has some things to tell you, so I'll just be on my way."

"I don't understand anything," Charlie said.

Maria chuckled. "Welcome to my world."

After she left, Ryan glanced down at the report. Stupid. He should have told her he was looking into the backgrounds of the people on her list. Doubtful she would have refused, but he should have included her in the decision to do so.

"Aaron wasn't married. He said he had once been engaged, but they called it off by mutual agreement."

Lifting his gaze to hers, he saw hurt and confusion on her face. Was that look because of learning her ex had been a lying bastard, or because her current boyfriend was interfering in her life without her permission?

"Maria's a whizz on the computer. If it's there to be found, she can find it. I asked her to run background checks on your list of possible suspects." He sighed. "Look, I'm sorry if I overstepped here. I guess I'm just used to doing things that need to be done, and I didn't think about how you'd feel about it." As an excuse, it was a true one, but he was still an idiot.

"He was married?"

Okay, maybe her upset wasn't with him. Relieved, he moved around the desk and took the seat next to her. "Not was, is," he said, taking her small hand in his. "Married Lindy Norwood four years ago." If she was hurt by that, the next thing he had to tell her was going to really upset her. "They have a five-year-old daughter." He waited for Charlie to do the math.

"So he got her pregnant, then waited until after the baby was born to marry her?"

"Appears so. That's not the worst of it, love. The whole time he was seeing you, he was going home to his wife and daughter." Her face paled. Jesus, he hated telling her that.

"He said his mother was sick, and that was why he had to make so many trips to South Carolina."

Ryan reached over and picked up the folder, and skimmed through Maria's report until he found what he was looking for. "His mother died ten years ago. His wife and daughter live in Columbia, South Carolina."

"Rat bastard." She pulled her hand away and stood. "He made me a home wrecker."

"Where you going?" he asked as she headed for the door.

"To kill him."

He caught up with her, wrapped an arm around her waist, and practically had to carry her back to his office. He kicked the door shut, then deposited her back onto the chair.

Kneeling in front of her, he put his hands on her knees. "Charlie, do you still have feelings for him?" He hadn't meant to ask that, but the question was out before he could stop it.

"Aaron?"

He nodded. That couldn't be jealousy causing his heart to pound as he waited for her answer.

"God no!" She leaned forward and covered her face with her hands. "I liked him at first, but the longer I was around him, the more I was . . ." she lifted her head and shrugged, "disappointed in him, you could say. I was surprised when he ended things, and I guess my feelings were hurt, but it only took a day or two before

I realized I was relieved. When I looked back on everything, I saw that he had been using me."

Ryan moved to the seat next to her. "How so?"

"To teach him how to be as good an aerobatic pilot as me. As soon as he thought he was, he was done with me." She gave him a cocky grin. "He's not though."

"That I can believe." The spark had returned to her eyes, and he wished he could make all this crap go away so that cute grin stayed on her face. Although her ex-boyfriend was a sorry excuse for a man, Ryan couldn't see any reason for him to go after her. He'd gotten what he wanted from her, and she hadn't tried to cause him any trouble. Still, his name would remain on the list.

"I need to call Mark Everson."

"Who?" Another name for her list?

"He's an aviation attorney. If the FAA pulls my license, I'm screwed. He'll find out who filed the false report on me."

"We already know who. I called Maria from the airport and asked her to find out."

The leg Charlie had been vigorously bouncing stilled. "Who?"

"Someone by the name of Travis Emery Parriman. That name mean anything to you?"

"Never heard of him. I've been thinking. What if someone else buzzed that family and they just got the tail number of the plane wrong?"

Although his gut told him that wasn't the case, it was one possibility. "Maybe. Thing is, there's no record of a resident of Escambia County by that name. Could be a tourist. Maria's working on finding the man."

She rubbed her fingers over her forehead. "Something just doesn't feel right about all this."

That he agreed with. "I think you need to call that attorney and bring him up to speed with what we know so far. I have to get busy with some other stuff, so use my phone. Maria will come get you shortly." He hadn't planned to tell her where he was going, but changed his mind. After dinner, he would tell her as much as he could. The thought of leaving her when someone was obviously out to hurt her didn't sit well. It was the same feeling he'd always had when leaving Kathleen, and look what had happened.

Don't even go there, O'Connor.

Standing, he pulled her up with him. "Maria's taking you over to Dani's house. I'll pick you up there."

"I still don't know who Dani is."

"The boss's wife and Maria's sister-in-law. You'll like her, I promise." Spreading his fingers over the back of her neck, he lowered his mouth to hers. She tasted so good, too good. He could get used to having her in his life. Inwardly swearing, he pulled away. "Forget about all this shit for this afternoon, cherub. Just have fun, okay?"

"I'll try," she said and licked her wet lips.

His gaze followed the path of her tongue. He left before he was tempted to find the broom closet and sink so deep into her that nothing else mattered.

Sheesh, Hot Guy sure knew how to kiss. Shaking off the daze he'd put her into, Charlie called David to get Mark Everson's phone number.

"Why are you calling him?" David asked.

"Because someone wants to see me lose my pilot's license. I need him to start looking into that complaint."

"I told you I'd take care of it. You don't need to involve him."

What was his problem? "I'm counting on you, David, but it would be stupid of me not to cover all my bases. Just give me his number."

"I'm in the hangar right now. I'll call you back with it later."

She frowned when she recognized the sound of the flight school phone ringing. "Okay, but call me soon."

Weird. Why would David lie about being in the hangar? She dialed information and after getting the number, called the attorney. His secretary said he was with a client, so Charlie left a message for him to call her. Still disturbed about David lying to her, she eyed the phone, debating whether to ring him back and call him on the lie. The only reason she could think of was that he didn't want her calling the attorney. Why would that be?

"Ready to go?" Maria asked from the doorway.

"Sure." Charlie grabbed her purse and followed Maria to her car. Girly afternoons weren't her thing, but she didn't see she had a choice. Ever since her best friend committed suicide, Charlie had avoided having girlfriends. Shannon's death had devastated her, and she didn't want to go through anything like that again.

Instead of being in the air where it was only her and her plane, she was grounded from instructing, and if she couldn't teach, she couldn't earn money for fuel, and with no fuel, she couldn't fly. It was enough to make her want to cry. The last time she'd cried was after her mother had blamed her for destroying their family. After the tears had dried, she'd sworn never again would she give anyone or anything the power to break her heart.

Life had been perfect when her daddy had still been alive, and even though it wasn't the same after her mom had married Roger, it hadn't been terrible either. Roger had been nice to her, and her mother was happy again. Charlie had at first been delighted to have a new sister, but that hadn't lasted long. Ashley soon made it clear that she found Charlie lacking, and where Charlie had hoped to have a new friend, she ended up instead being ridiculed and having dirty tricks played on her by a supposed family member.

Not wanting to mar her mother's newfound happiness, Charlie had never complained about Ashley. Besides, her stepsister was devious, and covered her tracks. She would have denied everything, and Charlie knew in her heart that Ashley would be believed over her. Everyone thought Ashley was perfect, even Charlie's mother, who often encouraged Charlie to be more like her stepsister. Charlie wasn't so perfect, as she proved by tearing her family apart.

Then she'd discovered airplanes, and if she lost her license, she would have nothing. That would shatter her. Whatever she had to do to keep that from happening, she would. Her plane was the only thing that hadn't betrayed her. It wouldn't go and die on her like her daddy had; it wouldn't accuse her of lying like her mother had. It would never put a noose around its neck, and it would never bully her or make fun of her.

"You seem a million miles away," Maria said, drawing Charlie back to the present. "Guess I can't blame you, considering everything going on in your life right now."

Ryan had said to enjoy her afternoon, and suddenly, she wanted to do that more than anything. For a few hours, she wouldn't think of rat-bastard ex-boyfriends, betrayals, and murderous plane saboteurs.

"Tell me about Dani and Sugar." As Maria turned off US 98 toward Pensacola Beach, Charlie made up her mind that she would give this girlfriend thing another try. She had the feeling that with Maria, what she saw was what she got, and she liked the woman already.

"Dani is Logan's wife. He's my brother. She's awesome, and you're gonna love her. She writes romance books. Sugar is Jamie Turner's fiancée. He works for us. We call him Saint because he doesn't drink or curse. Sugar's a trip. Real southern, but since she's from Charleston, that's no surprise."

"Sugar's an interesting name. Is it a nickname?"

"Ah, it's not the name she was given at birth, but it's her legal name now."

Based on Maria's hesitation, Charlie figured there was a story there. They turned onto a cobblestoned driveway, and she let out a low whistle. "Wow, that's an awesome house."

"Wait until you see inside."

A beautiful red-haired woman opened the door before they'd reached it. "Hey, sweetie," she said, giving Maria a kiss on the cheek and then turning to Charlie. "You must be Charlene. I'm Dani."

Charlie almost corrected her own name, but caught herself. Maybe it was time to start acting like a woman again. "I am. It's nice to meet you." As she entered the house, she tried not to stare, but sheesh, she'd never been inside a place so beautiful. The living room ceiling was open all the way up to the second story, and the back wall was nothing but glass with an amazing view of the gulf.

"Sugar's in the bathroom. Prepare to listen to her complain about how often she has to pee now that she's pregnant."

Charlie followed Dani to the kitchen island and took the stool next to Maria. The whole bottom floor of the house was open, and from where she sat, she had a great view of the beach. "Your home is beautiful, and I love the colors. The greens and blues are perfect for a beach house."

Dani turned and eyed the room as if seeing it for the first time. "I was in awe when I first saw this place. Still am. Logan chose the colors and décor."

"Really? I'm impressed."

"Wait until ya lay eyes on her husband. Talk about impressive. The man should be in the dictionary next to eye candy." The woman with honey-blonde hair and violet eyes walking toward them laughed. "He still scares me, though."

Sheesh, she was surrounded by beautiful women. Add Maria's glossy, almost black hair to the mix and all the hair colors were represented in one room. She wished she'd run a comb through hers before walking through the door. A little lipstick probably wouldn't have been amiss either. Realizing she was running her fingers through her hair, she dropped her hand to her lap.

"I'm Sugar, but they probably already told you that. I'm so tired of peeing that I'm fixin' to scream." She patted her barely visible baby bump.

Dani rolled her eyes. "Did I not tell you?"

"What?" Sugar asked, snatching a cracker and a slice of cheese from the platter in the middle of the island with one hand while the other scooped up half a dozen olives. "I hate olives, so why I'm craving them beats me." All six went into her mouth.

Maria laughed. "Why don't I just get the jar and pour them down your throat?"

An hour and two glasses of wine later, Charlie had forgotten that the women intimidated her, and was laughing hysterically as Sugar told the story of how she'd almost sent her husband to heaven via a beer truck.

"It was closer to seeing Jesus than I evah want to get for a long time," she said, then jumped up from the bar stool. "I gotta pee."

"Are all of you drunk?"

Charlie, holding her stomach from laughing so hard, looked up to see four men who could have stepped out of one of Dani's romance novels, only one of which she knew.

"Hi, love," Dani said and walked to one of them and kissed him on the mouth.

Wow, Sugar had been right. Logan Kincaid was crazypants eye candy. Charlie gave Ryan a little wave, and he grinned, sending her heart into a flutter. Nope, it wasn't him. It was just the wine sending butterflies into her stomach. He came and stood next to her, putting his hand on her shoulder.

One of the men, dark haired with hazel eyes, walked up behind Maria and wrapped his arms around her. "Miss me, Chiquita?" he asked.

She lifted her face and smiled at him. "Always."

"Where's Sugar?" asked the only one left without a woman next to him. "No, let me guess. She's in the bathroom."

"Yep," Maria said.

With his blond hair and blue eyes, and almost-pretty face, Charlie decided his nickname of Saint fit him. Ryan introduced her to everyone, and after a few minutes of talk, he asked if she was ready to go home. She nodded, swallowing past the lump in her throat at his words. It had felt as if she was one of them, that she and Ryan were a real couple.

Get those visions of forever out of your head, Charlie, my girl. Never gonna happen.

CHAPTER SIXTEEN

Ryan eyed Charlie, sitting quietly across the table from him. She had been quiet ever since leaving the Kincaid house. "I'm glad you enjoyed yourself this afternoon. I knew you'd like the ladies."

She shrugged. "They're all really nice."

The all-out belly laugh he'd caught her at when he and his teammates had walked into the Kincaid household had strangely made him feel jealous. She had never laughed like that with him. They had made love the night before, and being with her had about fried his brain. All he'd thought about all day was getting her into his bed again. But he sensed she held herself back and he wanted to see the real Charlie.

When they had walked into his house, and she had picked up Mr. Bunny, rubbing noses with him, that little tug in his heart had happened again. He almost ignored it, almost pushed it away. Then as he stood to the side of her while she nuzzled his rabbit, it occurred to him that he'd never taken her on a date.

He asked, she accepted, and now they sat across from each other in a ridiculously overpriced French restaurant. "This isn't working, is it?" he asked as he watched her move something he couldn't identify around on her plate.

As she lifted her gaze to his, he could tell she was about to swear he'd chosen perfectly. He reached across the table and took her fork from her hand and set it on the plate. "Never lie to me, Charlene. I don't even know what I'm eating, and as for what's on your plate, I couldn't venture a guess. I know a little place on the beach where they serve the best hamburgers in town. You with me?"

She laughed that wonderful laugh of hers. "I so am." With an apologetic glance down at her food, she pushed the plate to the side. "I'm sorry. This meal's going to put a serious dent on your credit card, and I should probably eat it."

Should he tell her he could afford years of them eating at the expensive restaurant? As Kathleen's jewelry business had been successful enough to pay the bills, they had socked his paychecks away, intending to use the money to buy a house when he opted out of the SEALs. Then there was the fact that Kincaid paid his men well, so his bank account was very healthy.

They got the burgers to go, and then walked to the nearby Pensacola Beach Gulf Pier. Ryan handed over a few bucks for their admission to get on the pier, and they found an empty bench. Railing lamps gave off a soft yellow glow, and he inhaled the tangy scent of the salt-laden air.

"I love the sound of the water," Charlie said. "This probably sounds silly, but I always feel at peace at the ocean."

"Not silly at all." She was beautiful in the moonlight, and he wanted to make love to her on a blanket on the sand some night.

They ate their burgers in silence, listening to the rhythmic roll of the waves crashing over the shore. The frothy whitecaps were almost iridescent and kind of hypnotic, and when they finished their meal, he put his arm around her, tucking her into his side. She leaned her head back on his shoulder and looked up at the moon. Her mouth was close to his, and he almost kissed her. But if he started he thought he might not stop, and after his earlier phone call from Maria, they needed to talk.

"You've been quiet tonight, cherub. Are you worried about losing your pilot's license?"

"Not really. Someone's lying, and the attorney will get to the bottom of it. I just don't need this crap less than two weeks before my air show. And I really don't need to be grounded from instructing. I'm more pissed about that than anything. My paycheck puts fuel in my plane."

"If you need—"

"No. I don't need your money."

He recognized pride when he saw it, and let the subject drop, although he vowed to find a way to help her if Haydon insisted on keeping her grounded. "I'm curious why your manager grounded you so fast. Shouldn't you be allowed to fly while the FAA investigates the complaint?"

"You'd think. I don't understand why David did that myself."

"Did you know he posted pictures of you on a website, claiming you're his girlfriend?" Maria had called with that latest information while Ryan was dressing for dinner. He had taken a quick look at the site and found photos of Charlie standing next to her plane, and others clearly taken around the airport. There was one that tinged his vision red, her wearing a halter top and shorts, washing her plane. She was bent over, scrubbing a wheel with a brush, and the camera was focused on her ass. He'd bet anything she hadn't realized at the time that Haydon was taking that particular picture.

"What?" She jumped up and faced him with her small hands fisted at her sides.

Spitfire. That was the word that came to mind, along with instant arousal. He wanted to strip her naked and lose himself in all that energy sizzling around her. Bad timing, but still . . .

Scissoring his lower legs around hers, he tugged, causing her to fall onto his lap. "Kiss me, Charlene."

"But—"

Ryan covered her mouth with his. When she sighed and wrapped her arms around his neck, he flicked the tip of his tongue over the seam of her lips, needing to taste her. Her lips parted, and he grunted his approval. There were still moments when he was struck by the differences between her and Kathleen—their size, their smell, their taste. Like now, at how much better Charlie fit on his lap. But it was happening less and less, and for that he was thankful.

"I could spend the rest of my life kissing you," he said when they came up for air. As soon as he realized what he'd said, he wished he could take it back. Where had that come from? He wasn't looking for a lifetime with any woman. Been there. Not doing it again.

The way her eyes softened at his words sent alarm bells ringing in his head. Was she falling for him? He'd tried to make it clear that all they would ever have between them was the here and now. For as long as the fun lasted.

He put his hands around her waist and lifted her to sit next to him. "Sorry, I got distracted. We were talking about you being David Haydon's girlfriend."

With a look that said he had her confused—hell, he was confused, so why shouldn't she be?—she turned her head away, staring down the pier. "First, I've never been his girlfriend, and if he claims I am or was, he's got a black eye coming. Second, just what do you want from me, Ryan?"

He wished he knew.

When Ryan stood and walked to the railing, Charlie stayed put. She watched as he placed his hands on the rail, ones that she personally knew could set a woman on fire. They sure had done that to her. She wasn't an expert on men. Far from it. Look at her one and only real boyfriend. He'd been married the whole time he was with her, the rat fink.

Unlike Aaron, Ryan was an honorable man, but he had issues, namely a dead wife who obviously still haunted him. A part of her sympathized with him, but a larger part of her wanted to scream at him, "Turn around and look at me. I would never betray you." She didn't make a sound, though, and he didn't turn around. What a pair they were.

"I'm leaving in a few days on an assignment," he finally said with his back still to her. "I'm not supposed to tell you this, but I trust you." He turned and caught her gaze with an intensity that made her catch her breath. "What I'm saying is that I'm trusting you with my life and those of others. I'll be leaving for Helsinki on an operation."

"I—"

He held up a hand. "No, just listen. What I do is dangerous. There's always the chance I'll come back in a body bag, but it's what I do. Then there's my wife, and my inability to deal with her death and her betrayal, meaning I'm on the wrong side of messed up. I have to tell you, I'm not happy that a pretty cherub means anything to me. But you do. You ask what I want from you, and the hell if I know. What I do know is I want you to be waiting for me when I get back."

Something had changed between them. Charlie curled into the embrace of Ryan's arms and breathed him in. The feel of him skin to skin, the sensuous slide of his hands down her back, even the sheets on his bed felt different. Silkier, softer.

What was between them was no longer a game; it had become real with his admission on the pier. She still didn't expect forever, but she gave him a little more of her heart anyway.

"I've thought about having you naked in my bed all night," he said, nuzzling her neck.

"I'm here. What are you going to do with me?"

He lifted his head, one corner of his mouth tilting up as if amused. "I'm going to love on you all night, girlfriend."

"Is that all?"

The orange streaks in his green eyes flared. "Is that all, she asks? By the time I'm finished with you, Charlene, you won't be able to talk, much less ask silly questions. That I promise."

His mouth was inches from hers, and her eyes followed his lips down until they covered hers. As he playfully nipped his way from one corner of her mouth to the other, Charlie cradled her palm on his face. From the smoothness of his skin, he must have shaved when he'd disappeared into his bathroom after they had returned.

Still shy with him, she tentatively brushed her tongue over his bottom lip. From the sound he made low in this throat, he liked that, and she grew braver. With her teeth, she gave a tug, causing him to chuckle.

"Impatient, are we?" He angled his head and thrust his tongue into her mouth, sliding it over and around hers.

They kissed, hot and wet, as if neither one could get enough of the other, and Charlie loved the taste of him, loved the way he seemed to like touching her—her hair, the curve of her spine, her breasts, her bottom. His hands were all over her, caressing, kneading, stroking.

It was the same for her. The feel of hard muscles under her palm, the expanse of his shoulders, his sex line that she finally found the courage to trace with her fingertips; she would never tire of touching him. And never had she been so needy and wanting.

"Please," she begged.

"Not yet, cherub." He kissed a path down to her breasts, then sucked a nipple into his mouth, swirling his tongue around it.

"Ahhh," she moaned when he lightly bit down.

He rocked his hips against her, rubbing his erection over her stomach. Just when she thought the breast he was giving his attention was too pleasure-pained to take any more, he moved to the other one. A few minutes later, he slid his face down, nipping and licking his way over her stomach, ending up between her legs.

"God, you taste so good, Charlie." His tongue swept over her skin, teasing her. Then his play turned serious. "I want you to come while my mouth is on you."

As if he'd given her a command she couldn't refuse, she shattered. It was so sudden and so surprising that she forgot how to breathe. Her vision blurred as tears burned her eyes. How had he given her such a powerful orgasm with barely a touch?

He climbed back up her body and took her mouth in a kiss that felt hungry, as if he would devour her whole. She would let him.

"I want to do the same thing for you," she said, wanting to taste him the way he had her.

"Not this time. I'm too close to losing control." He kissed one corner of her eye, then the other. "Remember we have all night, girlfriend. Trust me, we'll get around to that."

Whether he called her girlfriend, Charlie, Charlene, or cherub, his voice always seemed to curl around the one he chose at any given moment, as if his names for her were special to him. In doing so, he stole another little piece of her heart.

Reaching over to his nightstand, he opened the drawer and grabbed a condom. It was strange how it turned her on to watch him put it on. From the way his eyes seemed to burn hot as he watched her watch him, it turned him on, too.

When he was all rolled up, he put his hands on her thighs and spread her legs, then stilled. "If you want this as much as I want it, then it's entirely possible we're about to set the bed on fire." With that pronouncement, he lowered his big body over hers.

"I hope you're not too attached to your bed," she said. He laughed then, in a way she'd never heard from him before—as if he were truly happy.

He kept his promise. Throughout the night, they made love, slept, made love some more, and slept some more. At some point, she slid down his body the way he had hers and took him in her mouth. When he tried to pull away before he came, she wouldn't allow it.

He tried to apologize, and when she wouldn't let him, he'd surprised her by saying, "Kathleen never let me do that."

She didn't think he'd meant to admit that. He had been half-asleep when the words had seemed to slip out, and only seconds later, she'd lain there in the dark listening to his even breathing and wondering why his wife wouldn't have wanted the taste of him in her throat.

Charlie didn't know their story other than the little he had told her, but as she luxuriated in the feel of him spooned around her back, she couldn't help feeling sorry for them. For him because he'd loved a woman who had hurt him in the worst possible way. For his wife because she had tossed aside the love of a beautiful man who had loved her with all that he was.

When the sun tried to peek through the shades, Charlie was still awake. There was a part of her that had never been happier in her life, and there was a part that dreaded the end of her and Ryan when it came.

If she were smart, she'd get up, get dressed, tell him it had been fun, and leave before she really did fall in love with him. That she already was a little, she couldn't deny. But she didn't move, didn't get up, didn't get dressed.

She was apparently a fool, but how was gambling on the odds that Ryan just might fall in love with her any different than shutting off her plane and free-falling to earth? She would either survive or she wouldn't.

CHAPTER SEVENTEEN

Ryan hung up the phone when he got a recording saying that Cody Roberts's number had been disconnected. Where the hell was Dog? For some reason, their SEAL sniper had been on his mind lately. They'd talked a few times shortly after Kathleen's death, their conversations awkward, neither quite knowing what to say. Cody was the only member of the team who Ryan had even hinted to that there was more to the story of Kathleen's death.

At two months, the robber wouldn't have known she was pregnant, but he probably wouldn't have cared even if he had known. Ryan had installed cameras in the shop shortly after Kathleen opened her store, and everything from that day had been recorded. Knowing he couldn't bear to watch it, he hadn't asked to see the video. The cops told him that she had cooperated with the man, doing everything asked of her including opening the safe. The last thing the bastard had done before walking out the door was to put a gun to her head and pull the trigger. Although Ryan tried to console himself that she hadn't suffered, it hadn't helped.

The police theorized that the robber hadn't wanted to leave a witness. They'd never know as the strung-out crack addict had OD'd two days after killing her. Only half of Kathleen's jewelry had been found in the man's room, the rest undoubtedly sold to buy the drugs that did him in. Poetic justice, although Ryan wished he'd been the one to deliver the sentence. But he'd been deployed at the time, too far away to protect Kathleen and the child. The guilt for not being there to save her he likened to pouring battery acid down his throat. It had eaten away at him until there were days when he thought there would be nothing left. From one minute to the next, he bounced from heartbreak to anger at her deceit, and then he felt guilty all over again for being angry at her.

When he'd told Cody how she'd died, his friend had said, "Damn, man, I'd kill him for you if the bastard wasn't already dead."

Knowing Dog was serious, tears had stung Ryan's eyes, and he'd almost blurted the rest. It would have been good to get Kathleen's betrayal off his chest, and he could have trusted Cody to keep her secret. But Cody hadn't quite sounded like himself, so Ryan had swallowed his confession, not wanting to dump his problems on his friend.

He stared at the phone, wishing he'd made more of an effort to stay in touch with his buddy. "Where are you, man?"

"Who?"

Ryan glanced up at Maria. "Cody Roberts. I've been trying to get in touch with him, but no luck."

"Maybe he just needs some away time before he comes on board."

That would be just like Dog to disappear without a word. "What you got for me?"

She handed him a file, and he opened it and began to read. The complaint filed against Charlie was bogus. There was no Travis Emery Parriman at the local address given, and when Maria had called the phone number listed, a teenaged boy had answered and said he'd never heard of the name.

"How'd you get this so fast?" he asked when she handed the complaint to him.

Maria smirked. "I have my ways."

So who had filed a false report and why? The airport manager was fast moving up on the list of suspects.

He considered calling Charlie and telling her, but then she'd probably head straight to the airport to confront Haydon. Better to wait and tell her in person so if she did suspect her boss, too, Ryan would be there to control the situation.

"I also hacked into that website and removed all the pictures of Charlie that David Haydon put up on there."

Maria continued to surprise him. "I appreciate that." More than he was willing to admit. "I'll let Charlie know."

Jake poked his head around the doorway. "Chiquita," he said, "you weren't in bed when I woke up."

"Your talent for observation is astounding, husband. I came in early to take care of something for Doc, but I promise to still be there in the morning, and we'll explore some of your other talents." She gave him a quick kiss on the lips and an ass grab as she swept past him.

Jake's gaze followed his wife's retreating form before he turned back to Ryan. "She did that on purpose."

"Did what?"

"Made sure all I'd think about was her in my bed." He smirked. "Like that's not what I think about twenty-four seven. Ready?"

"TMI, man." He put the complaint about Charlie in his desk drawer and then stood.

Jake's gaze fell on the black leather bracelet. "That new?"

"Yeah."

"Let me see." After a long look at it, he let go of Ryan's arm. "Cool. What's it mean?"

"It's the Star of Life." He explained the meaning behind it. Before the conversation turned sappy and he started trying to explain what was going on in his head, he said, "Let's go evade some Russians."

Kincaid was always thinking of ways to keep his men safe when on an operation, and had built a large warehouse behind the K2 offices where mockups of houses and even villages could be erected. He also employed a crew of carpenters who created duplicates of mission locations as much as they could with what intelligence could be gathered.

The scene that greeted Ryan when he and Jake entered the warehouse was so close to the photos they had obtained of the house where their targets were being held—along with the nearby houses—that he felt as if he'd just crossed the border into Russia. Even though the buildings were plywood, and would fall over with a hard push, they looked real from where he stood.

"There's even trees," he said.

Jake laughed. "Kincaid's never been one to do things half-assed."

Ryan knew that from their time together in the SEALs. Their commander had always been two steps—hell, five steps—ahead of everyone else. But trees? When Kincaid's assistant, Barbie, walked into the warehouse to play the role of the wife, a pure white poodle on a leash prancing beside her, Ryan burst into laughter.

"Unbelievable," he muttered.

The upcoming operation would be his first since coming to work for Kincaid, and he definitely appreciated that the boss went to such great lengths to ensure his men would be as prepared as possible.

After a short strategy session, they put their plan to rescue the family and a damn poodle into motion. Throughout the day, they practiced over and over, and they would repeat the process the following day and the next. Ryan figured he would dream about yapping poodles all night.

He was determined to be back home in time for Charlie's air show. For that reason, he threw himself into the training and planning for the days leading up to their departure. Between being at work by dawn, and working past dark, his ass was dragging by the time he arrived home each night.

Charlie would have dinner waiting for him, and afterward, he'd fall asleep in front of the TV. As hard as he tried to stay awake and talk to her, he just couldn't. What she was doing with her days, he didn't know. He kept meaning to ask, but zonked out within seconds of his butt hitting the sofa.

On his last night in the States, Ryan took Charlie to a raw bar on the beach. Determined to spend time with her before he left while his eyes were open, he had slept an extra hour that morning, and had arrived home before the sun set.

"I know I haven't been much fun this past week . . . no, make that any fun, but I'll make it up to you when I get back." They were sitting side by side at an outside picnic table, and he put his arm around her and pulled her closer.

She rested her head on his shoulder. "It's okay. I understand the demands of needing to train."

"Which I know you'll be doing while I'm gone." That worried him, but he couldn't very well order her to keep her feet on the ground. They still hadn't learned who had made the bogus claim. It had been called in to the FAA, which had taken the false information over the phone. With his schedule the past days, he hadn't had time to investigate further.

Maria had turned her attention to their mission, doing her part to organize supplies and meets with their overseas contacts, and whatever else she could do to make sure her husband came home in one piece.

"That I am." Charlie sighed. "I know that worries you, but I refuse to be cowed by a nameless, faceless bastard who doesn't have the balls to face me. At least once we learned the report was bogus, I was ungrounded, and I started instructing again yesterday."

"I didn't know that." What a poor boyfriend he was turning out to be.

She nuzzled her face against his neck. "You've got enough on your mind, and I didn't want to bother you. I'm going to miss you, you know. You better not have any bullet holes in you when you get back, or I'm gonna be really pissed."

"I'll do my best," he said, unable to make any promises. "You better stay safe, too, if you don't want to see me pissed."

"I'll do my best," she echoed, then lifted her face.

Accepting her invitation, he kissed her. She sighed into his mouth, and he would have gone on kissing her if someone hadn't cleared their throat.

"Two dozen oysters on the half shell, and two beers, one with extra limes," the server said, setting a large, round platter lined with ice shards between them. "Your captain's seafood platter to share will be along shortly."

"I need hot sauce and some more lemons, please," Charlie said to the girl's retreating back.

"You're all the hot sauce I need," Ryan said, giving her a wink.

She snorted. "You say the most romantic things."

As they dug into the food, Ryan tried to remember if he had ever winked at Kathleen. Their partings had always begun and ended with her in tears, begging him to quit the SEALs. She had never understood that what he did defined him. Her greatest wish was for him to come work with her in her store. And it was her store, not his. Although he enjoyed making jewelry as a hobby, he would have slowly died doing it every day. She had never understood that either.

Somehow, he knew Charlie would never ask him to be anything other than what he was. Maybe it was because she lived on the edge the same as he did, and would understand his need for danger. He glanced at her to see her topping an oyster on a cracker with so much hot sauce that he wondered if she'd lose her breath when she popped it into her mouth.

"Am I going to need to give you CPR after you eat that?"

She turned to him, those beautiful blue-gray eyes of hers sparkling with mischief. "Are you hoping?"

"Oh yeah." If he didn't get them out of there immediately, he just might embarrass them both. He'd been on a tear, concentrating on the mission training, falling asleep early so he could get up early, to go at it again the next day. All because he wanted to return to his cherub in one piece. This one, though, she scared the hell out of him. When had he gone from it all being a game to wanting more?

Charlie popped the lemon-soaked oyster-on-a-cracker concoction—topped with cocktail sauce, topped over that with several dashes of hot sauce—into her mouth while holding Ryan's gaze. The man was doing seriously sexy things to her insides just by looking at her in that way he had.

"Do you want the rest of our dinner?" she asked.

"Someday, we should actually eat the food we've ordered." He kissed her again. "But not this time." Within minutes he had apologized to their waitress, paid the check for food eaten and not eaten, and added a generous tip. She knew that because she'd peeked over his shoulder when he'd scrawled his signature on the bottom of the receipt. His hand at her lower back as he escorted—pushed—her to his car sent a thrill through her. He wanted her as much as she wanted him.

"Charlie," he said as he turned onto the beach road, "I need you so damn much that I want to pull over, take you over those dunes, and find a place to make love to you."

Yes! "Pull over. Right now, Ryan."

He swerved so fast to the right, stopping at one of the beach access pull offs, that she could only marvel at his quick reaction to her words.

"You, me, making love over there," he said, pointing to a sand dune separated yards away from the others. "That will make me do my best to come home to you without a bullet stuck in my ass."

"You really know how to sweet talk, Hot Guy." A bullet hole anywhere on him would ruin her day. He laughed, then jumped out of the car, came around to her side, opened the door, reached in and slid his arms underneath her, and lifted her to his chest.

"Wow, you've gone caveman on me." But it sure was sexy. He gave a perfect caveman grunt, causing her to giggle.

"Do I get credit for not dragging you by your hair?"

"Definitely. Not that I have enough for you to drag."

"I love your hair."

The compliment warmed her, sure, but he didn't just say he liked her hair, or that it was pretty. He used the *love* word, and even though it was only the hair part of her he loved, a fierce longing for the whole of her to be loved by this beautiful man settled in her heart and refused to leave.

After walking over the dunes, they reached the one he'd pointed out. Coming to a stop, he let go of her legs but kept an arm around her back so that she made a slow slide down his body. When her feet touched the ground, he scanned the area.

"Good, there's no one on the beach." He looked down at the sand, a frown on his face. "I forgot the blanket."

"You keep a blanket in your car?"

"Only since I got it in my head to make love to you on the beach some night. Wanted to be prepared if the opportunity arose. Be right back."

She watched as he jogged away, while wondering how she was supposed to resist falling in love with him. If she was smart . . . to hell with being smart. Ryan wasn't anything like her ex, and although she still didn't see Hot Guy sticking around forever, she decided she was on the ride for as long as it lasted. That should have been a hard decision to make, but for her, it wasn't.

Because standing in the dark, listening to the swash of the waves hitting shore, she admitted to herself that she loved him. So she would take all that he would give her, and when it was over, she would have memories of loving a man who deserved her love. And although she thought the chance slim because of his history with his wife, there was always the possibility that he might look at her one day, and like a lightning bolt to his heart, he would know he loved her back. She thrived on risks, right?

There were no clouds overhead, and as she peered up at billions of stars twinkling in a velvet black sky, she pulled her T-shirt over her head, then slid her jeans down her legs. Too chicken to remove her bra and panties, she turned and walked down to the water, feeling daring. She had never done anything like that before and wondered why not.

Walking into the surf until she was thigh deep, she laughed when a wave almost knocked her over. The water was cold but not freezing, and she turned so that the oncoming wave would hit her in the back. In front of her, Ryan stood in water up to his knees, not a stitch on. As if she were metal to his magnet, she went to him.

"You're like a sea goddess, here to bewitch me," he said when she was inches from him.

"You have a glib tongue," she answered.

"I'm Irish. Glib is in my blood."

"I'm good with your being Irish, but I'm really fond of your tongue."

The white of his teeth gleamed in the moonlight when he grinned. "I think you should prove to me just how fond of it you are."

She took a step closer. "You have no clothes on."

"I'm doing something wrong if you're just now noticing that, cherub."

"Oh, believe me, I noticed."

Taking her hand, he led her deeper into the gulf, past where the waves were breaking. Although his chest and head were above the water, she was on her tiptoes. When he realized she was struggling not to swallow salt water, he laughed.

"Climb up me, little girl, before you drown." As she grabbed his shoulders, her feet leaving the ocean floor, he deftly slid off her panties.

She punched his arm. "You're a sneaky one."

"You've no idea. You know, the knights of old would be given a token from their lady before going into battle," he said, tugging her panties up his arm. "I think I'll keep these as my good luck charm."

"Ha! I don't think they gave them their panties."

"Actually, I don't believe they wore panties back then. A good practice, that."

"Men," she said. She wrapped her legs around his waist, and her arms around his neck. His arms circled her back, and they held each other as the water swirled around them. Without him to anchor her, the current would have swept her away, but he was so strong that she felt safe and protected. The heat from his body kept her warm.

"Kiss me, Charlene."

They kissed and petted and kissed some more under the moonlit night and the stars twinkling above. With him holding her close, she thought she could spend all night there in the Gulf of Mexico, doing nothing but loving him.

When the cold finally penetrated her skin and she shivered, he carried her out of the water and up to the dune where he had spread the blanket. With his large body covering hers, warming her again, he made love to her there on the sand, which was still heated from the daytime sun. His touches and kisses were tender, and as he whispered her name softly into her ear, she felt cherished. She squeezed her eyes shut against the tears burning in them and loved him back.

It was the most beautiful night Charlie had ever known.

Charlie walked alongside Ryan, their fingers laced together, as they approached airport security. Surprising her, he had insisted she come see him off. Ahead, Jake and Maria stood waiting for them. Jake had his wife tucked under his arm and was idly twirling a strand of her hair around his fingers. Charlie wondered whether Ryan would someday play with her hair like that, if she let hers grow.

Before they were noticed, Ryan pulled her off to the side. He turned and wrapped his arms around her, pulling her against his chest. "I'll call you if I can, but if you don't hear from me, it doesn't mean anything. You understand what I'm saying?"

She nodded, her nose rubbing over his shirt as she breathed him in, memorizing his scent. "No news is good news."

"Right. Take care of Mr. Bunny while I'm gone, and don't go and be getting him drunk, okay?"

She laughed when all she really wanted to do was grab his hand

and drag him back home where he would be safe. "Mr. Bunny told me to tell you that you're no fun."

The arms he had around her tightened. "I don't know what this thing is between us, cherub, but I do know it's something I want to explore. I'm counting on you to be here when I get back."

As if he had to ask. "I'll be here."

He leaned away and peered down at her. "As much as I want to, I know better than to tell you not to set foot in a plane until we figure out who's playing games with you. Deadly games," he added. "I'll be really pissed if I come home only to find out . . ."

That he couldn't bring himself to say the rest told her she really did mean something to him. She laid her head on his chest, right over his heart, so she could hear it beat. "I'll be here," she said again.

"If you need anything, call Maria. Even if you don't need anything but just want to talk to someone, call Maria. She'll know where I am, what's happening."

That was good to know, and she would definitely be calling Maria.

He put his finger under her chin, lifted her face, and stared down at her for a few seconds before he lowered his mouth to hers. Somehow, the man had slipped in on sneaky feet and stolen her heart the moment he had opened his door to her with a rabbit nestled in his arm.

I love you, she told him silently. Aloud, she said, "No bullet holes in your ass. Got that, Hot Guy?"

"Got it." Taking her hand, he walked them to Jake and Maria. Too soon, she watched him go through the security check, then she kept her eyes trained on him until the two men disappeared from sight.

"This is the hardest thing for me, watching the man I love head off on a mission, knowing I might never see him again," Maria said.

Charlie took a deep breath, trying to calm her racing heart. If she never saw Hot Guy alive again, it would put a hurt on her she might never get over. She slipped her hand into Maria's and squeezed. "Ryan said if I needed to talk to anyone while he was gone, that you were the one to call. Wanna go with me to some bar, I don't care where, just someplace we both can cry into our beer?"

Maria laughed. "It's nine in the morning."

"Your point is?"

Her new friend grinned. "Don't have one. Let's go get drunk and cry in our beer."

They ended up at a pancake house where they both cried into their coffee.

CHAPTER EIGHTEEN

Because the opportunity presented itself, Ryan pulled his cell phone from his pocket and called Charlie. "Just checking to make sure you're not getting my rabbit drunk," he said when she answered. She had argued against staying at his place while he was gone, claiming she didn't want to impose on him. Silly woman.

He had used the most potent weapon in his arsenal—a fucking rabbit—to keep her at his place, hidden from whoever wanted to hurt her. Mr. Bunny would get an overflowing bowl of Cheerios when Ryan got back; he wouldn't understand why he was getting the reward, and wouldn't care as he swallowed the treats whole.

She faked a very bad hiccup. "Well dang, I knew there was something I wasn't supposed to be doing." She made a *tsk, tsk* sound. "Mr. Bunny, give me back that glass of wine."

He smiled into the phone as he pictured her sitting on his sofa with his rabbit in her lap. He liked that image. It felt as if she was where she was supposed to be. "I miss you, Charlene," he said. The line went silent, and he wondered if he'd just said something she wished he hadn't.

Then he heard her exhale. "Miss you, too, Ryan. More than I should."

Before Ryan could respond, Jake lifted from the rock he'd been sitting on and walked to the edge of the water. Ryan's gaze followed his team leader's. As quiet as a cat sneaking through the night, a low-slung boat appeared just yards from the shore, as if by magic. "Gotta go," he said and clicked off. Not a good time to have his attention sidetracked by a woman, even if she was on his mind twenty-four seven.

He joined Jake and neither man gave way as the sleek, metal-gray boat slid its nose up the shore, stopping inches from them. "Nice toy," Ryan said.

Jake grunted. "I want one."

"Of course you do." It wouldn't surprise him in the least if one showed up at K2 in the near future. Kincaid was also fond of toys, the badder the better.

The hatch opened and the top of a head emerged. Then a face Ryan hadn't seen in over a year appeared, a shit-eating grin stretching from ear to ear.

"Damn Kincaid and his surprises," Jake muttered before walking into the water.

Ryan followed, a wide grin on his own face.

"Dog, my man," Jake said. "Where the hell you been hiding your ugly ass?"

One of the deadliest—and probably craziest—snipers the SEALs had ever known hopped over the side, landing gracefully in front of them. He turned, dropped his pants, and bent over. "You calling that ugly, Romeo?" he said, talking between his legs. "That hurts, man."

Ryan put his hands over his eyes. "Christ, Dog, I'll never be able to unsee that." The stunt was typical of Cody Roberts, master sniper and dog whisperer. Of them all, he thrived the most from living on the edge, and got off on shocking anyone dumb enough to invade his space. There had been times when he'd gone too far with his antics, but the others on the team understood what it could do to a man to look through the sights of a scope and put a bullet through the heart of an endless line of bad guys. So they made allowances where their sniper was concerned.

The man laughed, pulled up his pants, and turned back to them. "Surprise!"

"How the hell did you get your hands on this beauty?" Jake asked as he reverently slid his palm over the curves of the stealth boat.

Jake was so focused on the new toy he was making love to with his hand that Ryan was sure he missed the flash of pain—there, then gone—in Cody's eyes.

"You know I opted out not long after you two, right?"

Ryan nodded. He'd heard that, although at the time he'd been dealing with his own demons. Their team had been a close one, but they'd also paired off in a way. Evan Prescott and the boss, Romeo and Saint, Doc and Dog. A stab of guilt struck him that he'd been too wrapped up in losing Kathleen and trying to deal with her betrayal to be there for his friend.

Cody kicked at the water, sending a spray up Ryan's legs. "Kincaid showed up at my door not long after, offering me a job." He glanced at Jake, now with his body bent over the side of the boat as he practically drooled. Cody turned his back on Jake, his gaze settling on Ryan.

"Wasn't ready. Told him that. Next thing I knew, he'd pulled strings and I was in a secret location, learning all the ins and outs of a boat nobody had ever heard of." He leaned his back against the gray metal of a craft Ryan hadn't seen coming at them until it was less than a yard away. "I was a day or two away from putting my gun in my mouth and pulling the trigger."

That was Cody, saying shit that could knock you on your ass. Ryan was sure he was expected to be shocked. He was. "If you had done that, you fucking asshole, I would have dug you up and put another bullet in your stupid head."

"Save your bullet for the bad guys, Doc. I'm here, alive and breathing."

"So you are. It's great to see you." Ryan stepped over to his friend and gave him a man hug, and after a few hard slaps on the back by both of them, he hooked a leg around Cody's and pulled his feet out from under him. The man roared up out of the water and tackled Ryan. Damn, it was good to be together again, he thought as they tried to drown each other.

"Girls, you're getting me wet." Jake hauled them both up by their collars.

Soaked, water dripping from their faces, they exchanged a glance, the message between them understood. With the same precision of movements, they took their team leader down.

"I *will* get you both back," Jake said as the boat raced silently through the night.

Ryan, sitting behind the other two, grinned. "When we least expect it, of course."

"Of course. Damn, this baby's sweet."

"Stop fondling her." Cody slapped at the hand Jake was rubbing over the controls.

"But I love her so much I could just drool all over her."

"You do that, Romeo, and I'll kill you. You know I will."

"Didn't you get the memo, Dog Man? I'm not Romeo anymore."

"He's Tiger now. He went and got married and got respectable," Ryan said, then sat back, listening to their quibbling. The two of them had always been like that with each other, bickering like an old married couple.

As they continued toward the Russian coast—a test run to not only verify the time they had calculated to cross the Gulf of Finland, but to poke at the Russians and see if they got noticed—Ryan's thoughts turned to Charlie. He had asked her to wait for him. It was what he wanted, but after that, he didn't know. She said she would be there for him, and that was good enough for now. When he got home, they could spend time together, figure out what they wanted from each other.

Cody thumped a fist to the ceiling. "Heads up."

Ryan leaned over the back of Jake's seat and watched the video feed from the high-tech night-vision camera mounted outside the boat. Actually, there were four cameras pointed in different directions, he realized at seeing the screen split into four squares, a different scene in each. His gaze narrowed in on the one pointed at the Russian coast.

"There's the little cove I'll nose into to let you off," Cody said, tapping a finger on the bottom left of the screen.

The boat made a few circles so the cameras could record the area from all angles before turning back toward the coast of Finland. There had been no sign of Russian boats patrolling the area, which confirmed their intel. That eased Ryan's mind. The last thing they needed was a confrontation with the Russian navy. Although with the stealth boat, they could not only outrun anything that came after them, but easily hide as well. A little distance between their pursuers—if it came to that—and the *Sealion*, and they could disappear as if by magic.

Cody dialed in the preset coordinates for their hideaway, then said, "Prepare for liftoff." He gave a maniacal laugh as he pushed the throttle to its max.

Ryan was thrown back onto his seat, and he laughed along with the other two as they seemed to take flight. It felt great to be back in action. He'd not realized just how much he'd missed being Doc and being a part of a well-oiled team. Kathleen would have hated his new job, though. Their partings had always been emotional, her in tears and him feeling guilty for leaving her.

"It's the not knowing if I'll ever see you again," she'd once said, tears streaming down her face.

Their worry had been misplaced. They should have been worrying about her. How could either of them have guessed he would be the one to warrior his way through all his deployments with no more than a few minor scratches, but it would be her little corner of the world—one they thought safe—where death came calling?

Charlie defied death every time she set foot in her stunt plane and tested her skills and the aircraft to the max. Somehow, that put her on more equal footing with him than Kathleen had ever been. Instead of them both worrying about him, they could worry about each other.

"So you married Kincaid's sister and you're not dead. How'd you manage that?"

The conversation going on between Jake and Cody caught Ryan's attention, and he waited to hear what Jake had to say.

Jake laughed. "Very carefully."

Their speed slowed, and Cody eased the boat alongside a dock, then into a boathouse in the middle of nowhere. No houses dotted the shore; no lights from cars or anything else shone in the night.

"How'd Kincaid find this place?" Ryan asked.

Jake snorted. "He didn't find it. He had it built. There's probably sawdust still on the dock."

The boss was like some kind of magician. Want a boat only whispered about? Poof, you got it. Want a boathouse to hide it in? Poof. There it was, easy as pulling a rabbit out of a hat.

Ryan wondered if Mr. Bunny missed him.

"I promise, he'll be back soon," Charlie said to the rabbit that had spent the last two days staring at the front door. Other than the one phone call, she hadn't heard from Ryan. She had resisted the urge to call Maria to ask if there was news of the guys. Her new friend probably knew where they were, what they were doing, and if all was proceeding as planned. None of which Maria would be able to share with her.

A part of her wanted to be hurt that Ryan hadn't found a way to call, if only to be sure there hadn't been any more incidents with her plane. The little, insecure voice in her head mocked her, and tried to make her believe he didn't care enough to bother. She ignored that voice as best she could. If he was on a dangerous mission—and she believed he was—he was probably under some kind of blackout order. Was that what they called it when they went undercover? She'd have to ask him.

"Mr. Bunny, I miss him, too, but I have to go to work." She picked up the rabbit and carried him to his little bed in the kitchen. She'd already changed the water in his bowl and measured out his allotment of food. Grabbing her purse, she ran for the door, managing to get it closed before Ryan's pet could follow her out.

As she drove to the airport, she considered the meeting she'd arranged for that afternoon. The last thing she wanted to do was visit her stepfather in prison, but she needed to look him in the eyes when she asked if he'd hired someone to try and kill her. Her request for a visit had almost immediately come back approved. No surprise there. The man undoubtedly thought she was finally coming around.

Ha! He was the one in for a surprise. The creep should have gotten the message when she showed up to object at his parole hearing, but his monthly letters still arrived like clockwork. He'd even said in the first one after the hearing that he forgave her. There was nothing to forgive her for, and she'd stopped reading them.

"Dammit, David," she yelled when she turned into the parking lot and saw her aerobatic plane tied down on the tarmac instead of safe inside the hangar. Fuming, she went looking for her boss.

"I had to move it," he said, crossing his arms over his chest when he saw her coming at him. "And don't start poking at me. We had a Gulfstream come in last night and I had to make room for it."

For good measure, she poked a finger right into the middle of his chest, then pinched him.

"Ouch! Stop that, Charlie." He backed away.

Unable to argue that a paying customer outranked her, she spun and headed for her plane. "There better not be a scratch on her," she tossed over her shoulder as she left.

Circling the Citabria, she checked every nut and bolt, the tire pressure, the wings and struts, the aileron, and so on—taking her time going through the checklist. When satisfied all was as it should be, she tested her fuel. With an aircraft-fuel-testing cup, she collected a sample and checked the color and smell to make sure there was no dirty-water contamination.

"Lucky you, David. You get to live for another day," she said when finished. Normally, she preferred to practice in the early mornings before her first student arrived. Because she planned to fly her plane to an airport near the prison, she had instead decided to do a run-through of her upcoming performance on her way back to Pensacola.

Having cleared her afternoon schedule, the morning passed faster than she wished. As she made another check of the outside of her plane before leaving, her feet felt like blocks of cement were tied to them. She did not look forward to seeing her stepfather and began to list the reasons why the idea was a dumb one.

Stop being a coward, Charlie. Right, if she could perform death-defying stunts, she could certainly face one sorry excuse for a man. She climbed in, harnessed herself securely, made sure the cabin door and windows were closed, then worked her way down the preflight checklist.

"Let's go flying, baby," she said, patting the dash. The flight from Pensacola to Chipley, the closest she could land to Marianna, took a little under an hour. Many FBOs had courtesy cars, and Charlie had called ahead and reserved one of the two they kept available for pilots.

Keys in hand, she found the small car. Setting the directions she had printed the night before to FCI prison in Marianna on the passenger seat, she drove the twenty-three miles that would put her face-to-face with the man who had destroyed so many lives.

Getting in to see him involved showing a photo ID, having her picture taken, and watching as her fingers were rolled over a pad of ink. Although she expected some kind of search of her person, she was relieved that all she had to do was walk through a security scanner. Before she was ready, she was sitting in a chair, a phone to her right with only a sheet of Plexiglas that would separate her from the man she hated.

Her stomach rolled, and she wondered where the closest toilet was. Before she could find someone to ask, Roger Whitmore walked into view, a guard following behind him. Charlie squeezed her eyes shut. A few seconds passed before she could force her eyes open to see he held the phone on his side of the glass to his ear as he watched her.

Don't let him get to you, Charlie.

She pulled the black handset from its cradle and slammed it so hard against her ear that it took all of her willpower not to grimace.

"Hello, daughter."

A rage consumed her—one she had only known once before when she had learned Shannon had put a rope around her neck and stepped off the stool under her feet because of the man now smiling at her. The guard standing a few feet behind him scratched his nose, his boredom obvious by the blank look in his eyes.

She wanted to scream at the man to look, to see the evil in her stepfather's smile.

Don't smile at me like that. Please don't. Needing to find the strength to face the man on the other side of the glass, she thought of Ryan. He was such a good, honorable man, one her stepfather couldn't hold a candle to. If he were sitting next to her, he would put his hand on her knee and give it a reassuring squeeze. "You can do this, Charlie," he would say.

She looked right into the eyes of the man who had caused an innocent girl to take her life and had destroyed a family. Charlie's family. "I'm not your daughter. I'm here to ask you a question."

"You're doubting what you thought you saw and want to know if I really did what you claimed. I've been expecting this, Charlene, and I want you to know that I don't hold a grudge against you. Jesus said to turn the other cheek, and that is what I'm doing. I forgive you."

"I know what I saw." A black rage burned its way through her blood. If there wasn't a barrier between them, she would have clawed his lying eyes out. She forced herself to take a calming breath. If she wasn't careful, he would get up and walk away.

He was still a handsome man, more so than when he'd first gone to prison. Silver dusted the hair over his ears, giving him a distinguished look. His body was more muscled than it had been, most likely from prison workouts. As much as he tried to affect a kindly demeanor, his nature was there in those cold blue eyes. Sick eyes.

"You were a child, daughter, prone to hysterics. All you have to do is tell them you were confused because of your friend's death." The smile he gave her was inappropriate to the conversation. It was a sly one. "As her best friend, I imagine she talked to you, gave you hints she was depressed. Why didn't you try to stop her? At the very least tell someone you were worried about her?"

The son of a bitch was cunning. He had shot his arrow through the middle of the bull's-eye. The guilt of not anticipating that Shannon would take her life still rested heavy in Charlie's heart. But it was one thing for her to lay a guilt trip on herself. She'd be damned if she would let the man who held the blame for causing so much heartbreak point his finger at her.

"I'm not interested in listening to your lies. I heard a rumor that you've hired someone to kill me. Obviously cutting the brake lines on my car didn't work since I'm sitting here in front of you."

She had considered how to approach him, and if he were responsible, that should take him by surprise since no one had cut the brake lines on her Corvette. Her hope was that he would slip up and ask about her plane. Instead, there was genuine shock on his face. Either that or he was a damned good actor. Still, she thought his reaction was real.

"As I have written you in my letters, I've found Jesus and murder would be a sin. Besides, Charlene, why would I want you dead? I need you to recant your testimony, and you would be no use to me as a corpse."

The way he referred to her as a corpse chilled her blood. "Never going to happen," she shouted, unable to rein in her fury. He tapped on the Plexiglas when she put the receiver back onto its cradle and turned away, but she didn't look back. Once outside, she sucked in the fresh air in great gulps. All she wanted was to get in her plane and forget she had ever known the man sitting behind prison walls. When she got back to Ryan's, she was going to take a long, scalding shower so she would feel clean again.

She made one stop at a grocery store on her way back to the airport, grabbing the first package of cookie assortments she saw. After turning in the courtesy car and leaving the box of cookies on the counter as a thanks for the loan of the car, she walked out onto the hot pavement, and made her—lately—extracareful walk around the plane. The bright afternoon sun glinted off the metal frame of the windshield, and she put on her sunglasses. Still rattled by facing her stepfather, she realized she wasn't in the right frame of mind to practice. Instead of heading out over the gulf, she turned for home.

Two miles from Pensacola Aviation Center, the engine sputtered.

CHAPTER NINETEEN

The night was overcast, perfect for hiding in the shadows. As the almost-impossible-to-hear—unless you knew to listen for it—hum of the stealth boat faded away, Ryan followed Jake up to the tree line.

"He loves that boat, but it was killing him to drop us off without him hiding behind a rock or hanging out of a fucking tree, giving us cover," Ryan said as he moved up beside Jake for the one-mile jog to where a nondescript Russian car awaited them. They hoped.

"Dog's killed enough bad guys. It'll be awhile before Kincaid puts him behind the sights of a sniper rifle again."

Ryan got what was unsaid. Cody hadn't been joking when he'd said he was having trouble adjusting. Who could blame him? More times than they could count, the man had saved their asses by killing someone. A lot of someones.

They came to a dirt road and stopped without either of them saying a word. The black, older-model Volga coupe—a common Russian car—tucked away in the trees on the other side seemed safe enough. One never knew, though, what was watched and what wasn't. The nearby call of a nightjar sounded, then was answered by another. The tension in Ryan's shoulders eased a little. If the birds were talking, likely there was no one in the bushes or behind a tree with a rifle sight centered on the middle of their chests.

"You go around to the left; I'll take the right," Jake said.

They both had their guns down by their sides. Like smoke, Jake faded away. On silent feet, Ryan made his way to the back of the car, he and Jake reaching their half circle at the same time. "Seems abandoned," he said.

Jake let out a quiet breath. "Seems so. I'm driving."

"Says who?" Ryan said.

A key dangled in front of his face. "Says me, the one with the key."

"Not fair. You're taking advantage of your status as brother-in-law to the boss."

Jake snorted as he pulled on a thin pair of gloves. "Fucking A."

"Then after you, oh fearless leader," Ryan said with a bow and the wave of his hand. He slid onto the passenger's seat after putting on his own latex gloves to keep from leaving his fingerprints behind.

On the bench seat next to him was a map that had been left for them. Not that they didn't have one of their own, but verification never hurt. He reached to the back, snagging the pack he'd tossed there, and pulled out their map, a penlight, and the GPS already programed for their destination. Setting the GPS on the dash where they could both see it, he turned to compare the two maps.

"We've got almost two klicks of dirt road before we come to pavement," he said. "Let's just hope we don't meet anyone before we get on the highway. Hard to explain what we're doing out in the middle of nowhere."

"Since neither one of us speaks Russian, we'll just have to shoot them."

Ryan curled his middle fingers and stretched out his thumb and pinky, imitating a phone. "Yo, boss, would you do that magic thing you do and poof us some shovels? Got a few bodies to bury." He thumped Jake on the side of the head. "You're a bloodthirsty bastard."

"Dammit, my head's already caved in from Kincaid doing that all the time."

"Cause you're just so thumpable."

"You mean loveable."

"No, I actually meant thumpable. You never answered Dog's question. How did you manage to snag Maria without the boss killing you?"

Jake grunted. "Oh, he wanted to, but Maria made him promise not to hurt me."

"Lucky you."

"Because I'm not dead or because I got Maria?"

"Both."

"Yeah, I am."

There was a softness in his friend's voice that had never been there before he fell in love. Ryan tried not to envy him. He had loved being married, being half of a whole. It was hard not to be depressed knowing he might never have that again because his ability to trust had been destroyed. As he kept an alert eye on the road ahead and their surroundings, he wondered if Charlie would still be around in a year. Probably not. Women wanted commitment, and he was no longer capable of forevers.

She would eventually get tired of girlfriend status and want more from him. When she learned he could offer no more than that, she would move on. As she should. The thought of not having her in his life, though, made him want to punch something.

"Heads up," Jake said.

He'd also seen a car pass by ahead of them as they were coming up to the two-lane road. "Shouldn't be much traffic this late at night." That was good and bad. Hopefully most everyone was in bed asleep at that time of night, but it also made them stand out. Two men out and about at two in the morning in Russia would no doubt be considered up to no good.

They had deliberated about the possibility of being stopped, and after considering several options, a decision was made on how to handle the situation. Their cover story was that Jake was a British citizen by the name of Jason Beaumont, and Ryan was Rory O'Neil, Irish businessman. They were partners in a sporting goods company hoping to export Russian telescopes. They had picked that because one of the largest companies in St. Petersburg made first-rate telescopes, among other things.

The Russian company was large enough that it would take time to verify that the two foreign businessmen didn't have an appointment there. If stopped, they would claim to have gone out for dinner and drinks and then gotten terribly lost. Jake could imitate a perfect British accent, and Ryan could easily speak with an Irish brogue. Of course, Kincaid had performed his magic, and they both had papers proving the lie. They carried no other identification other than their forged documents.

Should their cover not pass muster, both he and Jake had Tasers in a pocket of their black cargo pants. If they had to, they would subdue anyone who tried to arrest them, then Ryan would give them an M9 shot to put them out for anywhere from ten minutes to half an hour. Depending on the circumstances, they would either make a run for it, or hog-tie their captives and stash them somewhere they'd be found the following day. Ryan just hoped it didn't come to that.

At the paved road, they turned northeast toward St. Petersburg. It would take about an hour to reach the location where they would hide the car and continue on foot. Using the penlight, Ryan took the time to go through his pack, double-checking the contents. He had ten syringes filled with the M9 serum, a dart gun also filled with the tranquilizer, and four small-animal tranquilizer syringes, along with a small bottle of Valium in a child's dosage.

Each man had guns with silencers, and knives sporting wicked blades hidden on their bodies. When he came to the shrink-wrapped, sterilized scissors and the baby blanket, he sent up a prayer that he wouldn't need to use them.

As he stared down at the little blue wrap, Ryan wondered what the sex of Kathleen's child had been. If it had been included on the autopsy report, he'd missed it. Of course, after reading the part stating she was pregnant, he hadn't comprehended much past that. His dream of having a family, of loving Kathleen forever, had come to a crashing end, with no time to prepare for the train wreck he hadn't seen coming.

"Your biological clock ticking or something?"

Ryan jerked his head up. "What?"

"You're fondling that blanket like it was a baby's cheek."

He glanced down to see that his fingers were, in fact, caressing the velvety material. "No, just hoping we don't end up delivering a baby before this is over."

After a few seconds of silence, Jake said, "When are you going to tell me what's eating at you?"

Never. "Don't know what you mean, man."

"Have it your way, but when you're ready, I'm here for you."

"I know," he said, also knowing he had just confirmed Jake's suspicion. Eyes burning, Ryan turned his face to the window. Houses were starting to appear, telling him they were getting close to their destination.

He glanced at the GPS. "One klick to where we hide the car." A little under a mile walk to the house. Fortunately, the Akulovs were being held outside the city limits in a quiet neighborhood where there shouldn't be any Russian police patrolling the area at that time of night.

They found the used car lot easily enough, and Jake parked the Volga in a spot between two other cars for sale. For a few minutes, they sat in the dark with the windows down, listening to the sounds, eyes surveying the area around them.

"Ready to rock?" Jake asked, easing the door open without waiting for an answer.

How the boss got such detailed intel was sometimes a mystery, but the For Sale sign Jake stuck on the windshield perfectly matched the other cars. As they slipped into the night, Ryan knew the vibes he sensed coming from his friend were excitement. He felt it, too. It was what men like them lived for. The training, the drills, the planning—all prepared them to look danger in the face and survive it. Nothing compared to the thrill of walking on the edge and living to tell about it.

No one but those who lived it would understand. Whether a warrior or a stunt plane pilot, they were a society unto themselves. He had known Charlie was like him in that way, it just hadn't hit home before then how alike they were.

He missed her.

"Shit. Shit. Shit." After her little temper tantrum, Charlie took several deep breaths.

The engine smoothed out, but she still listened to the raspy voice that had taught her everything she knew about airplanes and being a pilot. She was now approaching a mile before she could land. The checklist in hand, she calculated the glide speed necessary to reach the runway. Hopefully, she wouldn't need it, but she'd be damned if she would disappoint Captain Shafer.

A half mile to go, the engine quit.

Past the panic stage, she just aimed for the runway, knowing she was close enough to make it. After she landed, she sat in her plane and considered that she had told both David and Gary she planned to fly to Marianna for an appointment, and that on her way back she was going to make some practice runs to get ready for the air show. What if she had been in the middle of a stunt and lost her engine?

A shudder rippled through her. Of all the people on that list, those two would know how best to sabotage her plane. But why? What had she done to either one to cause them to want to see her dead? As for Gary, she couldn't think of a single thing. He was the best mechanic she'd ever known, and the man loved his planes. Sometimes he even spoke lovingly to them when he worked on them. Maybe he wouldn't think twice about losing a pilot, but he would mourn the loss of one of his planes, and the Citabria was on his list of favorites. It couldn't be him.

Although a pilot, David only logged enough hours in the air to keep the FBO brass happy. She thought she'd once heard they required him to fly in one of their aircraft at least three hours a month, but she wasn't sure about that. What she did know was that he grumbled about it whenever he took up a plane. So he wouldn't care about the loss of an aircraft, probably. His focus was on the FBO and bringing in the bucks.

There were all kinds of ways to do that—flight school tuition; fueling planes; rent fees for the planes, both on the tarmac and in the hangar—and that was all he seemed to care about. He wasn't a bad guy to work for, and she had always gotten along with him. The only time it had been awkward between them was when he had asked her out. Aaron had just broken up with her, and the last thing she wanted at the time was to jump right back into another relationship.

Even when she was ready to date again, David would have been a no-go. He was her boss for one thing, and she just wasn't attracted to him for another. For a week, he'd tried to get her to go to dinner, go for drinks, go for coffee. "Whatever you want," he'd said. Once he seemed to understand she wasn't interested, he'd stopped asking and she hadn't given it much thought since. That he had posted her picture on a website claiming she was his girlfriend was, to say the least, disturbing.

Should she confront him? She sighed as she scrubbed at her face in frustration, wishing Ryan wasn't away so she could talk to him about it. No answers were coming from sitting in her plane, so she started on the shut-down procedures. When she finished, she climbed out and spied Gary walking toward one of the flight school planes.

Trusting her instincts, she decided to talk to him, see if he had an opinion about what was going on. "Hey," she said, catching up with him.

"Hi." He kept on walking.

That was Gary, no interest in friendly conversations. "Listen, can I talk to you in confidence? I mean . . . what I mean is, I don't want you repeating anything to David."

"Why not?" They reached the Cessna, and he finally stopped.

"My engine shut down again when I was coming in for a landing. Lucky me, I was able to still land, easy peasy. Somebody's messing with my plane, Gary."

Troubled eyes met hers. "I know. I'll take a look at your engine, see what was done to it this time."

"I'd appreciate it. Thing is, I had intended to practice, but changed my mind. If I'd been out over the gulf, I would've never made it back."

Gary was whip thin, in his early forties, and gay, something he'd never tied to hide. He had been in a relationship with the same man for twelve years, and as far as she knew, he considered his life perfect. His boyfriend and his planes were all he cared about. It was one reason she trusted him. He had no motive to harm her, but even less so the Citabria.

"You think I'm messing with you?" His gaze swept over her plane. "I'd never do anything to hurt that beauty."

Charlie almost laughed. Yeah, screw her; just don't touch any of the aircraft under his care. "I know, and that's why I know I can trust you. Have you seen anyone near her, messing with her?"

He shifted his weight to his right foot. "No, and I've been keeping an eye out since all this shit started."

Although she was now positive she could strike him from her list of suspects, she still hadn't learned anything helpful. "Thanks. I appreciate that. I really didn't want to think it might be you or David," she said, watching his reaction closely.

A loose pebble seemed to catch his attention and he toed it toward him, then picked it up and put it in his pocket. Give the man a gold star for not giving anything away.

"He had a crush on you for a while there. Don't know if he still does."

He walked away, heading for her plane. Charlie stared after him. Had he meant to imply anything by that? She needed to talk to someone who could help her sort through everything. Since Ryan wasn't available, she dug her cell phone from her pocket and called Maria.

"Hi, it's Charlie," she said when Maria answered.

"Oh, I'm glad to hear from you. You doing okay?"

No, she wasn't. Someone was trying to kill her, and she missed Ryan, both things equal in her mind. Okay, maybe the killing part took first place, but she sure missed her boyfriend. "Yeah, I am," she lied. "Listen, I was wondering if you might have some time in the next few days. I need to work some things out in my mind, and I could use—"

"Drinks. In two hours?"

"Uh, sure. Thanks."

"Great. My house. In fact, since both our men are gone, why don't you spend the night, then I won't have to worry about you driving home. We'll order a pizza and consume vast quantities of wine. If you bring a bathing suit, we can do all that while we float aimlessly in my pool."

"Sure, I'd love that." Charlie swallowed the lump in her throat. She'd been okay with depending on no one but herself for so long, but since Ryan had walked into her life, it seemed things were changing.

"See you soon," Maria said, then clicked off.

Since she didn't want to talk to David until she had a chance to work things out in her mind, Charlie headed for her Corvette. In a hurry to be gone before anyone stopped her, she jogged past several cars until she came to hers. As she pulled the door closed, she heard David calling to her. Pretending she hadn't heard him, she jammed her key into the ignition and backed out of the space, then took off.

When she reached Ryan's, she scooped up Mr. Bunny and held him to her. Even though he was a living, breathing, warm thing, he didn't come close to her need to be held in Ryan's arms.

After getting her bunny fix, she set him down and headed for the shower. "You coming?"

She glanced over her shoulder to see him sitting expectantly in front of the door. The rabbit was going to make her cry if he didn't stop that. Returning to the living room, she picked him up and carried him with her to the bedroom, closing the door behind her.

"There you go," she said, setting him down on Ryan's pillow. When she'd agreed to stay over at Maria's she'd forgotten about Mr.

Bunny. Unable to bear the thought of leaving him alone all night, she made a quick call, relieved when Maria said to bring him with her.

"You just got invited to a slumber party," she told him. "Whadda you think about that?" After a quick shower, she decided she had time to fold the load of clothes she had washed that morning. Most were hers, but there were a few of Ryan's. It seemed a personal thing to be folding his T-shirts and boxers, but she couldn't resist rubbing one of the soft shirts over her cheek. It no longer smelled of him since being washed, and she wished she had thought to keep one out.

Mr. Bunny hopped over and sniffed at the folded pile of clothes as if he knew they belonged to Ryan. She pushed his nose away. "You're gonna get fur on them." Although she felt like she was snooping, she opened several of his drawers before she found the one for his boxers. The one above it held T-shirts, and as she started to put them away, she spied the edge of a frame and pulled it out.

It was the picture of Ryan and his wife. *Kathleen.* It was a pretty name, a feminine one, unlike Charlie. It really was time to stop trying to be one of the guys. She had proven herself hadn't she? Charlie or Charlene, she was a good pilot, and no one could deny that. Besides, she loved the way Ryan said *Charlene*, especially when he whispered it in her ear during intimate moments.

Had he hidden the picture away so she wouldn't see it, she wondered as she trailed her finger over the silver frame. Again, it struck her how happy they both seemed, and she felt jealous of the woman. Not that he'd once loved her, but that he held on to her memory. Would there ever be room in his heart to love another woman? Tucking the photo back under his shirts, she closed the drawer.

She scooped up the rabbit. "Let's go *par-tay*, Mr. Bunny."

CHAPTER TWENTY

A six-foot-tall block wall circled the target house, with no bushes around the dwelling to provide cover. Ryan held the nightscope to his eye, focusing on the guards. "Dumb asses. They're standing together outside the front door, having a smoke break. You're clear to go over," he whispered into the thin wire inches from his mouth.

Jake responded with a snort. "I was hoping for a challenge."

Swinging the scope to the back wall, Ryan watched his teammate's head pop up, then his body appear as he nimbly swung his legs over, and then dropped to the ground. Jake ducked low and ran to the back corner of the house.

"Red rover, red rover, come on over."

"What are we, in grade school?" After one last check to make sure the guards were still more interested in their cigarettes than their surroundings, Ryan tucked the scope in his pocket, then made his way to the spot where Jake had gone over.

Back at K2, when they were training for this moment, there was—as far as Ryan could tell—a duplicate of this wall down to the last brick. Having spent most of the week climbing the thing, practicing the most efficient way to get from one side to the other, his respect topped the charts for Kincaid and his boss's obsession with intel and training.

Once over, he headed to the opposite corner of the house from Jake, his silencer already in one hand, the Taser in the other. The husband and wife slept in the back bedroom, and he slipped down the side of the house to the first window, where he gave prearranged taps on the glass. Tap, tap, tap. Tap. Tap, tap. *We're here.*

"Let's do this," he said into the mike.

"Roger."

He made his way to the front corner of the house, opposite to where he knew Jake had stationed himself. Now all they had to do was wait, and hope the idiot guards soon got back to their duty of actually walking the perimeter of the building. Five minutes later both guards laughed, something was said in Russian, and then the crunch of footsteps on gravel sounded.

Bringing up the Taser, he grinned. Two lazy guards were about to be taught a lesson. A shadow of the man's body caused by the porch light preceded him, and Ryan rolled his eyes. No one on his team would ever make that kind of mistake. *You're just making this too easy, dude.*

At the moment he calculated the man to turn the corner, he pulled the trigger on the Taser.

"Oomph."

That was the only sound the man made as his legs gave way. Ryan caught the guard's twitching body and eased him to the ground. Quickly removing one of the syringes, he stuck the needle into the man's jugular, where the M9 should take effect immediately, which it did. Removing the Taser's electrodes, he jogged to the other side of the house to subdue Jake's man. Once the two guards were knocked out, they hog-tied both of them, then dragged them to the front door. It had taken less than three minutes. Now to get the family out of Russia.

Jake thumped his fist on the door, using the same signal as Ryan had on the window. The door cracked open and a man's face peered out.

"Freedom awaits you, my friend," Jake said, the words also prearranged.

The go-between was the daughter's doctor. He had been the one to make overtures to the American government on behalf of the Akulovs, and had carried messages back and forth once the Americans agreed to come for the family. Could he be trusted? It seemed so, but there was always the possibility he had set them up. Because he knew when they would arrive at the house, both Ryan and Jake wanted to be gone as soon as possible.

Once the code words were given, Akulov opened the door. Ryan grabbed the feet of the first guard, and with Jake at the man's head, they carried him inside, following the Russian man down a hallway to a broom closet. The process was repeated with the second guard.

Jake took a dead bolt, some screws, and a small drill from a pocket of his cargo pants and installed the lock on the outside of the door. When the men did wake up, they would have to bust their way out.

Mr. Akulov nodded as if reassured, then stuck out his hand. "Demetri Akulov. How do I thank you for saving my daughter's life?" he said with a heavy Russian accent.

"Just doing our job, man, just doing our job," Jake replied, exchanging handshakes.

That was true, but Ryan knew his friend, and picked up on the catch in his voice. "We need to go, Mr. Akulov. Where's your wife and daughter?" And the damn dog.

When the man opened the door to a bedroom, the dog announced his location with a series of yaps as he ran toward them. The white bundle of fur bounced like a windup toy as he circled them, barking his little head off.

"Who let the dog out?" Ryan muttered as he dance-stepped away from the nipping teeth.

"Put him under," Jake said, then walked into the room.

When Ryan pulled a syringe from the pouch at his waist, Mr. Akulov grabbed the dog and stepped back. "Not kill him, please. Would break Sasha's heart."

"I'm not going to kill your daughter's pet. This is just something to make him go to sleep for a little while, I promise," he said, looking the man in the eyes, letting him see the truth in them. The man nodded as he held out the dog, allowing Ryan to give the animal the shot, then there was blessed quiet when the dog conked out.

"Doc, I think you better come here."

He didn't like the tone of Jake's voice. "What is it?" he asked, entering the room, stilling at the sight of a hugely pregnant woman. No way was she only seven months. "How many months?" he demanded, turning on Akulov, who had followed him in. "When is this baby due?"

The man had the good grace to appear abashed. "Baby come in two weeks. If I tell your government that, they not have send you."

Perhaps, perhaps not. If the man had information they badly wanted, they probably would have sent someone. It wouldn't have been them, though, because Kincaid would have refused if he'd known. Ryan knelt in front of the woman. "Do you speak English?"

She looked at her husband, who nodded. Did she need permission to speak? Ryan tried to imagine Maria or Charlie asking permission to talk. Yeah, that would happen maybe never.

"I," she pointed to herself, "one day be American."

That was said with pride, causing Ryan to smile. "And you will be. I need to touch your stomach." He held up a hand. "May I touch your baby?"

Akulov said something, translating Ryan's words, he assumed. She pushed her stomach out to him. "I need you to stand up." He took her hands and pulled. "She's dropped," he said to Jake. "If we're lucky, she has another day or two before the baby decides to come."

"Let's just get her to Finland. After that, I don't care when that baby decides to make an appearance."

Ryan couldn't agree more. He turned to the young girl, the reason Akulov had set everything in motion. She was a beautiful child—blonde, blue-eyed like her father, and her skin as pale as an albino. If he had to guess, she needed that heart transplant sooner rather than later.

"Hi, sweetheart," he said as he pulled a small, white stuffed poodle toy from the left pocket of his cargo pants. When he handed it to her, she giggled as she grabbed the toy and hugged it to her chest.

"Time to go," Jake said.

Akulov knelt and pulled two duffel bags from under the bed. When Jake glared at them, the Russian man glared back. "They say we bring two, yes?" He passed the sleeping poodle to Ryan, then thrust the bags at Jake, who took them with a resigned sigh. Lifting his daughter in his arms, he said something to his wife. She stood and curled her fingers around the back of his belt. "Go," he ordered his American saviors.

"I never thought I'd miss Afghanistan, but I'm suddenly beginning to," Jake muttered as he led them out of the house.

At the back gate, Jake set down the duffel bags. "Explain to them what happens next," he said, then vaulted over the wall and disappeared.

"He's going to get the car," Ryan said, wishing the operation was done and over with. Snoring poodles, ready-to-drop-their-kid women, children who would die without a transplant, and a husband-slash-father who was worried enough about his family that he could prove to be unpredictable were not Ryan's idea of fun.

He tucked the dog under one arm and rested the animal's weight on his hip, freeing his other hand so he could palm the gun stuck into the waist at the back of his pants. "Do you have a key for that?" he asked, eyeing the lock, figuring he would have to either shoot it off or hoist an about-ready-to-deliver woman over a six-foot-high wall.

"Yes. Yes. I do." Akulov pulled a key from his pocket and slid it into the lock.

Ryan stepped forward, blocking the opening. "Stay behind the wall until the car pulls up, then as fast as the three of you are able, get inside the backseat. Okay?"

Akulov gave a vigorous nod, then translated the instructions to his wife and daughter. The child impressed Ryan. Other than giving her dog worried looks, she hadn't complained or cried.

"Stay where you are until I tell you to move." He handed the dog to Akulov, then stepped past the gate and surveyed the street from left to right. All seemed quiet. Strangely, he didn't like the quiet. Give him rocket-propelled grenades and heavy-caliber mortars aimed at his head any day over this eerie silence. At least then he knew where the enemy was.

The sound of an approaching engine had him slipping back behind the wall, his gun at the ready. The Akulovs squeezed together so close behind him that he could feel their body heat on his back. The car came up the street, then stopped in front of the gate.

"Go, go, go," Ryan said after he confirmed it was Jake in the Volga. When they hesitated, he picked up the girl and carried her to the car, setting her on the backseat. The parents followed and once they were inside, he went back and grabbed their two bags, tossed them on the floor at Akulov's feet, then closed the door. He ran around to the passenger side, jumping into the car.

"Let's haul ass," Jake said, doing just that.

Ignoring the conversation in Russian going on between the family, Ryan reached into the backpack at his feet and pulled out the satellite phone. "We have them," he said when Kincaid answered.

"Any trouble?" the boss asked.

"Piece of cake. Well, unless the stork decides to land before we make it back to Finland. Wife's due in two weeks, maybe sooner. Looks like the baby's dropped."

"Two weeks? We were told she was only seven months."

"The family lied about that. They were afraid if we knew how close she was, we wouldn't come for them."

"We wouldn't have."

"Too late now. I'm about to call Dog, tell him to pick us up in an hour."

"Car coming up behind us," Jake said.

"It's probably nothing, boss, but there's a car behind us. Better go."

"Call back when you can."

Ryan returned the phone to the backpack, then turned to watch the oncoming car. It seemed to be going fast, and the hair on the back of his neck itched. They wouldn't run; that would just give them away. Hopefully, it was someone out for a late night, in a hurry to get home. When it was only a few yards from them, blue lights mounted on the roof flashed.

"Shit," Jake said.

Taking a rabbit to a slumber party was like toting around a baby. Charlie set the carrier with Mr. Bunny inside on Ryan's living room floor, then returned to her car to get his litter box and the bag of rabbit food. He'd had a great time playing with Maria's cat. The two animals had been the evening's entertainment, and the more wine she and Maria drank, the harder they had laughed at the silly creatures' antics. Who knew a cat and a rabbit would decide they were best friends?

If it hadn't been for the bit of news Maria had given her, it would have been the perfect girl time, something she hadn't had since isolating herself after Shannon's death. As soon as Maria had told her that three years earlier, a woman had filed a complaint and taken out a restraining order against David Haydon, he had moved to number one on Charlie's list.

She had wanted to get in her car and go straight to his house to confront him, but Maria had sensibly convinced her that wasn't a good idea. "Besides, before we do anything about this, I want to dig deeper, see if there's more to find on him," she'd said.

Charlie nudged the litter box against the wall next to the back door. What was she supposed to do? The air show was fast approaching, and she needed to practice. Maria had tried to talk her into withdrawing until they found out who was messing with the plane, but Charlie refused to consider it. Flying was what she lived for, and no one was going to take that away from her. Then there was the money she would make from the show. She desperately needed it, especially since she had racked up repair bills on her plane.

Since she wasn't stupid, however, she'd decided to move the stunt plane to Emerald Coast Aviation. It wasn't as close to her apartment, and when she had called to see if they had hangar space, she managed not to grimace at hearing the rental fee. Although it would put another dent in her budget, she didn't hesitate to give them her credit card number. Obviously, she couldn't move the flight school's Cessna, so she'd decided to take a leave of absence until the air show was over.

"What's a girl to do?" she asked Mr. Bunny as she let him out of his carrier. Apparently worn out from his cat-rabbit playtime, he hopped into the kitchen and curled up in his little bed. "You're no help," she told him, then grabbed her purse and keys.

On the way to Pensacola Aviation, she practiced what she was going to say. Although she wanted to demand David tell her if he was the one trying to sabotage the Citabria, Maria was right. They needed to know more about him. Her friend had promised to get right on investigating him further as soon as she got to work. She had also reminded Charlie that even if he had a history of stalking women, that didn't mean it was him doing those things to her plane, which meant Charlie still had to be suspicious of just about everyone. That sucked.

When she pulled into her usual parking space, she saw David walking around the stunt plane. Throwing the Corvette into park, she almost fell on her face trying to hurry out of the car. Leaving her purse behind, she clicked the lock button on the remote, then headed for her boss, head down like an angry bull.

"Get away from my plane," she fairly snarled when she was a few feet from him.

He turned toward her, a frown on his face. "What the hell's wrong with you?"

Be cool, Charlie, a warning voice said in her ear. Right, cool. She could do cool. "Nothing." She forced a laugh. "After everything that's happened, I guess I'm getting paranoid. Sorry about that. You're just making sure she's not been messed with, right?"

Brown eyes narrowed to slits. "You think I'm the one doing that?" He threw up a hand when she opened her mouth to respond. "Screw you, Charlie."

When he stomped off, she hurried to catch up with him. "That's not what I think." Well, it was, but there was no proof, so she couldn't accuse him of trying to kill her. Not yet. "I'm sorry. I'm just a bundle of nerves between all the crap going on and the air show coming up." She grabbed his arm. "Would you just stop for a minute? I need to talk to you."

He heaved a sigh, but he stopped. "What?"

"Why didn't you want to give me the phone number for the attorney?" Well, that had slipped out before she could stop it, but it had been preying on her mind. At his puzzled look, she said, "When I called and asked for the aviation attorney's number, you said you were in the hangar and couldn't give it to me."

His cheeks flushed red as if he was embarrassed. "Oh, that."

"Yes, that. What was the deal, David?"

He stuck his hands in his pockets and stared down at his feet. "Okay, this is going to sound stupid, but I wanted to take care of it for you."

"You mean like being some kind of hero and taking care of my problems?" She had thought he'd gotten the message that she wasn't interested in him. Maybe she hadn't been clear enough.

"Something like that." He shrugged. "But it's all cleared up now, right?"

"Yeah, the complaint has been dismissed." Maybe she was a fool, but she believed him.

"So we're good?"

"We're boss-employee good, and that's all we'll ever be." He nodded, and she was grateful that had been dealt with.

"Are we done here, Charlie?"

"No, there's one more thing." This was going to be harder than she'd thought. "I'm moving my plane this morning. And I'm taking a leave of absence from instructing until after the air show. It's gotten to the point where I'm starting to feel afraid every time I get in the Citabria and start the engine. I can't go on like that."

"You're moving your plane?"

"Yeah, I am."

"Where to?"

"I don't know. Alabama, maybe." No way she was telling him or anyone else where. "There's some hangar spaces available at a few FBOs I'm looking into. It's just temporary until I feel safe enough to bring her back here, okay?"

He swiped a hand through the top of his crew cut. "Okay, I get moving your plane. I would probably do that, too. But you can't just stop instructing without giving me some kind of notice."

"Actually, I can. There's no contract that I've signed saying otherwise." As far as she knew, none of the instructors had contracts, which worked in her favor. "It's just until after the air show. Not even two weeks. Give my students to the other instructors if they don't want to wait for me to come back."

"You're a pain in the ass, Charlie, you know that?"

"I know, and I mean to do whatever I must to keep on hearing you say that." She still hadn't ruled him out, but she had just moved him to the bottom of her list.

"If you're not back instructing the day after that damned air show, you're fired," he said as he threw up his hands and stormed away.

"As long as I'm still breathing, I'll be here," she called after him. She'd better still be breathing because she'd promised Ryan she would be waiting for him.

CHAPTER TWENTY-ONE

The Russian police car was inches from their bumper, its lights on bright. "He's blinding me," Jake snapped.

The Akulovs had gone deathly quiet, and Ryan turned to check on them. They were slouched down in the seat, huddled together. "Stay down," he told them. Angling toward Jake, he said, "You thinking of trying to outrun him?" The car's engine was supposed to be souped-up, but who knew what souped-up meant to a Russian.

"Tempting but no." He turned on the blinker as he slowed. "He's probably already called the stop in, so let's do this fast."

Ryan dug into his backpack and retrieved three of the M9 syringes. Hopefully there was only one cop in the car, but he couldn't see past the bright lights to tell. Jake reached into a pocket of his cargo pants, brought out his Taser, and tucked it next to him. Ryan stuck his between his legs. Their guns stayed hidden. No way were they going to shoot a Russian cop.

"Not stop," Akulov said, pushing on Ryan's shoulder. "They take us away."

"No one's going to take you, Mr. Akulov. Just stay down and be quiet."

"Ooooooh."

At the low moan from the backseat, Jake glared at Ryan as if he were to blame. "Tell me that was the damn poodle and not a pregnant woman having contractions."

"Sure, man, it was the damn poodle."

That earned him another glare from his teammate. "Not funny, Doc."

Rapid Russian from the backseat had him turning again. "What's she saying?" When they ignored him, he glanced at the girl. She stared back at him, her eyes wide with fright. "It's going to be okay, sweetheart." Although she nodded, Ryan figured she didn't have a clue what he said and was only responding to his calm voice.

"Mr. Akulov, what is your wife saying?"

The man's eyes were as wide as his daughter's. "Her . . . she . . . the water, it came."

"Her water broke?"

"Yes!" the man exclaimed, as if Ryan had just said something brilliant.

Perfect. Just perfect. "Okay, she still has some time. Ask her to try to be quiet," he said as Jake pulled to a stop. "Tell your wife and daughter not to be afraid at what they see. We're not going to hurt anyone, okay?"

"Okay."

The headlights stayed on from the police car, keeping them from seeing if there was more than one person inside. A full minute passed as they sat there, waiting.

"What the fuck is he waiting for?" Jake muttered as he stared into the rearview mirror.

"Running the plate, I'd guess."

Another low moan sounded from the backseat.

"The plate's clean. If he doesn't hurry up, he can help us deliver a baby."

Ryan glanced into the side-view mirror. "Worst-case scenario, he's waiting for backup."

"One more minute and I'm going back there."

"I got a better idea." He turned to Mr. Akulov. "Sir, listen to me." He explained what he wanted, and when the man began to shake his head, he said, "She's the only one of us the cop won't be suspicious of. At least ask her if she can do it."

Jake watched the girl's face as her father spoke to her, and when she met his gaze, he smiled. "Okay, Sasha? Da?"

She smiled back at him. "Da. O-ke."

"Tell her to only go halfway to the car," he reminded Akulov. After a quick conversation, the girl opened her door and Ryan was sure they all held their breath as she ran toward the cop car, yelling that her mother was having a baby. At exactly halfway, she stopped, hollered something, then started back for their car.

"What did she just say?" he asked.

"Please come. Please come help my mother," Akulov said.

The child had performed her role perfectly, and before she reached them, the cop was getting out of his car and heading their way.

Jake pulled the Taser from under his leg. "Show time."

"Tell your wife to cry out as if she's in pain," Ryan said.

At the woman's loud shriek, the cop increased his pace. Ryan leaned over the seat as if helping Mrs. Akulov. "Remember," he said quietly to Mr. Akulov, "we're just going to put him to sleep. Tell Sasha to back away when the officer arrives."

Akulov spoke to his daughter, who stood by the open door. When the cop poked his head in, Ryan Tasered him before he had a chance to open his mouth. Before he could fall into the car, Jake was out the door and behind him, pulling him back. Ryan tossed the Taser—the electrodes still attached to the man—to Jake, then grabbed a syringe. Once the cop was tranquilized, he and Jake carried him to the police car, hog-tied him with plastic ties, then put him in the backseat.

"I'll follow you," Jake said.

Ryan got in the police car, and as he drove, he watched for a place where he could hide the car. Three miles down the road, he saw a stand of trees and turned into them, parked, then jogged to the Volga.

"There are headlights a ways behind us," Jake said when Ryan returned. "Let's see how fast this thing can go."

Turned out it could go pretty fast. Ryan fished the satellite phone from the backpack, and called Dog.

"Dammit," Jake said, looking into the rearview mirror.

Ryan glanced over his shoulder to see not just one, but two cars behind them, blue lights flashing. "Coming in hot. ETA ten minutes," he said when Cody answered. "Boil some water." He grinned when Jake snorted.

"Copy coming in hot, ETA ten minutes." There was a pause, then, "Repeat the last."

"Woman in labor on board. Don't you boil water for that?"

"This baby can do a lot of things, but boiling water ain't one of them."

Cody clicked off, and Ryan returned the satellite phone to the backpack, then leaned forward and slipped his arms through the straps.

He twisted in the seat. "Mr. Akulov, you and your daughter need to change places with me." They were coming up to the dirt road, and Jake wouldn't slow his speed over it. Hopefully, the bumps wouldn't cause Mrs. Akulov to deliver her baby, but the SEALs had taught him to prepare for all contingencies. When the man protested, Ryan said, "Do you know what do to if the baby starts coming?"

"No, I . . . I do not, but she needs me."

"I'm a medic, sir. Right now she needs me more than you." He slipped over the seat, picked up Sasha, and lifted her to the front. "When the car stops, you need to take your daughter and run to the boat. Move to the front. Now!"

Akulov said something to his wife, then handed the poodle to his daughter before he scrambled over the seat. Whether it was the command in Ryan's voice or that the man realized his wife would be in better hands with him, Ryan didn't care. At another moan from Mrs. Akulov, he punched the knob on his watch to light the dial so he could check the time.

The last thing he wanted to do was deliver a baby in the middle of an operation, but babies didn't always care about one's wishes. When Jake slowed only enough to take the turn on all four tires, Ryan lifted the moaning woman onto his lap.

"What you do?" her husband demanded—sounding jealous—as he craned his neck to see his wife.

"Trying to absorb the bumps in the road so she's not bounced around so hard that your baby decides to make an appearance." Like he would decide it was a great idea to seduce a moaning woman on the verge of giving birth while in the middle of an operation. Idiot men in love.

Jake must have heard the irritation in his voice. "Listen up," his teammate said, landing a hard punch on Akulov's shoulder with one hand while the other hand expertly steered them toward Cody's stealth boat and out of danger. "Tell Sasha to hold tight to her dog when you run with her to the boat that's waiting for us."

"My bags—"

"We'll get your bags, sir, and your wife. You just do what we tell you."

Ryan shut out the conversation from the front seat and lit up his watch again when the woman in his arms buried her face against his chest and moaned. Certain she was drawing blood, he ignored how her fingernails dug into his skin. "Four fucking minutes, Jake," he said.

"I'll get us there in time, partner."

Although Ryan's arms grew tired from holding Mrs. Akulov a foot above his lap so she didn't bounce along with him, he didn't lower her even an inch. The baby was not going to be born on a dirt road in the middle of nowhere if he had anything to say about it.

"They've gained on us," Jake said. "Almost there. Be ready to haul ass."

Ryan reached up and thumped Jake on the side of the head. "I was ready to haul ass a mile back."

"Dammit, Doc, you do that one more time, your ass is grass."

Ryan did it again. "I'm not afraid of you. Trade places?"

Jake did what he always did when amused by one of his teammates. He snorted. "Not happening, man. Ever." He laughed as if he were having the most fun of his life. "Oh, Miss Scarlett, I don't know nothing 'bout birthin' babies!"

The Gulf of Finland came into view when they turned a corner and Ryan squinted. "Where's the damn boat?" Just as the words were out of his mouth, the *Sealion* appeared as if by magic, and reached the shore at the same time as they did.

The car screeched to a halt. "Go, go, go," Jake ordered, reaching across Akulov and pushing his door open. "Go!"

Ryan decided that was good advice. Following Akulov, who was holding his daughter and the poodle, he ran toward the boat, keeping his pregnant patient close to his chest. The two bags belonging to the family came flying by him—tossed by Jake—and landed on the bow.

Gunshots sounded behind him, and he turned to see Jake crouched in front of the Volga firing back at the four men shooting at him, two of them in uniform, two in plain clothes. KGB? Cody pulled father and daughter aboard, then took Mrs. Akulov from him, tossing Ryan a high-powered rifle and ammo in exchange.

Ryan pitched his backpack onto the boat, then pushed it away. "Get them out of here!"

"You better get your ass back on board in time to deliver that baby, Doc," Cody said before he disappeared below and the stealth backed silently into the night.

"That's the plan," he muttered as he belly-crawled back to the Volga.

It was mind-boggling amazing to take off in her plane without the sickening feeling that something was going to go wrong. As Charlie flew the Citabria out over the gulf, she thought of the day she had flown there with Ryan as a passenger. She tried not to worry about him, but failed miserably. Maria had sworn that everything was going as planned, but Charlie needed to hear his voice, needed to know he was okay. If only he would call.

Yet, his job took him into dangerous situations, and that was something she would have to get used to if they stayed together. That he wouldn't be able to call her would be the norm, but she could live with that if they had some kind of commitment.

Getting ahead of yourself, Charlie. All he'd asked was that she be waiting for him when he returned, not to mention she had an air show to get ready for. After that, they could spend some time together, see how things went. Clearing her mind, she went through her routine, pleased with the Citabria's performance.

After returning to her new hangar, she made sure the plane was towed inside—safe and secure—before she left. Maria was bringing her cat, Mouse, over for cat-rabbit playtime after work, and Charlie headed for her apartment to check her mail and pick up a few more clothes before going to Ryan's.

Although she loved staying at his place, he wouldn't want her there forever. She supposed when he returned and was there to take care of his rabbit, he would want her to move back to her apartment. More questions that couldn't be answered until he returned.

A parking spot was open right in front of her door, and she pulled the Corvette into it. As she walked up the sidewalk, she flipped through her keys to find the one to her house. When she reached the door, she took the three envelopes from the mailbox. Once inside, she set the mail on her small desk, then went to her tiny closet and grabbed a few hangers with jeans on them, dropping them on the bed. She took some extra T-shirts from a drawer, then opened the one holding her underwear, collected a handful, and piled everything on the bed with the jeans.

Returning to her desk, she opened the envelopes, each a bill not due for a few weeks, then she picked up her brown organizer. When she opened it, she flipped through the dividing tabs to reach the To Be Paid section. She frowned.

What the hell?

Even she would admit she was a bit obsessed about things belonging in their place, down to how she filed her bills and important papers. Because her one-room apartment was short of storage space and her desk was actually a small table, she'd learned to be neat and organized. The papers in the accordion folder were definitely not organized. Someone had gone through them!

Making a slow spin around the room, she looked for anything out of place. One of the throw pillows on her love seat was lying flat on the cushion instead of tucked up in the corner the way it should have been. Had someone sat there and gone through her papers? Why? She had nothing valuable, nothing that could possibly be of interest to anyone.

First things first. She went to her door and slid closed the dead bolt; then going back to her dresser, she opened each drawer, viewing the contents with new eyes. Someone had searched through them, too, and although they had tried to keep everything in its place, her clothes weren't aligned as precisely as they should be.

At least her only computer was a laptop and it was at Ryan's apartment. Except for the papers at her desk, the only other personal items she had were in a metal case on her closet shelf. To get to it, she had to drag a kitchen chair over. Taking the case with her to the love seat, she flipped up the hinges. It had a combination lock, but she'd never bothered to use it. That would change, even if there weren't anything valuable inside.

Before she took out the contents, she tried to remember what had been on top, but it had been some time since she had opened it and couldn't remember. A photo of her mother and father with her between them, holding their hands, stared up at her.

Tears burned her eyes, and she angrily swiped at them. She had been too young to remember that day or who took the picture, but her mom looked so happy. Not like the bitter, hateful-word-slinging mother of Charlie's recent memories. The massive stroke that had taken her mother's life a year after Roger had gone to prison had stolen any chance of reconciliation.

She trailed a finger over her daddy's face. As an only child, she'd had all her parents' attention and had never doubted she had been loved. She still remembered how her father would pull her and her mom into a hug, saying, "My two precious girls."

Sometimes life just sucked. If he hadn't been on that highway at that one second in time, he would have made it home safely, and her mother would have never married Roger. Best of all, Charlie never would have had Ashley as a stepsister. And she wouldn't have ended up wondering if she was still loved by her mother.

One second had been all it took to change her life forever, and the ripples of that event would have made her daddy sad. Charlie swiped the sleeve of her shirt across her face, wiping away the tears. She set the photo aside to take with her, and continued on with her inspection.

It took three passes through the items in the case before she realized the one thing missing. A picture of her mom and her stepfather on their wedding day, her and Ashley sitting in front of the just-married couple, all of them with happy smiles on their faces. It had been the first and the last time Ashley had smiled whenever Charlie was anywhere near. She had never understood Ashley's instant hate toward her—because as ugly as the word was, that's what it had been.

Aaron had picked up the photo one night. "Who's that?" he'd asked.

"My stepsister, Ashley Whitmore."

"She's pretty. She live around here?"

"Yeah, we grew up in Pensacola. Last I heard, she's living in her father's house on Scenic Drive." His interest in the picture had disturbed her enough that she'd put it away, and now it was missing.

Her cell phone buzzed, and she set the case aside and went for her purse where she'd dropped it on the desk, her heart pounding out a name. *Ryan,* it beat out in excitement. Seeing Maria's name on the screen, she tried not to let her disappointment show when she answered.

"What's wrong?" Maria said to Charlie's lackluster greeting.

"Someone's been in my apartment," she answered. That was better than telling her friend there was someone else she wished had called.

"Are you still there?"

"Yes, but don't worry, whoever was here is long gone, and I've dead-bolted myself in."

"I need to make a call, then I'll come over. What's your address?"

After giving it to Maria, Charlie grabbed the afghan folded over the arm of the love seat and wrapped it around her. It wasn't cold, yet she was freezing. Who had been in her apartment and why take that particular picture?

Aaron once had a key, but she had taken it back when he broke up with her. Had he made a copy? As for the photo, she had kept it on an end table for a while, but had put it away after he had asked who the pretty girl next to her was. She had already noticed whenever they were out together that he never missed checking out a pretty woman. For him to be looking at a picture of Ashley with interest in his eyes had raised red flags that Charlie had chosen to ignore. With her new knowledge of the kind of man he was, that was regrettable. She should have trusted her instincts. It made her sick to think that she had been *the other woman.*

Charlie wrapped her arms around her stomach and rocked forward. Oh God, she needed Ryan. Someone pounded on her door, the sound penetrating the fog that clouded her mind. Keeping the afghan wrapped around her shoulders, she went and stuck her eye to the peephole. Even though she had only seen the man once before when she had been at Dani's house, her body slumped with relief. She fumbled with the lock, finally getting the door open.

"I'm Logan Kincaid, Maria's brother. Can I come in?"

"Of course." She stepped back, and as he entered, Maria came running up the sidewalk. When her friend reached her, she wrapped her arms around Charlie. "Oh, thank God. You're safe now. I was so freaked out." She pulled Charlie inside, closing the door behind them. "I called Logan. He'll know what to do."

The next fifteen minutes seemed like some kind of bizarre movie reel as the most intimidating man she had ever met questioned her. Yet, having him in her little apartment calmed her. Who would be stupid enough to mess with guys like him and Ryan? The other one she had met, the one they called Saint, walked in.

"Hey, Maria," he said, giving her a peck on the cheek. "Sugar's in the car. Why don't you take her and Charlie to your house while we see what we can find here? I'll pick her up later." He set a small case on her desk. "It's a fingerprint kit," he said to Charlie's unasked question. "I'll clean up after myself, okay?" He gave her an angelic grin, and she could only nod in response to the beautiful, blue-eyed man.

Maria grabbed Charlie's hand and pulled her toward the door. "You're spending the night at my house again. We'll pick up Mr. Bunny on the way. Between him and Mouse, they're going to make Sugar laugh so hard, she's gonna pee all night."

Charlie glanced over her shoulder at the two men, one dark and intimidating, one fair and no doubt scarier than he appeared. They were there for her, but only because of Ryan. Without him, she would be facing all the crap going on in her life alone. She had forgotten what it was like to have anyone on her side, and when Logan Kincaid met her gaze, she mouthed, "Thank you." As she followed Maria out, she tried swallowing, but the lump in her throat refused to go away.

CHAPTER TWENTY-TWO

Ryan crawled up next to Jake. "Why the hell didn't you run for the boat?" He peeled off his gloves and stuffed them in a pocket.

"Oh, I thought I'd just stick around and have a little fun," Jake said, then winced. He pointed to his thigh. "Fuckers shot me. I fell down. Tried to get up. Fell down again. Beginning, middle, end of story."

"You missed your calling, man. That was bestseller shit there." Ryan took aim and shot the gun out of one of the uniformed cops' hands when the man left the cover of his open door. "Let's see. We have orders not to leave any dead bodies behind, which definitely cramps our style. Got any ideas?"

"Happens I do." Jake dug into one of his several pockets and brought out a grenade and two smoke bombs. "You throw the grenade just close enough to scare the shit out of 'em at the same time I toss these. Then you help me into the water."

So they would do what they did best. Swim. "First, we gotta wrap your leg," Ryan said. He pulled a roll of gauze from a pocket.

"That hurts," Jake grunted as Ryan worked on his leg. "Next time somebody shoots me they better find a different place or I'm gonna be real pissed."

"You've been shot in the leg before?"

"Last year. Ready to swim?" he said when Ryan tied off the knot.

"One thing to do first." Ryan leaned over the hood of the Volga and shot the rest of his rounds into the ground in front of the first car to keep the Russians from moving forward. "On the count of three," he said, taking the grenade.

Jake used the grill of the car to push himself up. "One. Two. Three."

The grenade hit the ground halfway between them and the Russians at the same second the two smoke bombs exploded. Hoisting the rifle strap over one shoulder, Ryan slipped his arm under Jake's and they melted away, into the Gulf of Finland. They were in the water, yards from shore when the smoke cleared. By the time the Russians would have been able to see them, he and Jake had slipped under and disappeared.

"It's like finding sexy mermaids, but not," Dog said as he leaned over the side of the *Sealion*, peering down at them.

"Take him," Ryan answered, pushing Jake up. "He was shot." As both he and Jake wore tracking devices, they had been easy to find.

"Yeah, take me," Jake gasped, reaching for Cody's hand. "Doc tried to drown me."

Ryan laughed. "A bullet in his leg apparently doesn't shut him up."

After they both were pulled on board, Ryan, dripping water, went straight to the woman curled into a fetal position on the bench. "How far apart is she?"

"Three minutes," Cody said, as he pushed the throttle of the stealth boat forward and turned for the coast of Finland.

"You're doing good, Mrs. Akulov," Ryan said, and waited for her husband to translate. They had about sixty-five miles before they reached the boathouse, and it was going to be close as to whether the baby would be born on land or in a speeding stealth boat. If nothing else, the kid would have a good story to tell someday.

"Just keep holding her hand and talking to her, Mr. Akulov." Next on his patient list was the girl, and he grabbed his medic's bag. "Hey, Sasha, darlin'. Can I listen to your heart?"

She glanced at her father, who translated for her. With a shy smile, she nodded. Ryan lifted the poodle from her lap, putting him on the bench beside her. The dog twitched and his eyes fluttered. Just great, the little yapper was waking up. While Sasha stroked the animal's fur, whispering soft words to him, Ryan listened to her heartbeat, then took her pulse. It was abnormal, but that wasn't surprising considering her condition, and with all the excitement and worry for her mother. She was also too pale, and that concerned him, but other than observe her, there wasn't much else he could do.

Next, he moved to Jake. "How ya doing, partner?"

"Hurts like a son of a bitch, but I'll live."

"Your pretty wife's gonna be happy about that."

"My pretty wife's going to be pissed I got shot again."

Ryan removed the gauze he'd wrapped around Jake's leg. "There's no exit wound, so it's going to be straight to the hospital for you. Can you move your toes?"

"Yeah. Doesn't feel like it hit any nerves."

His greatest worry was infection from being in the water. Since they all stayed current on their tetanus shots, that would help. The wound began to bleed when it was uncovered. Ryan took a pair of scissors from his bag and cut open Jake's pants. After cleaning the wound as best he could with saline, he bandaged the leg with a sterilized wrap. He held up a bottle of pills and raised a brow.

"No. Give me the satellite phone so I can call Kincaid, then go take care of your real patients."

Not surprised at the refusal of the painkillers, he got the phone and gave it to Jake. "Holler at me if you start bleeding."

"Yeah, yeah."

Leaving Jake to take care of business, Ryan returned to Mrs. Akulov. "How far apart now?" he asked her husband.

"Close. They come close."

A whimper had him glancing at Sasha. Her chest heaved in and out as she stared with wide eyes at her mother. "Sweetheart," he said, "the man driving our boat loves dogs so much we call him Dog. Why don't you take . . ." he glanced at Akulov.

"Valentin. Her dog is Valentin." Then he translated Ryan's words for Sasha.

"Why don't you take Valentin to him. He would love to pet him."

Cody glanced over his shoulder and met Ryan's eyes, then shifted his attention to Sasha. "Hey, sweetheart. You bring that dog to me so I can admire him, okay?"

After her father translated, she looked at Ryan as if asking permission. He nodded, picked up the woozy animal, and placed him in her outstretched arms. "Go on now," he said as he gave her a gentle nudge.

"She have baby here?" Akulov asked, his gaze shifting to Jake.

It was beginning to look that way. The man wasn't happy about having an audience for the delivery. Ryan lifted his chin toward his teammate.

"Kincaid will have an ambulance waiting for us," Jake said, then stretched out on the bench seat and put an arm over his eyes.

"You tell him you need one, too?"

No answer, which meant no. At hearing a little girl laugh, he glanced forward to see Sasha sitting on the floor, her pet on her lap, as both of them stared up at Cody in fascination as he made funny noises. The man barely tolerated adults outside of their team, but had always been able to win the affection of any dog he came across. Apparently, that now extended to children.

Turning his attention to Mrs. Akulov, Ryan timed her contractions. Her head was in her husband's lap, and tears were streaming down her cheeks, but her moans were quiet. Ryan assumed she was doing her best not to upset her daughter. Less than a minute on the last contraction. He took the container of sterile wipes from his bag and cleaned his hands and forearms.

All of a sudden, she pushed up. "Теперь!"

"She said *now*," Akulov said, his voice strained.

For the next few minutes, Ryan shut out everything around him and concentrated on his patient. "I see the head. Tell her to push." Tears streamed down her face as she grunted and pushed. One more hard push from her, and he was holding a baby.

"You have a boy," he said, getting a smile from the mother and a laugh from the father. He grabbed the towel he'd put next to him, wrapped it around the baby, and tilted him at an angle, gently rubbing his tiny back. At a cry, Ryan breathed a sigh of relief. Using the Apgar score—activity, pulse, grimace, appearance, and respiration—he evaluated the baby.

"A healthy boy," he said, and laid the baby on his mother's chest, then sat back, feeling a mix of emotions.

It was his first delivery and it really was a miracle like people said, but there was an ache in his heart. He swallowed hard, remembering his rage the day he read Kathleen's autopsy report and learned she'd been two months pregnant. Yet, even though the baby wasn't his, he felt a sadness that she had never had a chance to hold her child in her arms.

It also occurred to him that if she hadn't been murdered, they would almost certainly be divorced. He'd never considered that, hadn't been able to think past her betrayal. Even so, at least he might know what happened to them if she had lived, understood where they had gone wrong. The sadness that hit him as he watched the Akulovs coo over their baby, he didn't want. He felt like his heart was torn in two, one half belonging to his past and Kathleen, the other half claimed by a blue-gray-eyed cherub. If he was to move forward—and he wanted to—he had to find the answers that would let him put his wife to rest.

The baby let out a loud cry, and Sasha jumped up and ran to them, the poodle wobbling along behind her. As the family exclaimed over their new addition, Ryan moved to the front.

"How long before we get to the boathouse?" he asked Cody.

"Five minutes."

"Good." He decided to let the paramedics cut the umbilical cord. Going to where Jake was pushing himself up, he sat next to his teammate.

"Next time there's a damn poodle and a pregnant woman on any mission, I'm calling in sick," Jake said.

Ryan laughed. "Nothing to it. Just another day at the office."

"Easy for you to say. You're not the one with a bullet in your leg."

"Why didn't you tell Kincaid you'd been shot?" Ryan eyed the bandage but didn't see any new blood.

"So he could tell Maria, and then she'd worry?"

Ryan didn't say, "At least you have someone to worry about you." Then he thought of Charlie and wondered if she was worried about him.

CHAPTER TWENTY-THREE

He was coming home! Strewn over Ryan's bed were the only clothes Charlie had at his place. Why hadn't she thought to bring something nicer than T-shirts and jeans from her apartment, or better yet, gone shopping for something sexy?

All Maria had said when she called was, "They're landing this afternoon at three thirty. I'll meet you in front of security."

Her friend had sounded so excited that her husband was coming home, and Charlie got it because her heart had gone into overdrive at the news she would be seeing Ryan soon. She had raced to his place, showered, washed her hair, and now stood with a towel wrapped around her, trying to decide which T-shirt to wear. She finally picked the one that said, *Feel safe at night, sleep with a pilot.*

Although she didn't know anything about where he'd been other than he had landed in Finland, or what was involved, she had the sense it had been a dangerous mission. She wanted him to feel safe, and the T-shirt seemed appropriate. Never mind she was dying to feel his arms wrapped around her, both while sleeping and not.

Ryan's rabbit popped out from under the pile of clothes, his nose twitching. "He's coming home, Mr. Bunny. He's coming home!" The refrain bounced around in her head like the melody of a song.

Once dressed, she went into the bathroom and applied a little makeup, then blow-dried her hair. She hadn't been this excited since she'd gotten her pilot's license. He was coming home, and she couldn't wait to see him.

Maria squeezed Charlie's hand at the sight of a limping Jake walking toward them. "Stupid idiot, he went and got shot again."

"Did you know that?" Charlie asked.

"No, 'cause he didn't tell us when he reported in. And why not? Because he knew I would yell at him so loud he wouldn't have needed a phone to hear me." She let go of Charlie's hand and headed for her husband.

Charlie searched the faces of the people walking behind Jake. Where was Ryan? They probably hadn't been able to sit together, and Ryan must have been at the back of the plane. So focused on watching for him to appear, she didn't notice when Jake and Maria stopped next to her.

"Sweetie, he's not coming," Maria said, giving her a hug.

Not coming? What did that mean? Had he been hurt, too? Tears stung her eyes at the thought of Ryan hurt and alone in some hospital in a foreign country. "How bad was he hurt? Where is he? I'll go to him." Jake and Maria exchanged uneasy glances, and Charlie's heart fell, landing with a heavy thud in the bottom of her stomach.

"He's dead," Charlie whispered, and clutched her stomach as it took a sickening roll.

"No, no, he's fine. He booked a flight to Boston when we landed in New York."

Charlie stared at Jake in disbelief, and he gave Maria a look that as much as said, "Help me out here."

There was pity in Maria's eyes, and Charlie hated that. "He called my brother, asked for some time off. Said he needed to go home for a few days to take care of some stuff. I'm sorry, Charlie. I didn't know until Jake just told me."

Stunned, Charlie didn't know what to say. He hadn't even bothered to call and tell her not to show up at the airport. He was the one who had asked her to wait for him, and here she was waiting for a man who hadn't cared enough about her to make one lousy phone call.

"Did he . . ." She snapped her mouth shut. If he'd sent her a message, Jake would have told her by then. She stared at the floor, wishing it would just open up and swallow her. How pathetic she must look to them, showing up to welcome a man home who had better things to do than come back to her.

"Listen, I've got some errands to run, so I'm taking off." She had to get away before she suffered the ultimate mortification and broke out crying.

"I'll call you later," Maria said.

"Yeah, sure." She waved a hand as she walked away. A few steps down the concourse, she stopped and turned. "Welcome home, Jake."

"Thanks." His smile was soft, as if he were sad for her.

He had Maria tucked up under his arm the same way Ryan liked tucking her into him. It was too much. The tears she'd been trying to hold back pooled in her eyes. She turned away to leave.

"Charlie," Jake called.

Unable to bear seeing the couple again, nestled into each other, she stopped but didn't turn. "Yeah?"

"I'm sure he'll call you tonight."

"Probably," she said, although she didn't believe it.

The only place she knew to go where she could rid her mind of Ryan O'Connor and the ache he had put in her heart was the sky.

Charlie adjusted her airspeed to enter a snap-roll maneuver. To do the stunt, she would have to depart from controlled flight, stalling one wing during an accelerated pull up. It was a sudden stall, roll, spin, recover heart-thrilling maneuver, and one of her favorites.

It was a beautiful day in Northwest Florida; the sky was an azure blue and the gulf below an emerald green. Fluffy white clouds floated lazily overhead as if they had all the time in the world to get where they were going.

As she set up for the maneuver, she cleared her mind of everything but her and her plane. Why she could vanquish all her problems so easily when flying was something of a mystery, but from the minute her wheels lifted off the runway, she felt like she could breathe again. It was always like that. If she was sad, she flew. If she was angry, she flew. If she wanted to get a certain green-eyed hot guy out of her head, then time to go flying. As she prepared for the stall, her mind cleansed of all the crap going on in her life, she laughed from the joy filling her heart. This! This was all she needed for life to be good.

She came out of the roll, applied the opposite rudder, and released the back pressure to unstall the wings. As she leveled out the Citabria, she saw two navy F/A-18 Hornets circling off to her left, the pilots watching her. They both tipped their wings in a salute. Charlie grinned, and unable to resist showing off, she climbed until she was above them, inverted her plane, and flew over them like Tom Cruise in *Top Gun,* her all-time favorite movie.

Although she was breaking every regulation in the book, she didn't care, nor, it seemed, did the navy pilots. Each gave her a thumbs-up, and one blew her a kiss. As they rolled away and flew off, Charlie watched them until they'd disappeared, envious of their planes. How she would love to be behind the controls of an aircraft that flew at Mach speed.

No way her troubles could catch up with her.

Ryan walked out the door of Boston's Logan International Airport and hailed a taxi. He'd told no one he was coming, not even his mother. Instead of sending Charlie a text when changing planes in New York, letting her know that he was on his way to Boston, he should have called and told her everything.

So call her now, you dumb shit. Taking out his phone, he clicked on her name and stared at it, wondering what to say. How to explain that he wanted a future with her, but until he put Kathleen and the past behind him, his wife would always be between them. Charlie deserved better from him.

He missed her. His finger hovered over the Call icon.

"Where to?" the taxi driver asked.

He stuck the phone back into his pocket, and before he thought better of it, he gave his parents' address. Then, "No, take me to the Marriott on Long Wharf." The hotel was reasonable, but more importantly, close to where Kathleen's jewelry store had been.

If he showed up at his mom and dad's door, they would be thrilled to see him, but there would also be questions he wasn't ready to answer, especially from his mother. She had eyes that could see into her children's souls. What he had in his, he didn't want her to see.

He would take the first few days home to do what he needed to do, then spend some time with his family. After checking in, and throwing his go bag on the bed, he opened the curtains in his room and looked out at the harbor marina. He tried not to think that he had possibly ruined whatever he and Charlie might have had. In a corner of his mind, he held on to her promise to wait for him.

The next morning, and after a sleepless night, Ryan showered, shaved, and dressed. The last time he had slept well was with Charlie. Before he left his room, he called her, got her voice mail, and disconnected without leaving a message. What he needed to say couldn't be left on a machine.

His first stop was at Kathleen's father's house. "Hello, Donal," he said, hiding his shock at how much the man had aged. The last time he'd seen Donal had been at her funeral, and although that had been only a little over a year ago, his father-in-law looked ten years older.

"Ryan?"

Of course he was Ryan. Why was that a question? "Can I come in?" he asked when Donal stared at him as if not pleased to see him. They had always gotten along, so why did he not feel welcome?

"Of course. Of course." Donal stepped back, his slippers scraping over the tiled foyer.

Offered a cup of coffee, Ryan accepted and followed his father-in-law into the kitchen, a place he'd spent many hours. Now it felt as if he were a stranger to the old man. The tingle at the back of his neck that he'd long ago learned to trust sent off warning signals. Any doubt he'd had that Kathleen's father knew more than he'd let on vanished. The two of them had been close, as much friends as father and daughter. Somehow Ryan had to find a way to get the man to reveal Kathleen's secrets.

"I'm sorry I haven't kept in touch," Ryan said. "After she died, I didn't know what to do with myself, but that's no excuse."

Donal turned sad eyes on him. "I understand, son. I didn't know what to do with myself either."

They sat at the worn table where the three of them had spent hours talking or playing Hearts. They had even laughed together at this very table over Donal's blatant cheating. As they each sipped their coffee, Ryan tried to think how to ask his questions so he would get answers.

"I miss her," he said. And even as he said it, it hit him that he missed Charlie even more.

"As do I." Donal traced the pattern of the checkered, vinyl tablecloth. "You didn't just drop in out of the blue, did you?"

Donal had migrated to America as a young man and his Irish accent was still there in his speech. A wave of homesickness rolled through Ryan. They'd had such happy days: him, Kathleen, her father, his family. That time was gone, though, and if he was to move on, he needed answers. He decided to just spit it out.

"You knew she was pregnant, didn't you?"

Donal's eyes met his before his gaze shifted back to the strawberries in the middle of the green squares of the tablecloth. "Why are you asking this now, son?"

So, he did know. "Because I have to know why." When there was no response, Ryan tried again. "Because it's eating me alive, and there's this girl back in Pensacola that I like a lot. I loved Kathleen with all that I was, you know that. But it seems that wasn't enough for her. If I can't understand why, then I don't know if I'll ever be able to trust again."

The strawberry next to Donal's coffee cup got traced twice over before his father-in-law sighed, then sighed again. "*Tá tú ag briseadh mo chroí, buachaill.*"

Ryan tried to translate, but gave up. "What does that mean?"

"I said, you're breaking my heart, boy. I loved my daughter. I love you. Which one of you do I remain true to?"

That was an easy question to answer. Ryan covered the old man's hand with his. "As much as I wish otherwise, Donal, she's gone. I'm still here. Your answer won't hurt her now."

"Talk to Patrick," he said as the nail of his index finger dug through the middle of the strawberry, leaving a two-inch scratch.

Why would Patrick know who had fathered Kathleen's baby? "I don't understand. If Patrick knew something, he would have told me."

Tears rolled down Donal's cheeks as he met Ryan's eyes. "Ask yourself what the one reason would be that he kept such a secret. It probably won't help, but they both were sick with regret that they allowed such a thing to happen."

"Patrick?" That was the only word he could get out before his throat closed on him.

Donal nodded. "I'm sorry, son. You were such a good husband to my Kathleen, and I prayed you didn't know."

Ryan felt as if he'd been sucker punched, losing all the air from his lungs. His own fucking brother? Without asking, he stood and blindly made his way to the bathroom. When there was nothing left but dry heaves, he stumbled to the sink and rinsed out his mouth, then splashed cold water over his face.

A knock sounded on the door. "Are you all right, son?"

No, he wasn't fucking all right. He swallowed, trying to clear his throat. "Had to use the john. Be there in a minute."

Forcing himself to spend another few minutes with Donal, he finally said his good-byes, promising to come again in the near future. It was a lie. He would never come again. Not that he blamed Kathleen's father for what had happened, but he had to mentally cut ties with anything to do with his wife, including her father.

She had betrayed him with his brother, and he didn't know which of them he hated more. A stranger, someone he didn't know, who wasn't supposed to be loyal to him; that he could have accepted. Maybe never understood, but he could have gotten past it.

A few blocks from Donal's house, he pulled over and took out his cell phone, flipped to Patrick's number, and punched Call.

"Well, if it isn't Squirt."

His older brother had called him that as far back as Ryan could remember. Where before it hadn't bothered him, now he wanted to reach through the phone and wrap his fingers around Patrick's neck until the lifeblood was squeezed out of him.

"Yeah, it's me. When you get off?"

"My shift's over at seven, why?"

It was close to impossible, but Ryan forced his voice to sound normal. "I'm in town. Meet me for a beer at O'Reilly's."

"The hell you say? Mom didn't tell me you were coming."

"She doesn't know I'm here, so keep it that way." He hung up before Patrick could ask any more questions. He returned to the hotel, parked his car in the garage, then walked down to the wharf. As he aimlessly wandered the downtown streets of Boston, he tried not to imagine Kathleen in Patrick's arms, kissing his brother, letting Patrick know her in the ways only a husband should. It was impossible to block out what his imagination conjured.

He probably should have told his cop brother to leave his gun at home. Before the night was over, one of them might be tempted to use it.

Leaving the wharf, he walked past his hotel and up two more streets to where Kathleen's shop had been. Over the door, there was a sign of an outstretched palm, with the words *Madame Loka's Palm Reading*.

Something ugly coiled inside him as he stood on the sidewalk and stared at the garish purple and green paint covering the bricks. The last time he had seen the storefront, the bricks had still been red as bricks were supposed to be, and the classy sign with Kathleen's name on it, followed by a pair of entwined rings, had still been there. A woman dripping diamonds walked by him and entered the shop.

Ryan turned away and spent the rest of the day walking the streets of Boston, stopping for a few minutes at each place he and Kathleen had been to . . . the restaurants, the shops, the theatre. As he left each place behind, he left a bit of his rage, handing over those pieces at each stop to her ghost, because although he couldn't see her, he could feel her.

"Why?" he asked her when he finally came to their favorite restaurant. Not expecting an answer and not getting one, he returned to his hotel. He almost called Charlie, but he needed to finish what he'd started before he tried to make things right with her.

CHAPTER TWENTY-FOUR

By the time he walked into O'Reilly's, Ryan was strangely calm. Although he still needed to hear from Patrick's mouth why he had violated every rule that existed between brothers, there was nothing Ryan could do to change it. The day he had spent exorcising his wife's ghost was something he should have done long before. If he had, he would be home, holding Charlie in his arms, and more than anything, that was where he wanted to be.

Patrick was already in a booth along the back wall, two mugs of beer on the table. Ryan slid onto the seat across from his brother, and unable to meet his eyes, he picked up the beer closest to him and downed half of it.

"Liquid courage."

"What?" Ryan jerked his gaze up to Patrick. There was sadness, maybe even regret in his brother's eyes.

"Liquid courage. You know, but you don't know how to ask me." Patrick spun his mug in a full circle before lifting it to his mouth. "I stopped by Donal's before coming here. I check on him a few times a week. He said you were there this morning asking questions."

It was going to be that easy? He had thought his brother would try to deny his affair with Kathleen. Ryan studied Patrick. It would be obvious to anyone they were brothers, but Patrick was bigger, his hair redder. His green eyes were always flashing with humor, one of the reasons women loved him. Was that why Kathleen had been drawn to him? Had he made her laugh in ways Ryan hadn't been able to?

"She was pregnant."

Tears pooled in Patrick's eyes. "I know."

"This morning, when I found out it was you, I thought about killing you."

"And I wouldn't blame you if you had. Mom would be pissed at you, though."

Ryan laughed, surprising himself. "Yeah, then she would've killed me for killing you."

"Nah, you were always her favorite."

"Bullshit. We were all her favorite." Ryan sucked in a deep breath, then let it out. "Why, Patrick? I have to know."

His brother raised two fingers when their waitress walked by. "It wasn't supposed to happen. I want you to know that."

"No shit, *brother*." Ryan drained the rest of his beer, renewed anger vibrating through him.

"Every deployment, you asked me to keep an eye on her, and I always did. If I could, I'd be there when she closed her shop, make sure she safely got to her car. The last time you were gone, I stopped by to walk her to her car one afternoon. It was the day after Erin and I broke up, and Kathleen knew as soon as she saw me that I was upset. She decided I needed a shoulder to cry on and insisted we go somewhere for dinner and talk. That was—"

"That was Kathleen." And it was. She was drawn to anyone in need. Hell, there were too many animals to count that she had rescued and found homes for. People, animals, didn't matter, and he had loved that about her. He wasn't so sure he did anymore.

"Are you sure you want to hear this?" Patrick asked.

"It's not that I want to. I need to. I have to understand. I've been fucked up for the past year, Patrick. I can't . . ." He paused when the waitress arrived and set two more mugs on the table. "I can't let her go until I know why she cheated on me. Believe me, I've tried." Patrick winced at the word *cheated.* Ryan didn't give a damn if he was making his brother uncomfortable. He was the wounded party here.

"I guess I'd feel the same, if the tables were turned." Patrick took a deep swallow of his beer, then wiped the foam from the top of his lips with the back of his hand. "We intended to eat at the Golden Dragon, but when we got there, there was a wait. So we got some stuff to go and went to my place 'cause it was closer. We were just going to talk is all."

Ryan let out the breath he didn't realize he'd been holding at hearing they hadn't gone to the home he shared with his wife. If Kathleen had been with Patrick in their bed, he would have lost it. Why that made a difference, he didn't know, but somehow it did. "Go on."

"Isn't it enough to know it happened? You don't need the details."

"How did you get from talking to fucking my wife?"

Patrick sat back as if struck. "It wasn't like that."

Yes, it was. "Then explain to me what it was like. Tell me why."

"We ate, drank some wine, talked about me and Erin, drank some more, then we talked about you and she started crying. She missed you, Ryan. She didn't understand why the SEALs were more important to you than she was."

He'd heard that from her plenty of times. "They were never more important to me than her."

"Are you sure about that?"

No, but he could honestly say she was *as* important to him. He'd promised he would opt out as soon as she got pregnant. He just expected he would be the one to get her that way. "So she was crying," he said, refusing to answer the question.

"I tried to comfort her. I was the one who was supposed to be crying on her shoulder, not the other way around. We were both a little drunk, both hurting. Before we knew what was happening, it happened. It was a terrible mistake on both our parts, and we knew it."

"Did she tell you when she found out she was pregnant, and how the hell did that happen? The condom break?" Because they had been trying to have a baby, she hadn't been on the pill.

Patrick's cheeks flushed. "I wasn't wearing one. It just . . . it just happened so fast. If it helps, we were both horrified after. She said she was going to tell you when you got home and beg your forgiveness."

"I might kill you after all, Patrick." Suddenly, he didn't want to hear any more. He wanted Charlie. Needed to wrap himself around her and lose himself in her sweet body.

Patrick pushed his empty mug aside. "If it will make you feel better to beat the shit out of me, I won't try to stop you. Truthfully, it might even make me feel better if you did."

Ryan slid out of the booth. "I don't give a damn about making you feel better, brother." He reached in his pocket, pulled out a twenty, and put it on the table. Ignoring Patrick's plea to stay, Ryan walked out of the bar. When he reached his car, he fished his cell phone from his pocket and called Charlie.

"I need you, cherub," he said when she answered.

Charlie squeezed her fingers around her phone. Although she heard the hurt in Ryan's voice, she tried not to respond to it. It didn't work. "Do you want to talk about it?"

"No." A sigh. "Yes, but not on the phone. Can you come to Boston?"

There was a question she wasn't expecting. "Why didn't you call me, tell me you weren't coming home? Do you know how I felt when I stood at the airport waiting for you and you didn't get off the plane?" She laughed, the sound not pretty to her ears. "No, of course you don't."

"I sent you a text, telling you I was detouring to Boston."

"Yeah, you did and it got hung up in cyberspace somewhere and didn't show up until this morning . . . after I stood there like a pathetic idiot, watching for you to get off the plane."

"Jesus, Charlie, I'm sorry. I should have called. I just . . . I didn't know what to say to you."

"Well, that makes me feel better."

"Okay, I deserved that and anything else you want to throw at me. Come to Boston and yell at me, beat your tiny fists against my chest, bash me over the head with a hammer, I don't care. Just come, and when you're done punishing me, I'll tell you everything."

"I don't think I should." The man was killing her, but she had to look out for Charlie. No one else was around to do it, and a part of looking out for Charlie was protecting her heart. Not that it wasn't already a screwed-up hot mess.

"Please, baby." When she didn't answer, he said, "No, you're right, I shouldn't be asking. I know you have your show in a few days, and you need to concentrate on that. Listen, I have to go, but when I get home, we're going to talk, Charlie. About us."

Her heart hammered against her chest with longing, but she ignored it. "We'll see. Did you get the answers you were looking for?"

He laughed, and it sounded bitter. "You know that old saying—be careful what you ask for? Well, I asked for it and I fucking got it."

Not knowing what to say to that, she remained silent.

"Sorry, I'm not myself right now. Have there been any more problems with your plane?"

"Not since I moved it to a different hangar and refused to tell anyone where."

"Good, but don't let down your guard, okay? You'll call me if anything else happens, right?"

"Right. You take care of yourself, Ryan, and try to enjoy your visit with your family."

Another bitter laugh. "My family's half the damn problem. Remember, call me if you need me. Even if you just want to talk, call me, okay?"

"Okay." She clicked off, then stared at the phone. What had he meant by his family being half the problem? From what he'd told her, he was close to his parents and siblings. It wasn't until tears dropped onto the screen of her phone that she realized she was crying.

Damn him.

Charlie peered at the digital clock for the thousandth time, or for what felt like that many times. She groaned at seeing it was after midnight. Go to sleep, she ordered herself as she pulled the pillow over her head. It didn't work. Three hundred and fifty-seven sheep counted later, she gave up. All she kept hearing was the pain in Ryan's voice when he'd said he needed her. Before she could talk herself out of it, she turned on the lamp, then got out of bed and went to her desk, turning on her laptop. Twenty minutes later, she had a flight booked for the following morning, even managing not to gag at the cost of the last-minute ticket as she entered her credit card number.

So what if she had to live on ramen noodles for the next two years? Ryan needed her, and fool that she was, she couldn't turn her back on him. After she packed a carry-on, she set her alarm, climbed back into bed, and fell instantly to sleep.

When the blare of her alarm woke her, she jumped out of bed, heading for the shower. Although she'd expected to regret her rash decision in the middle of the night, she felt strangely invigorated and excited. After a shower, she dressed in a pair of jeans and a T-shirt that said, *Pilot inside.* It was the tamest one she had, and if she ended up meeting Ryan's family, she didn't think her shirt should say, *Will fly for sex.*

When she knew Maria would be up, she called her friend. "Ryan called last night and asked me to come to Boston. I'm probably stupid for doing it, but I booked a ticket."

"If you felt strongly enough to spend the money on a ticket, then you were right to do it. I don't know his story, but he was so sad until he met you. What time are you leaving? I'll take you to the airport."

"You don't have to. I'll call a taxi. I just wanted to tell you where I'd be."

"What time?"

"Eleven fourteen." Charlie squeezed her eyes shut against the swell of gratitude for her friend.

"I'll be out front at nine forty-five."

"Thanks. Really, thanks. Do you have his Boston address?" It hadn't occurred to her until then that she had no clue where to go after landing in Boston.

"Not off the top of my head, but I'll have it when I pick you up. Pack up Mr. Bunny and I'll take him to my house."

"Thank you, Maria, for everything."

"That's what friends are for."

After hanging up with Maria, Charlie debated calling Ryan to tell him she was coming. Not sure if she would change her mind and get right back on a plane for home, she decided not to.

At dinner, Ryan sat in the same chair that had been his as a kid. Knowing his mom would insist on him staying home, he'd checked out of the hotel. His parents had been ecstatic to see him, and he hadn't realized before how much he had hurt them by cutting them out of his life the past year. As his mother fussed over him, and his dad went for manly questions—asking him about being in the SEALs—he let his mom wait on him only because it made her happy. He answered all his dad's questions, telling him amusing stories about his teammates.

His oldest sister, Megan, alternated between concerned looks at him and goofy glances at her husband. It made him wish Charlie were sitting next to him so he could give her goofy grins. His other sister, Colleen, lived in Northern California with her wine-making, rich husband. How that had come about he still wasn't sure, but he hadn't seen her in two years and he missed her. She had been his coconspirator in all things that got the two of them grounded as children.

As Megan's gaze flickered between him and Patrick, her eyebrows furrowed in the way they had in his teen years when he was up to no good. She had always been the one to tattle on them.

Patrick studiously avoided looking at him, and that pissed Ryan off. Who the hell was he to act like the wounded one? About the time Ryan decided to reach across the table, never mind how it would upset his mother, and land his fist on his brother's nose, the doorbell rang.

Their mother rose. "Anyone expecting company?" No one answered as they darted glances between him and Patrick.

"What's going on here?" his father asked.

Ignoring his dad's question, Ryan leaned over his plate toward Patrick. "Look at me, damn you."

Before he could say more, the last voice he expected to hear said, "Is Ryan O'Connor here?"

She'd come. Sweet Jesus, she had come. He pushed away from the table so quickly that his chair turned over. If he didn't get out of the house, away from his brother's presence, he didn't know what he would do next.

"Yes, he is. Come in," his mom said.

Ryan grabbed the keys to his father's car as he walked past the bowl on the foyer table. "She's not coming in." He stepped around his mom. "We'll stop by tomorrow. You can meet her then." Even knowing the rest of the family had followed him and now stood behind his mother didn't stop him from wrapping his arms around Charlie and pressing his face against her neck.

"You're here," he stupidly stated the obvious.

"You needed me," she answered, as if that was the only excuse she needed to travel halfway across the country at a moment's notice.

He picked her up so that she straddled him, carried her to his dad's car, lowered her onto the seat, and buckled her in. Because he couldn't resist, he kissed her. Hard.

"Who is she?" he heard Megan ask.

His mom ran toward them, waving one hand, a tote bag in the other. She handed it off to him. "This is hers." She gave him a fierce hug. "You better bring her back tomorrow, or you'll be cleaning toilets for the next six months."

Cleaning toilets had been a childhood punishment for their sins, of which there had been many committed by all the siblings, but especially by him and his brother. "I promise," he said, returning her hug. "But you can't make me scrub a toilet now. I'm bigger than you."

Before the rest of his family could descend on them, nosy people that they were, he tossed the bag onto the backseat, then jogged around the front of the car and slid onto the driver's seat. As he backed out of the driveway, he tried to decide where to take her. He wanted someplace private where they could clear the air between them, then hopefully pass the night away making love. On his walk, he had noticed a quaint bed-and-breakfast near the wharf. Best of all, he and Kathleen had never been there. He turned the car toward downtown, hoping they had a vacancy.

Charlie hadn't said a word since showing up and asking for him. Afraid to start a conversation he didn't want to have while driving, he risked reaching over and taking her hand. When she didn't pull away, hope spread its way through him. She didn't have to tell him he'd almost lost her. He knew it. But she had come, and he would hold on to that.

And she wore the earrings he'd made for her. Another sign that he still had a chance with her? All he had to do was find the right words to explain everything, then convince her he was ready to put the past behind him.

CHAPTER TWENTY-FIVE

Charlie still wasn't sure she hadn't made a mistake coming to Boston. She supposed before the night was over that she would know the answer. As Ryan drove to wherever he was taking them, she concentrated on the passing view. Never having been to Boston, she thought she should at least pay attention. Get her money's worth, if nothing else.

Her return ticket was for the following afternoon, and she had no choice but to be on the flight if she was to have time to be ready for her performance. Somehow—and much to her surprise—the air show paled in comparison to her hope of making things right between her and Ryan.

Because he was silent, she stayed silent, too. After twenty minutes, downtown Boston came into view, and still, he hadn't said a word. Just held her hand as if he would never let go. Even though tension radiated from him, the silence between them wasn't uncomfortable. He began to rub his thumb over the top of her hand, sending shivers up her arm, and because she wasn't ready to forgive him, she did her best not to let him see how much his touch affected her.

At a quaint building near a marina, Ryan turned into the parking lot. He pulled into a space, then turned off the ignition. "Will you stay here with me tonight?"

Where else was she supposed to go? She glanced at the sign. "I've never stayed in a bed-and-breakfast. Always wanted to."

"Is that a yes?"

"My flight home doesn't leave until tomorrow afternoon. Guess I have to stay somewhere, right?" She knew she wasn't responding the way he wanted her to, but she couldn't help it.

"One room or two?"

What she wanted was for him to just take charge, but she understood he was giving her the choice of whether or not to spend the night with him. "One." She didn't know what the following days would bring for them, and maybe she was stupid, but she wanted this night with him.

"Thank you."

As they walked toward the entrance, Ryan took her overnight bag from her, while his other hand rested on her lower back. "I hope they have a room available," he said.

Turned out they did. As Ryan unlocked the door to their room, her nerves notched up. He followed her in, and she turned in a circle, taking in the décor. She knew nothing about antiques, but she felt as if she'd walked through a time warp, back a hundred years maybe. There was even an old-fashioned pitcher and washbowl, something she'd only seen in magazines. The bed had an iron headboard, a colorful quilt, and fat, fluffy pillows.

Ryan set her bag on a suitcase stand, the only piece of modern furniture in the room. He walked to the French doors, opened them, and stepped out onto a balcony. She followed him and stared out over the harbor. The water sparkled like colored diamonds from the red, yellow, blue, and white lights coming off the boats and nearby businesses.

"It's beautiful," she said.

Instead of taking in the view, he was focused on her. "Yes, beautiful."

There were two wicker chairs on the balcony, and she sat before her legs gave out. How could he make her tremble just by looking at her like that? He settled in the other chair and put his feet up on the railing.

For a few minutes, they watched the boats bobbing in the marina. There were a few large yachts, but most appeared to be smaller pleasure boats. She would not speak first. He had said he needed her, and she had heard the pain in his voice, so she had come to him. As far as she was concerned, they could sit all night staring at the view, or he could tell her what had happened. Out of the corner of her eye, she studied him. Usually clean shaven, he sported a bristly stubble, and he just looked . . . lost. That was the word. He was lost.

Another five minutes passed before he said, "It was my brother."

Shocked, she turned her head toward him. He couldn't possibly mean his wife had had an affair with his brother. "Your brother what?"

"The ba . . . baby. It was my brother's."

Oh, God. No wonder there had been such pain in his voice when he'd called her. He'd even stumbled over *baby*, as if he could barely get the word out. She couldn't blame him—wasn't even sure which was worse for him, the betrayal of his wife or that of his brother.

As the story poured from him, she didn't know what else to do but just listen. By the time he finished, tears flowed down her cheeks. For him. For her. How could he get past something like that? Would she ever matter to him as much as his wife had? He had a history with Kathleen—according to him, they'd been together since the third grade. Theirs had been a once-in-a-lifetime love, for goodness' sake. How was she supposed to compete with that?

"That's it," he said. "My sad story."

That was putting it mildly. "What're you going to do about your brother?"

"I don't know. I don't think I can ever forgive him."

He couldn't possibly know how much those words hurt deep in her heart. "Until you do, you won't ever be able to let go of her." And that was the crux of the matter from her perspective. She was really proud that she had managed to keep her voice steady.

Standing, he began to pace the small confines of the balcony. Not knowing what else to say, she brought up her legs and rested her head on her knees. God, she was tired, both physically and emotionally. She lifted her head to see him standing at the railing as he stared into the night.

Enough was enough. She couldn't do this. It had been a mistake to come. Quietly slipping away, she went into the room and climbed onto the bed, curling up on her side with her face toward the wall. Too wrung out to even cry, she closed her eyes. Minutes later, the bed dipped as he slid up behind her, spooning her. Unable to help herself, she tensed.

"What you just said, you're right." His arms came around her and he pressed his mouth against her neck. "I'm sorry, Charlene."

When she didn't respond, he pulled her closer, until a piece of paper wouldn't have fit between them. He was killing her. There was no place she'd rather be than in his arms, but she couldn't be with a man who loved a ghost.

"Will you come with me tomorrow to my parents' house?"

"No. I can't." She turned to face him. "I can't do it, Ryan. You need to figure out what you want, and you especially need to find a way to forgive your brother. It's not a journey I can take with you."

The orange streaks in his eyes flared. "Do you care about me at all, cherub?" He tugged on the silver chain, pulling his ring out from under her shirt. "I know this thing between us started as a game, but I don't want to lose you. I am though, aren't I?"

She wanted to deny it, wanted to take him however she could have him. But she would hate herself for settling for second best, and in the end, he would lose all respect for her. The only thing she could do was to be honest with him.

"I'm halfway in love with you, Ryan. Whether you lose me or not depends on you." She put her finger over his lips when he began to speak. "I'm not jealous you loved your wife, but I'm sure as hell jealous of her ghost. If you can't let her go, and a part of that is forgiving your brother, then there is no us."

His beautiful eyes filled with tears. "I know I have to let her go, but I don't know if I can forgive Patrick."

"Then you'll never be free of her. I'm sorry for you."

"Can I stay with you tonight?"

She wanted to tell him no, but she couldn't say the word.

"Do you want me to go? If that's what you—"

"Stay."

A shudder passed through him, then his mouth covered hers. His kiss was hot, demanding, possessive. There was nothing tender about it. At that moment, if her life had depended on it, she wouldn't have been able to resist him. How much he really did need her, she didn't know, but she needed him. Wanted him. Burned for him. If that made her a fool, she didn't care. Not then. If she felt differently in the morning, she would deal with it.

"Make love to me, Hot Guy."

Ryan wasn't sure he heard her right. Why wasn't she ordering him to leave, to get out of her life and leave her in peace? He was a hot mess, and without any consideration of what was going on in her life, he'd called and begged her to come to Boston. Then when she had, instead of showing her how happy he was to see her, he'd gone and dumped his pathetic story on her. Yet she was still here, looking at him with those soft, blue-gray eyes of hers.

She'd given him an ultimatum. Forgive his brother or lose her. Because he couldn't bear the thought of not having her in his life, he would try to do as she asked. Somehow he would find a way to do the impossible.

Her small hand came up to cradle his cheek. "Please, Ryan."

"Yes," he whispered. He stood and removed his clothes, then slid his arms under her and picked her up.

She wrapped her arms around his neck. "Where we going?"

"I spent most of the day walking the streets of Boston before ending up at my parents'. I need a shower so I'll smell good for you." He nuzzled her neck. "I figured you could join me."

Wanting to take care of her, he sat her on the counter, then undressed her after turning on the water to warm up. Although he was as hard as an iron bar from wanting her, he didn't want to take her in the shower. Instead, he bathed her, using the scented soap and shampoo provided by the bed-and-breakfast.

She hummed, rippling like a cat being petted as he rubbed the . . . "What do you call this thing?" He held up the sponge he'd taken out of a cellophane wrap.

"A loofah. I'm not sure I've ever smelled like a strawberry," she said, eyeing the label of the shampoo bottle.

"I love strawberries. Did you know that?" He licked the skin at the bottom of her neck. "Mmm, delicious." At her giggle, he smiled. If he didn't find a way to make things right with her, he would be the biggest idiot in the world.

After pouring more of the liquid soap onto the loofah, he knelt in front of her and began to wash the bottom half of her. His face was even with her curls, and unable to resist, he trailed his tongue through her folds, then up. When he touched her clit, her hands grabbed on to the top of his head.

"Ryan?"

"Hush, baby." Her taste was strawberry sweet, and as he lapped at her and inhaled her scent, he wrapped his hand around himself. If he didn't take the edge off, he would come the second he slid into her. It wasn't long before she gasped as a shudder moved through her, and he let go, too.

"Charlie," he said between harsh breaths, then he buried his face against her stomach, squeezing his eyes shut. "Charlie."

She reached behind them and turned off the water, then knelt in front of him. "No matter what happens tomorrow, this night is ours, okay?"

It was more than okay, and although he wanted to demand that she promise they would be together after tomorrow, he didn't. "Okay," he said, and scooped her up, carrying her to the bed.

"We're wet," she said, laughing.

"Just makes it easier to slip slide all over you. Or I could lick you dry. Your choice."

His cherub huffed out a breath. "That's like asking if I want to win a million dollars or win a million dollars."

"Some of both then," he said. As he slid over her warm body, he licked away at the droplets of water on her silky, sweet-smelling skin. She deserved so much more than life had given her, and for that night at least, he would show her how special she was.

He pushed up on his elbows and stared down at her, his breath catching at the hint of sadness in her eyes. Although he wanted to tell her not to be sad, that he would find a way to make things right for them, he wouldn't promise something he wasn't sure of.

"Just so you know, Charlene, there's no one else in this bed with us. It's just you and me here tonight." That, he could promise her.

"Just you and me," she whispered, then pulled his head down.

Their mouths met, explored, tasted each other. Their tongues swirled around each other's, scraping teeth, their noses bumping as the intensity of the kiss increased. The need for her that swelled through him rocked his soul.

You're mine, Charlene Morgan, he wanted to tell her, but he didn't have the right to say it. Not yet. So he showed her with his mouth, with his caresses, and with his body what she meant to him.

As he positioned himself to enter her, he froze. "I'm an idiot. I don't have a condom, cherub, but I'm clean." Not only had he not been with anyone since Kathleen, but K2 required physicals, so he was double sure.

"I've been tested since I broke up with what's his name. I'm good." She grinned up at him. "Even better, I'm on the pill."

"Then let's make some magic, okay?" He liked how she'd referred to her ex, and if it bothered him to think of her with someone else, how must it feel for her to have Kathleen's presence between them? But he'd promised her there were only the two of them in this bed, and he pushed the stray thought away.

"Yes, please."

When he slid into her, he sighed and stilled. The sensation of having her wrapped around him, all hot and wet, was so pleasurable that he couldn't even think of words good enough to describe it. She nuzzled her face against his neck and scraped her teeth over his skin.

"Charlene," he said as he began to move. "You feel so good."

"And you feel . . . impressive." She giggled.

"And you think that's funny? I'll show you impressive, then dare laugh."

With great effort and control, Ryan made love to his girlfriend slow and easy. If that one night was all they had, then she would damn well remember it and him. He made her come three times before he couldn't hold back any longer, and when he let go, he came so hard and long that white spots danced in front of his eyes.

"I think I'm permanently cross-eyed," he said when he could talk again. She didn't laugh, didn't say anything, just held him tightly to her. He pretended not to notice her tears dampening his skin.

Throughout the night, they alternated between sleep and making love, sometimes hard and fast, sometimes in the slow haze of a half-asleep state. Each time, he felt her tears afterward. She was breaking his heart.

CHAPTER TWENTY-SIX

The cup of coffee sat untouched in front of her. After she had changed her afternoon flight home to a morning one, Ryan had insisted on waiting with her until it was time to go to her departure gate. His coffee was untouched, too.

Charlie wished he would leave.

If he would go away, she wouldn't be able to smell him. She wouldn't have the desire to reach up and feel the bristle of his unshaven face against her palm. She wouldn't keep thinking about how dangerous and sexy he looked with a day-old beard. He reached over and trailed the back of his knuckles down her cheek. She wished he wouldn't do that, she thought, as she closed her eyes against the burn in them.

"I'll be back in time for your air show," he said.

Charlie shook her head. "No, stay here with your parents. You said you haven't seen them in a year, and they'd be disappointed if you left so soon."

"I'll call you every day then."

Again, she shook her head. "Please don't. Don't call me, don't come to see me."

"Ever?"

There was anger in his voice, but she didn't care. "Not unless you can look me in the eyes and say you've forgiven not only your brother, but your wife, too. You once promised you would never lie to me. If the day comes when you can do what I need, then come to me, and I'll believe you."

He stared hard at his coffee cup as he twirled it in a circle. Then he turned his uniquely colored eyes on her, the orange in them flaring like a lit match. "No, I'll never lie to you, Charlene." He stood and stuck his hands halfway into his pockets. "The barbarian inside me wants to throw you over my shoulder and carry you to my lair, no matter how you feel about it." He leaned down and kissed her hard, then he walked away without looking back.

Tears streaming down her face, Charlie watched him until he disappeared against the crowd of people hurrying to their gate. When she could no longer see him, she swiped at her eyes, then, towing her carry-on behind her, got in the security line.

After dropping her things off at her apartment, Charlie went straight to Emerald Coast Aviation, made a preflight check, oversaw the fueling of her plane, then took to the air, the one place she could put Ryan out of her mind.

For the air show, she would start with an inverted flight, simply flying low and upside down past the grandstand. The stunt started from a wingover, putting her in the upside-down position, then she accelerated to cruise speed, keeping the plane's nose elevated higher than the tail.

She went through each aerobatic maneuver she had planned without once thinking of Hot Guy, something she marveled at when the plane's wheels were back on the ground. The moment she rolled to a stop, there he was, back in her mind. Maybe she should just take to the air twenty-four seven.

After she landed and had climbed out of her plane, she turned her phone back on. Four beeps, one after the other, sounded, signaling messages. Ignoring them for the moment, she made sure her plane was towed back into the hangar. Waving good-bye to the girl behind the counter, Charlie clicked on her messages as she walked to her car.

The first was from Maria, and Charlie hit Call Back. "It's Charlie," she said when her friend answered.

"Where are you?"

"Here. Pensacola." She got in her car and turned on the ignition long enough to roll down her windows.

"Oh, I thought you'd still be in Boston."

Charlie didn't want to talk about Boston or the man she'd left there. "Nope. I'm back."

"Right. Subject off-limits."

"For today, anyway. How's Mr. Bunny doing?" She even missed his rabbit.

"Having a ball playing with Mouse. You gonna come get him?"

"If you want me to, but I moved back to my place."

"He's fine with me if that works better for you."

"Yeah, I think it's best." She didn't want to give Ryan any reason to come see her unless it was to tell her he'd done what she had asked.

"No problem. The reason I called is we picked up three sets of fingerprints that weren't yours. One was Ryan's, and since you said he was in your apartment with you, that was expected. Of the two others, one we got a hit on and the other we didn't. The one we can't identify is possibly a woman's. I can't tell you that for sure, but some studies indicate that women tend to have a somewhat higher ridge density than men. Nothing conclusive, so best guess it was a woman. The third one belonged to Aaron Gardner."

"My ex," she said.

"How long's it been since he was in your apartment?"

"Over a year. Wouldn't his prints be gone by now?"

"Not necessarily. Unfortunately, there's no way to know how old they are. As for the one that might be a female's—"

"There's been no female in my place other than you and me. Well, except for whomever those belong to." It was embarrassing to admit she didn't have any female friends. She needed to get out more. Make some friends.

"And we can't say for sure those are female prints."

Charlie sighed. She didn't need this crap, wondering who had been in her home, nosing through her stuff. "So I don't know any more than I did before?"

"I'm sorry."

"Not your fault. I really appreciate everything you've done." And she did. After years of being alone other than the short time she'd let Aaron into her life, it was nice to have friends who cared about her. More than nice.

"I wish we could point to someone with certainty. I don't like that someone's been in your apartment without you knowing. Just don't let your guard down, okay?"

After promising she'd stay alert, Charlie ended the call, then checked her next message. It was from David, wanting to make sure she would be back at the flight school on Monday as promised. She called him, got his voice mail, and assured him that she would be there. After spending the money on her plane ticket to Boston, she should go back to work immediately, but she just wasn't up to it.

The third message was a text from Ryan. Even as she told herself not to open it, her finger did just that.

I can still smell you on my skin.

You're killing me, Hot Guy. She saved the text. When she'd told him not to call or come see her, it hadn't occurred to her to tell him not to text her either, so in all fairness, he wasn't breaking the rules. God, she missed him.

Should she answer? No, she wouldn't make it easy on him. But he was thinking about her, and that had to count for something. Before she changed her mind and answered him, she hurried on to the last message.

As soon as she heard the voice, she almost clicked off. Why was Aaron calling her? When the message ended, she frowned. For what reason would he want to see her? They had nothing to say to each other, the lying, cheating bastard. She still hadn't gotten over the shock of him being married, and she was almost tempted to call him back and tell him what she thought of him. But she didn't really care anymore, and the realization was freeing. She didn't care about him one way or the other. Deleting his message, she started her car and turned for home.

For dinner, Charlie opened a can of vegetable soup. She supposed she'd be eating a lot of canned soup for a while until she replenished her bank account. The oyster crackers she liked to have with soup had just become an extravagance, so she limited herself to five.

"Pitiful," she muttered. As she ate, she tried to decide if the cost of the ticket to Boston had been worth it. Who was she kidding? She'd do it again without a thought. The night with Ryan had been magical, and if there was never a repeat—no, she wouldn't cry—she had a dang good memory.

She cried.

No longer hungry, she put the remainder of her dinner in a plastic bowl and the three uneaten crackers back in the bag. Although she told herself not to do it, she got her phone and pulled up Ryan's text. She was staring at it, lecturing herself not to respond, when there was a knock at the door. The only person she could think of who might stop by was Maria.

She went to the living room and put her eye up to the peephole. Really? "I'm not home," she said.

"Please, Charlie. Open the door."

"Go away, Aaron. We have nothing to talk about."

"I miss you, baby."

A rage burned through her, and she unhooked the chain. So angry when she opened the door, she pushed him back. "You don't have the right to miss me, jackass. Go home to your wife." When his mouth opened and closed, reminding her of a blowfish, she pushed him again. "Yes, your wife, who you neglected to mention. Or that you had a kid, who I feel really sorry for, by the way, for having a loser father like you." The lock of blond hair that she'd once adored fell over his forehead. Instead of wanting to brush it back like she used to, she wanted to pull it out by the roots.

"I can explain."

Just like that, her fury fizzled out. He wasn't worth her anger, wasn't worth a miniscule thought in her head. "There's nothing you can say that I care to hear, Aaron. Go away."

She turned to go back in her apartment, and he grabbed her arm. "Come on, runt, just listen, okay? Five minutes is all I ask."

Calling her *runt* wasn't winning him any points. "Five minutes is five minutes too long." She jerked her arm away.

His brown eyes flashed with anger. "You always were a bitch, Charlie. Always thought you were such a hotshot pilot. You'll be sorry—"

"I'm sorry all right. Sorry I ever met you."

"You're gonna wish you'd listened to me." With that, he turned and strode away, shooting her a bird over his shoulder.

"Screw you, too, asshole."

Why should she listen to anything he had to say? As she closed and locked the door, unease slithered down her back. In her anger, she'd not given a thought to him being on her suspect list. Maybe she should have heard him out.

Parked in the driveway of his parents' house, Ryan slipped his cell phone back into his pocket after texting Charlie. He probably shouldn't have sent it, but she hadn't included "no texting" in her list of don'ts. And dammit, he could still smell her on his skin, and it was driving him crazy.

As he walked up the sidewalk, his dad stepped out. "Ah, there's my car."

"Sorry," Ryan said, dropping the keys in his father's hand. "I guess I should have asked to borrow it."

"That's the polite thing to do, but you seemed to have other things on your mind at the time." He put his arm around Ryan's shoulders. "Where's the woman you left with? Your mom wanted to meet her."

"Maybe next time. She had to return home." Or maybe never if he couldn't do what Charlie needed from him. It felt as if someone had stuck the point of a knife in his heart at the thought of no cherub in his life.

"Probably for the best considering we're about to have a family sit-down."

As far back as Ryan could remember, his family had sit-downs whenever there were important things to discuss. He wondered what was up. More times than not, growing up, it had been because one of them was in trouble. Since they were all adults now, it must have something to do with his parents. Maybe his dad had finally decided to retire. He had more than enough years in on the force, but had always sworn he'd go stir crazy without his job.

As they walked into the living room, Ryan tensed at seeing Patrick sitting on a chair facing the sofa where their mother sat. Even though knowing a family sit-down would include Patrick, Ryan still had the desire to plant his fist in his brother's face.

And that was Charlie's whole point, wasn't it? If he couldn't forgive his brother, he'd never be able to put his wife to rest. He wanted to do it for Charlie, he just didn't know if he could because that would also mean forgiving Kathleen.

"Sit, son," his father said, pushing him toward the couch.

Ryan took a seat next to his mom, and she took his hand, squeezing her fingers around his. His dad settled on the love seat next to Megan. Unease rippled through him as Patrick exchanged glances with the others.

"What's this about?" he asked.

Patrick cleared his throat, then cleared it again. "I told them."

"What? Told them what, Patrick?"

"Everything."

Anger burned through him so intensely that he thought his skin might be on fire. He'd kept the secret of Kathleen's betrayal for so long, not wanting to besmirch her memory in his family's eyes. It was his choice, not his brother's, whether or not to tell them. The tears rolling down Patrick's face infuriated him.

When Ryan tried to stand, intending to beat the shit out of his brother, his mother held on to his hand. Because he loved his mom and respected her above all others, he let her pull him back down. It was that or drag her along with him to get to Patrick.

"It didn't mean anything, I swear."

Ryan stared at his brother, so many responses to that statement crowding his mind that his throat closed up on him. *It didn't mean anything that you, my own brother, fucked my wife? It didn't mean anything that you got her pregnant? It didn't mean anything that you let me spend a fucking year wallowing in misery, wondering what I had done wrong because you were too much of a coward to face me like a man?*

Finally settling on the one that now mattered, he said, "You had to know why I crawled into a hole like a damned hurt dog, licking my wounds this past year, and you let me. You let me, Patrick."

Before he really did kill Patrick, he pulled away from his mother's grasp and left the room. He had no destination; he just walked. It wasn't until he came to the ladder leading up to the tree house his dad had built for his kids that Ryan was even cognizant of his surroundings. The tree house was still there?

It had once been a place he and Patrick had taken over, doing their best to keep their sisters out. Hadn't worked, though. Colleen and Megan had been determined little things. In the end, the four of them had spent hours up there, laughing over dirty jokes they wouldn't dare repeat in front of their parents, telling each other secrets, doing all the crazy stuff kids did in a tree house.

Ryan climbed up. The twelve-by-twelve-foot wood floor hadn't rotted, and the beanbag seats weren't covered with dust. Did his dad keep the place clean? In his heart, Ryan knew it was his father who still cherished the hideaway of his kids.

He stood on wood that had held him as a boy, unafraid his adult weight would be too much. In his mind's eye, he saw the ghosts of the children they had once been as they laughed and played in the treetop. As adults, even when separated by time and distance, the bond between remained. No matter their hurts, no matter their anger, they would kill to protect each other, and they would just as willingly die for each other.

When you can forgive your brother . . . Charlie's voice suddenly filled his mind. No, he wouldn't kill Patrick, but how to forgive him?

"Son?"

Ryan glanced over his shoulder to see the top of his dad's head. The tree house belonged to Michael O'Connor's children, and he wouldn't step any higher without permission. Love for the man who had loved him back without reservation for as far back as he could remember—the man who respected his son so much that he wouldn't set foot on the floor he himself had built without Ryan telling him he could—brought tears to Ryan's eyes.

"I think I would be hurting more if not for Charlie," he said, knowing it was true. He turned and opened his arms, welcoming his father's embrace.

As his dad climbed up and hugged him, Ryan watched over his father's shoulder, unsurprised, as first his mom, then Megan, then Patrick followed him up, crowding into space only meant for children.

"You sure this tree house can hold us all?" he asked, half crying, half laughing.

"Son, when I build something, I build it to last. You understand?"

He did. Whether tree houses or families, Michael O'Connor was a master builder.

"I love you, Dad," he said.

"And you, your brother, and your sisters are my heart, Ryan. You gotta let go of your hurt, boy."

Before Ryan could respond, his mom was there, hugging him and his dad. He turned and buried his face against his mom's neck. "Tell me how to forgive them," he said, trying but failing to hold back his tears.

"I'm sick over what Patrick did, believe me," his mom said through her own tears, as she wiped his away. "But he's still my son as are you. Your father and I love you both, you know that. For our sake, please just listen to him. If you want to beat him up after that, I won't stop you."

"I'll even help you do it," Megan said, glaring at Patrick through watery eyes.

She would, too, and as Ryan glanced around at his family, all of their cheeks wet, even his father's, the love in his heart for these people almost brought him to his knees.

The only O'Connor not joining in the family hug was his brother. Patrick stood near the ladder. "I'm sorry, Ryan," he said, his voice trembling. "So damn sorry. If I could do it over again . . . God, I wish I had it to do over again. It's killing me knowing I did something so unforgivable. I don't blame you for hating me. I hate myself."

The funny thing was, Ryan didn't hate his brother, could never hate him. He just didn't like him right then. But what was the saying? It took two to tango. Either one of them could have said no—both of them absolutely should have, but hadn't. Patrick wasn't perfect, but neither was Kathleen. Who was?

As the fire burning through his blood cooled, Ryan's thoughts turned to Charlie. She was who mattered to him now.

When you can forgive your brother . . .

He finally got it. He had to forgive his brother and his wife. Not for Charlie, but for him. It was the only way he could move forward, and she was the way forward. Slashing the back of his hand across his face, he cleared away his tears, then held out his hand.

With hesitant steps, Patrick came to them, and Ryan pulled him into their family's embrace. "I forgive you," he said, meeting Patrick's gaze. At his brother's surprised expression, he said it again, meaning it. "I forgive you, but if you ever touch Charlie, I will kill you." Even as he said the words, he knew she was a stronger woman than Kathleen had been, and that Charlie would never hurt him the way his wife had.

"Who's Charlie?" his mother asked, openly sobbing.

"My future. I hope."

"I think I'd feel better if you gave me a black eye," his brother said.

Megan narrowed her eyes at Ryan. "Charlie's a female, right? I mean, you're not gay, right?"

"If he was, he would still be my son," his mother sobbed out.

"This family is going to be the death of me," his father said.

"Someone's trying to kill her," Ryan blurted.

Before he could blink twice, his family began to make plans for every single one of them to travel with him to Pensacola to help save the woman he loved.

And as soon as he caught up with the stubborn woman, he was going to tell her that he loved her, and only her.

CHAPTER TWENTY-SEVEN

One would think a former SEAL and two cops—his dad and his brother—should be able to find the bastard out to get Charlie. That didn't even take into account a mother and sister on a mission to see him happy again, and if that meant a stunt plane pilot needed saving, then nothing was going to stop them from coming, too.

"A stunt plane pilot? Are you kidding?" his mom had asked, a wide grin on her face.

"Oh, I like her already," his sister said.

By the time they'd gotten organized and booked six tickets on the first available flight early the following morning—Megan's husband not wanting to miss out on the rescue—Ryan was ready to put a hurt on someone. He needed to get back to Florida so he could keep Charlie safe. Because he'd been wrapped up in his own problems, he had made the stupidest mistake of his life by letting her go home without him.

They had landed in Pensacola early on the morning of Charlie's air show. He'd almost texted her to expect him, but she'd said not to come near her until he could look her in the eyes and say that he'd forgiven his wife and brother.

Maybe it was male pride that had him showing up at the airfield—the O'Connor family in tow—without calling to warn her, but dammit, he was just following her orders. He would stand in front of her and tell her what was in his heart.

Having neglected to ask Charlie where she'd moved her plane to, their first stop had been Pensacola Aviation Center. Neither the airport manager nor the head mechanic were there. Both had left earlier for Jackson Field in Alabama, where the show would take place.

The airport in Alabama was an hour away, and as Ryan raced west on I-10, his concern for Charlie increased with each mile. "Try this on for size," he said, getting the attention of his family. "Someone wants to hurt Charlie, that I don't doubt. Maybe the previous incidents were a kind of test. See what he-she-they could get away with, the added benefit being to shake her up, rattle her."

"Who does she suspect?" his dad asked.

"We made a list." He ran down the different names and reasons.

Patrick leaned forward from the backseat and put his hand on Ryan's shoulder. Although he was still working on getting back on solid ground with Patrick, Ryan was happy to have his brother at his back. The large hand on Ryan's shoulder was familiar and comforting.

"Of those, who hates her the most?" Patrick asked.

"I'd have to say her stepsister, Ashley. She blames Charlie for sending her father to prison, and then to make matters worse, Charlie testified against him at his parole hearing." Knowing they would ask, he told them the circumstances and Charlie's role, along with the history of the stepsisters. "She's made no secret of the fact that she hates Charlie for ruining her life. Charlie said that Ashley was one of the most popular girls at school, but when her father was arrested, her boyfriend broke up with her and her friends shunned her, so she quit school. Last Charlie heard, Ashley was waitressing to earn a living."

"Charlie's a hero," his mother declared. "Imagine the courage it must have taken to stand alone against her family and do the right thing. Do I have to keep calling my future daughter-in-law Charlie? Is that a nickname?"

"Whoa there, Mom. Getting ahead of me on that one."

Megan snickered. "If you're not careful, she'll propose to Charlie for you."

"Charlene, her name is Charlene."

"Oh, that's a lovely name." His mom punched his dad. "Do you remember that pretty girl you liked before you met me? Her name was Charlene."

"I don't remember liking any girl but you, *A mhuirnín*."

"Good answer, Dad," Ryan said as it hit him how he'd known the Gaelic word for darling—hearing his father say it to his mother over the years.

His father chuckled. "I'm not stupid, you know. Back to your woman, son. Since her stepfather has more reason than not to want Charlene alive, the only one of those people on her list that has a real motive is the stepsister. Hate can devour a person, driving them to do things they wouldn't normally do, even murder. It sounds like you want to pin it on her boss. I'm not so sure. Even though he has one incident of stalking a woman that you know of, but—"

"But if his behavior hasn't escalated, I can't see him deciding to kill her just because she wouldn't go out with him," Patrick said, cutting in.

"What about the ex-boyfriend?" Sean, Megan's husband, asked.

"I don't know." Ryan moved into the right lane to pass a slower-moving car.

"They should start giving tickets to drivers poking along in the fast lane," his cop father said. "We'll get back to the boyfriend in a minute. Before Patrick," he turned and wacked Patrick on the side of his head, "so rudely interrupted me, I was going to say that although I don't see her boss as a killer, there is one thing to think about. This Ashley, does she have access to Charlie's—"

Ryan's mother reached forward and tapped her husband's shoulder. "Charlene sounds so much better, dear."

At his father's huge sigh, Ryan glanced at him, getting a grin and a wink from his dad. Damn, he loved his family—boisterous, interrupting people that they were.

"Of course, love, she shall be Charlene henceforth," his father said.

"To answer the question you were trying to ask," Ryan said, "no, she doesn't have access, but even if she did, Charlie . . . Charlene swears she wouldn't know how to sabotage a plane."

"Then if it's her, she has help."

Ryan nodded. "Yeah, if it's Ashley trying to hurt Charlie, she's got someone helping her."

"Charlene," his mom corrected.

Charlie, Charlene, cherub, girlfriend—didn't matter. All that did matter was finding her and making sure she stayed safe. "In Afghanistan, I learned to trust my instincts. Mine are telling me that whoever is helping her, it's Ashley behind this, and taking Charlene out while doing what she loves best and in front of thousands of spectators . . . she would get off on that." He eased his grip on the steering wheel before he broke it in half.

The line of cars trying to get into Jackson Field was at a dead stop. After a few minutes of impatiently waiting for it to inch along, Ryan unbuckled his seat belt. "One of you get behind the wheel. I'm going on foot."

Not surprised when his dad and Patrick joined him, he jogged with them down the road toward the ticket stand. The line there was also long, and frustrated, he joined the end of it.

"I'll be back in a minute," his dad said, leaving him and Patrick to wait.

Ryan glared at the backs of all the heads in front of him. "Maybe I could pay someone to let me cut in ahead." The line moved a few feet. He needed to get inside that fence ASAP. They moved forward again. At least the line was moving faster than the cars trying to get in. When they were back in Boston packing, his dad had given each of them handheld radios so no matter what, they could stay in touch. Ryan's crackled to life.

"Come to the gate, son," his dad said.

Patrick rolled his eyes as he pushed Ryan out of the line. "The old man's doing his Irish magic again."

Sure enough, his dad stood talking to a cop in uniform at the entrance. When Ryan and Patrick jogged up, the officer waved them through. "What'd you tell him?" Ryan asked as they pushed past the people milling around.

"That I was a cop—did the bonding thing. Then I told him your girl was one of the stunt pilots and you were supposed to be her passenger. I didn't want to tell him the truth and have a hundred cops swarming the place, scaring off our bad guys. Those people are going down today if I have anything to say about it."

Ryan was in complete agreement. He fished his cell phone from his pocket, scrolled to the file he had saved, and showed his dad and Patrick pictures of Charlie, Ashley, Haydon, and the ex-boyfriend.

"Who's that?" Patrick asked of the last photo.

"The stepfather. He's in prison, so don't be looking for him. We need to split up. I'll find where all the planes are staged. Patrick, you start searching the crowds for any one of those people, and Dad, you . . . hell, I don't know. Do whatever you think best."

His father bumped shoulders with him. "Go find your girl, son. I know what to do."

To Ryan's left was a large hangar, and as he headed for it, he heard a plane taking off. Heart in his throat, Ryan ran faster. He had to get to her before she left the ground. As the plane lifted off, he glanced over at it, breathing a sigh of relief that it wasn't hers.

Then he heard another engine revving from the direction of the runway. The plane barreled down the asphalt, and when it was even with him, the world revolving around him stopped as the crowd of people and their voices faded away to nothing.

Charlie!

The red Citabria passed by, wheels leaving the ground. As he stood, watching her take to the sky, he'd never felt so helpless in his life. *Land, Charlie. Please land.*

"Have you ever seen her perform before? She's amazing."

Ryan jerked his head toward the man standing next to him. "Haydon, I have one question, and you'd better tell me the truth because if I find out you lied to me, I will kill you. That's not a threat. It's a fact."

The man's eyebrows shot up. "Huh?"

"Are you the one who's been messing with her plane?" Ryan stepped close to him, crowding him.

Haydon threw his hands out as he backed up. "Hell no, man. What's going on?"

Another plane took to the air, and Ryan followed its progress, stalling a moment. He hadn't seen any guilt or fear on the man's face. His gut said it wasn't Haydon, so Ryan decided to risk laying it all out to see if he could add anything. As quickly and efficiently as he could, he told Haydon everything.

"And I was on her list? Man, Charlie's my best instructor. No way I'd risk the money she brings in." His cheeks flushed and he glanced away. "About putting her picture up as my girlfriend, I guess that was stupid."

"Yes, it was and if you ever do anything like that again, I will hurt you." No concern there for his best instructor, just the money mattered. Ryan was tempted to put the man's ass on the ground on general principle. "We need to radio her, tell her to land."

"We can do that in the tower." As Ryan followed him, Haydon said, "Charlie's ex-boyfriend came by not too long ago. There was a woman waiting in the car for him. Asked him if that was his new squeeze. Sure as hell didn't know he was married, so maybe it was his wife."

Ryan got his phone back out and brought up Ashley's photo. "Was it her?" He turned the screen so the man could see it.

Haydon squinted, studying the picture. "Not sure, but it could be. The hair looks the same, but I wasn't close enough to get a good look at her face."

Ryan was no longer operating on instinct. He knew down to his bones that it was Ashley and Charlie's ex. As they climbed the steps to the tower, he radioed his dad and Patrick, telling them the two were definitely who they were looking for.

After a brief conversation with the air show controller, the man tried to call Charlie. She didn't answer. "We've lost contact with her," the man said.

Ryan knew then that he had failed her. He blindly stumbled out of the tower and down the steps, only stopping when his father's arms wrapped around him.

"I've lost her," he said, choking out the words.

Charlie circled as she waited for her turn to fly by the grandstand. She should be hearing chatter on the radio, but there was nothing but dead silence. "Jackson Field tower, this is Citabria November Three One Golf Hotel."

No response. She tried again and still got nothing back. Dang radio. Now what? She knew she should land, but she was up next. "We'll just do this first one, then I'll take you down, baby" she said. Disappointed that she wouldn't be able to show the crowd what her plane could do, she rolled from a wingover into an inverted position, flying by the grandstand upside down. Once past, she made a slow roll to bring herself upright. Because she'd been flying so close to the ground, she accelerated to gain altitude. Flying in her aerobatic plane never ceased to thrill her—whether for herself or in front of a crowd—and as she pointed the nose up, she laughed as adrenaline surged through her.

"If only Ryan could see us now, baby, wouldn't he be impressed?" She patted the dash. The Citabria rewarded her affection with a cough. Then a sputter. Then the engine quit.

"Oh God, not again."

She tried everything she'd learned from her training to start the engine.

"Shit," she yelled at the stupid plane when it decided to fall to earth. The one thing she was thankful for was that she wasn't taking a nosedive into the crowd. That would've haunted her through all eternity.

CHAPTER TWENTY-EIGHT

Ryan held on to his father, needing his dad's support as Charlie's plane plummeted nose down toward the ground. "I never told her I loved her." His father held him in strong arms that had always been there for him.

"She knew, son. She knew it."

His mother and sister were suddenly there, wrapping themselves tightly around him and his dad. Unable to watch his cherub's plane crash, he lost himself in the arms of his family's love.

"Look! Ryan, look!"

He couldn't look. Why was Megan even asking that of him?

"She parachuted. Wow, my future sister-in-law is floating to the ground like she has wings."

What??? He dared to lift his gaze to the sky and there she was, steering her parachute away from the burning wreckage of her beloved plane. He pushed away from all the arms wrapped around him and started running, his only intention to catch her. And when he did, he would tell her what he thought of her scaring thirty years off his life.

Static crackled over his radio, then Patrick said, "I've got the assholes messing with your girlfriend. It was the ex and her stepsister.

Hardly had to threaten them before Ashley was pointing her finger at the boyfriend, and Aaron pointing his right back at her."

Ryan couldn't care less. "Hand them over to dad," he answered, then turned off the handheld.

He didn't catch Charlie. She touched the ground before he could get to her. But when he did, he swept her off her feet, pulled her up against him, and swung them in a circle. The parachute wrapped around them, tripping him. On the ground, entangled in red-and-white nylon, he rolled on top of her.

"Cherub, my rabbit misses you but not as much as me." He kissed her then, long and hard, and then some more.

"You're here," she said, with wonder in her voice.

"Silly girl. Where else did you think I'd be when my girlfriend has trouble?"

Someone tugged on the parachute, then lifted it, exposing him and Charlie to curious eyes. He glanced up, saw his family peering down at them with too much interest. "Go away nosy people," he said, laughing. When the nylon fell back down around them, he went back to kissing his girl.

"My plane crashed," she said when they came up for air, tears pooling in her beautiful eyes.

Ryan kissed her nose. "I'll buy you a new one."

Charlie stood next to Ryan, watching the interrogation of her step-sister through the one-way mirror. He wrapped his arm around her, tucking her tightly against him the way he liked to have her.

"The bitch deserved to die," Ashley said, defiant even in the face of an attempted murder charge. "She ruined my life when she told her lies about my father."

As she listened, Charlie was surprised that she felt only pity for

Ashley. Her stepsister could have had it all if she hadn't let bitterness consume her life. Although still beautiful, there was now a hardness in the lines around Ashley's mouth, and the hatred shining in her eyes put Charlie in mind of someone possessed. Maybe she was.

Ryan gave a grunt of what sounded like disgust. "My dad recently said hatred could devour a person. I'd say that's what happened to her. Didn't take long to show her true colors, did it?"

No, it hadn't. For the first thirty minutes of the interrogation, Ashley had tried to blame Aaron for everything, but the officer questioning her had pushed the right buttons, and she lost her temper. Charlie didn't think Ashley even realized the hole she was digging for herself.

"She really does believe I lied about her father, which I guess justifies in her mind what she tried to do to me."

"There is no excuse for what she tried to do." He turned her to face him. "Don't go feeling sorry for her, cherub. If she'd had her way, I would have lost you."

"I don't." But she did a little. He wrapped his arms around her and hugged her as if he needed reassurance that she was safe and in his arms. Charlie hugged him back, pressing herself against his big body. They had come close to losing each other, both from Ashley's nasty game and from Ryan's inability to let go of the past. Although he had yet to say he loved her, she had heard the catch in his voice when he'd said he almost lost her, and maybe it was wishful thinking, but she thought she had seen love in his eyes when he had tangled them up in her parachute.

Although anxious to leave so she and Ryan could be alone, they stayed to hear Aaron's interrogation. Aaron confessed to breaking into her apartment with Ashley, their aim to find the diamond ring Charlie's father had given her mother. After her father's death, her mom—when she was still everything a mother was supposed to be—had slipped the ring off her finger one day and given it to Charlie. Because a three-carat diamond was valuable, Charlie kept it in a safe-deposit box. The only thing they ended up taking was the picture Aaron had once asked about.

During his interrogation, he'd put all the blame for sabotaging Charlie's plane on Ashley, even though it had been his hands doing the dirty work. He confessed to making a copy of Charlie's house key and to stealing a key to the hangar.

"It was just a game," he told the officer. "Ashley was really pushing me to do it, but I never did anything to Charlie's plane that would make her crash. Just little things to give her a scare."

Next to her, Ryan's hands fisted at his sides. Charlie slipped her fingers around his and felt the tension in his arm ease. She wasn't sure it was normal for victims to be able to listen to interrogations, but apparently, Logan Kincaid had made a phone call at Ryan's request, and now here she was, listening to her ex-boyfriend make light of sabotaging her plane. At first she hadn't wanted to, but Ryan had told her it would give her closure. Although it made her sick to listen to the two of them try to justify what they had done, Ryan was right. After she walked out of this place, she would never think of the two pathetic people again.

"I was intrigued enough with the woman in the photo to search her out," Aaron admitted to the detective when asked how he had met Ashley. Yes, Aaron had felt sorry for poor Ashley after he'd learned how Charlie had ruined her life. According to him, Ashley had convinced him that Charlie deserved to suffer because of the lies that had sent Ashley's father to prison. Along with his supposed sympathy for poor Ashley, he'd been promised the ring and anything else of value they could find when they broke into her apartment.

That made Charlie laugh since, other than her plane, her car, and the ring, she owned nothing of value. The joke was on him, the asshole. He admitted to the detective that having a wife and daughter, along with several girlfriends, was damned expensive, and he needed the money. That there had been *girlfriends* plural made Charlie sick that she'd been one of them.

"You never told him your side of the story, what Ashley's father did and the repercussions?" Ryan asked.

"No. I'm not sure why. Maybe without realizing it, I didn't trust him?"

He peered at her, one brow lifted. "Are you asking me?"

She didn't know if she was asking or telling. No, she did know. "You were the first person I trusted enough to tell. You, Ryan."

His gaze caught hers, and he brought her fingers to his lips and kissed them. "Thank you."

"I went to her house and tried to warn her not to fly in the show, but she didn't want to listen," Aaron said, his voice an unwelcome intrusion as far as Charlie was concerned. She didn't much care anymore what he had to say.

The same cop who had questioned Ashley said, "When you went to see Charlene, were you hoping to get back together with her?"

Aaron looked into the one-way glass as if he knew Charlie was watching. "Yeah, I guess I was. She's a hotshot aerobatic pilot and it was good for me to be around her. I broke up with her because my wife found a picture on the Internet of me with my arm around Charlie at an air show, and I panicked. Once things calmed down at home . . ." He leaned forward as if getting closer to the mirror. "I missed Charlie. I thought she would be glad to have me back, but when I went to see her, she attacked me. That was too bad, because I was going to tell her what Ashley was up to, but after that, I figured she deserved what Ashley had planned for her." He shifted his gaze to the officer. "I want to file an assault charge against Charlie."

Ryan growled. "Tell me you've heard enough, cherub."

Charlie wished they'd let her in the room so she could punch Aaron in the nose. "More than enough. Let's get out of here."

"Then let's go home before I break this glass so I can get my hands around that bastard's throat."

He kept her tucked next to him, only letting her go when they reached the car. "Tomorrow we're spending with my family, but tonight, you're mine," he said as he held the door open. She was his long past tonight, though. For a lifetime, if she would have him.

On the way, they stopped at Maria's and picked up Mr. Bunny. When they got home and let the rabbit out of his carrier, the animal zoomed around the living room like a race car on an oval track, pausing only long enough to touch one or the other of them with his twitching nose before taking off again.

"He's crazy," Charlie said, laughing.

"Not as crazy as me." Ryan scooped her up and carried her to his bed. "Do you know why?" he asked after he lowered her down, then fell on top of her, catching his weight on his arms.

"No, but I'm sure you're going to tell me."

He lowered his mouth to hers and kissed her, hard at first, then gentling the kiss to feathery brushes over her lips.

"And tell you I will. I'm crazy in love with you, Charlene Morgan. You and only you."

As Charlie stared into those beautiful eyes that had the ability to captivate her, she put her hand on his cheek. "You are?"

"Oh yeah, girlfriend, I am." He smiled then, the orange streaks in his eyes light and bright. "I forgave them both. My brother and Kathleen. That's what you said you needed from me, and I wanted to do it for you. But the funny thing is, when all was said and done, I did it for me."

"Oh, Ryan." She wrapped her arms around his neck and held him close. She hadn't been sure he could let go of his hurt, and she hadn't dared to hope. That he'd understood it was what he needed to do for himself, not her, brought tears to her eyes.

"Is that all you have to say?"

"I'm so happy for you."

"And?"

The orange streaks flared darker as his eyes pierced her in what seemed like annoyance. It hit her what he wanted her to say, and unable to resist, she toyed with him. "And I think Mr. Bunny wants on the bed." The rabbit was stretched up on his hind legs, paws on the comforter, peering at them.

"Charlene!"

The man gave good growl. Grinning, she relented. "And, I love you."

"Damn, that was like pulling teeth to get that out of you." He returned her grin. "We've gone steady long enough, don't you think? How about we try an engagement next?"

Charlie wondered if her heart could withstand its fierce pounding without splitting in two. Up to the day he had appeared at the air show, kissing her like he couldn't live without her, she hadn't dared to hope for a happily ever after for them.

At her hesitation, he narrowed his eyes, and she couldn't resist teasing him. "Do I get a new ring if I say yes?"

"You do. One I'll make just for you, *A mhuirnín*."

"Then yes, I'll get engaged to you." She wondered if her heart would ever stop fluttering when he grinned at her like that. She hoped not.

"Does that mean I get phone sex for real now?"

"Sheesh, Hot Guy, you really do have a one-track mind."

"I keep telling you that, Charlie."

He made love to her then as if she were a priceless work of art, cherishing her body until she was begging, another thing he seemed to like. Much later, she fell asleep with a heart full of love and Ryan wrapped around her, and her last thought was that she had soared and touched the stars.

Agitated, Charlie twisted around her finger the sapphire-and-diamond engagement ring Ryan had made for her. Refusing to tell her where they were going, Ryan had taken her on a commercial flight that ended up in Orlando, Florida. A limo had been waiting for them when they walked out of the airport, and after a thirty-minute ride, they'd ended up at a Citabria dealer in Sanford.

The brand-new, cherry-red aerobatic plane sitting on the runway in front of her was the most beautiful thing she'd ever seen. "I can't let you do this, Ryan." Oh God, to own that beauty.

He stepped behind her and wrapped his arms around her. "You don't like it?"

Was he crazy? "Of course I do, silly. I'll look for a used one, something I can afford to make payments on." He chuckled into her ear, sending shivers down her spine. The man was entirely too potent.

"Here's the thing, *A mhuirnín*. It's my wedding present to you. And before you say I can't afford it, I can. There's even enough left over for us to go house shopping. If you want to make me happy, you won't say no." He nuzzled her neck. "Come on, cherub, make me happy."

Charlie burst into tears. She turned and threw her arms around her fiancé. "Yes, I'll make you happy."

Halfway back to Pensacola, the intercom clicked on. "Kid's play," said the passenger sitting behind her.

Charlie grinned. "You remember what happened the last time you said that, Hot Guy?"

"Yeah, you left my stomach two miles behind me. Do it again."

Until she learned her new plane—all its quirks and secrets—she wouldn't put either one of them at risk doing anything dangerous, but a few dives and wingovers would be safe enough.

"Tighten your harness then."

"Yee-haw," he yelled after she crested the arc she visualized in her mind, then dived straight down.

She burst into laughter as happiness swelled up inside her. Dang, she loved her Irish Hot Guy with the funny-colored eyes. She pulled the nose of the plane up, and then crested the next invisible arc.

"Yee-haw," she yelled in unison with Ryan as they dived, leaving both their stomachs behind.

Acknowledgments

With each book, I write the acknowledgments, and each time there are names I've included in previous books, and then there are new ones. I am and will forever be humbled by the support and encouragement I receive from family, friends, fans of my books, and other authors. There are some of you I will never meet, but it doesn't make our friendship any less meaningful.

Without readers, I wouldn't be writing this. At the beginning of this book, I dedicated this story to the fans of my K2 Special Services series, and I mean it when I say y'all rock. Your e-mails, comments about these guys on Facebook, telling your friends they need to read this series—for all of that, I thank you from the bottom of my heart. The best way to thank any author who has carried you away for a few hours to another place, who has made you laugh or cry, is to write a review. If you've done that for any of my books, then I wish you were in front of me so I could give you a hug. Since that's not possible, I hope you will settle for two words. Thank you.

To the very first friend (and critique partner extraordinaire) I made at the start of this journey: You know I love you, Jenny Holiday. I know you claim you're not a romantic suspense author, but you're dang good at helping me come up with evil plot ideas. To Lindsey Ross and Felice Stevens, my late-night partners in crime, thank you for all the belly laughs. The two of you will be forever in my heart. To Leslie Lynch, my 2013 Lucky 13 Golden Heart® sister, thank you so much for answering all my questions about pilots and airplanes. Anything I got wrong is entirely on me.

I am truly honored to be published by Montlake Romance. To Maria Gomez, Melody Guy, Jessica Poole, Scott Calamar, and all the other members of the fabulous Montlake Romance team, thank you for all that you do for your authors. Love you guys! So much!

Courtney, it's become a tradition to save you for last . . . isn't that what you do with the best? So to Courtney Miller-Callihan of Sanford J. Greenburger Associates, thank you for everything. It's such a fun ride that we are on together. Heart you!

About the Author

Photo © *2015 Cat Ford-Coates*

A native of Florida, Sandra Owens now lives in the beautiful Blue Ridge Mountains of North Carolina. As a romantic suspense author, Sandra often burns dinner because she's about to crash a plane, or some such mischief. She recently told her husband (who happens to be her very own hero because he eats that ruined food without complaint) that if men in dark suits wearing reflective sunglasses knock on their door, he shouldn't panic. All can be explained. She hopes. "It was just research," she will claim when those scary men ask why she was all over the Internet asking questions that brought her to their attention.

Sandra has gone from riding a Harley while managing a Harley-Davidson dealership to writing about seriously hot heroes and their feisty heroines. A true daredevil, she has skydived, been a passenger in an aerobatic plane doing death-defying stunts, and will ride insanely outrageous roller coasters. She regrets nothing.

You can connect with Sandra on Twitter @SandyOwens1 and Facebook at SandraOwens.94043. Her website is: www.sandra-owens.com.